Deadly Pretense

The Force of Truth Book Two

ENDORSEMENT

Deadly Pretense

The Force of Truth Book Two

Kim Teague

ELK LAKE PUBLISHING INC

PUBLISHING THE POSITIVE
Plymouth, Massachusetts

Cover and Interior Design: Derinda Babcock

Editor(s): Peggy Ellis, Deb Haggerty

PUBLISHED BY: Elk Lake Publishing, Inc., 35 Dogwood Drive, Plymouth, MA 02360, 2021

Library Cataloging Data

Names: Teague, Kim (Kim Teague)

Deadly Pretense / Kim Teague

338 p. 23cm × 15cm (9in × 6 in.)

ISBN-13: 978-1-64949146-6 (paperback) | 978-1-64949-147-3 (trade paperback) | 978-1-64949-148-0 (e-book)

Key Words: Mystery, Suspense, CIA, Murder, Lichtenstein, Kidnaping, Contemporary, Romance

Library of Congress Control Number: 2021932590 Fiction

Deadly Pretense

The Force of Truth Book Two

Kim Teague

ELK LAKE PUBLISHING INC
PUBLISHING THE POSITIVE
Plymouth, Massachusetts

DEDICATION

To my sisters—Becky, Adrienne, and Chris—
and to my mother, Carolyn.
I love you all.

ACKNOWLEDGMENTS

Many wonderful people supported me in the writing of this book. My heartfelt appreciation goes to:

My Elk Lake Publishing family, especially Deb Haggerty, Linda Rondeau, Cristel Phelps, Peggy Ellis, and Derinda Babcock—for your skill, wisdom, and patience.

Sherry Bradbury and Pam Fortney—for giving valuable insight on this project.

My sweet friends in our Tuesday Bible study—for your prayers and encouragement.

Mavis and Lloyd Lane—for cheering me on.

My daughter, Bethany—for inspiring this story with your skill and creativity both in front of and behind the camera.

My son, Corban, and my daughter-in-law, Caroline—for your sweet encouragement.

My husband, Barry—for your loving support and for being excited with me.

Most of all, thanks to Jesus, the author of life, eternal and abundant.

CHAPTER 1

JANUARY 20
MONDAY, 9:05 A.M.
K STREET NW, DC

Special Agent Ben Anderson eased his chair closer to a mahogany table in the Liechtenstein ambassador's office. He'd met Ambassador Schrader once before. Though she spoke flawless English, her accent required concentration.

"Gentlemen, I'm pleased the FBI has agreed to assist our embassy." She poured coffee from a silver pot into china cups.

Ben glanced at his team member Joe Peterson. A step above their usual chipped mugs.

"Our embassy has excellent security here in the United States," she continued. "However, I felt the need to obtain additional assistance due to a threat which concerns both our country and yours."

Ben raised an eyebrow. "What kind of threat?"

"Two days ago, I received a note inside a blank, open envelope." She handed a sealed bag to him.

The clear plastic revealed a plain white index card containing one typed sentence. "Stop the research exchange now—or someone will get hurt." Scenarios swirled through Ben's mind. He passed the bag to Joe, then turned to the ambassador. "Let's start with information about the research exchange."

"For the past year, research analysts in Liechtenstein have partnered with Caldwell Research Institute here in Washington. The focus of the study is economics—job creation, financial stability, long-term employment, to name a few. We are developing workshops, conferences, forums— things to benefit *both* our countries. In just weeks, we'll move from the planning stage of the project to the actual execution. Economists from CRI will fly to Liechtenstein, and economists from Liechtenstein will visit the United States." She clasped her hands. "Liechtenstein has much to contribute. Our country has one of the lowest unemployment rates in the world. The United States also has invaluable resources to offer us. For someone to believe this type of exchange is not in everyone's best interest makes no sense."

"Have there been other incidents of concern?"

"Not here at the embassy, but our principality recently uncovered bribery and threats regarding government appointments to offices. The same day I found the envelope, I received word someone had tampered with the brakes of a vehicle scheduled to transport Prince Alexander in Liechtenstein." She shuddered. "It's only by the grace of God he wasn't killed. I can't imagine this note is related to those things, yet the timing of this message raises questions."

"Where did you find the note?" Joe asked.

"I attended a lecture at CRI this past Saturday. Everyone received a program with information about the institute, along with the order of events for the evening. After the lecture, I left the program in my seat for a moment while I spoke with friends. When I returned home to the embassy later in the evening, I found the note inside my program." She paused. "The president of the institute, Frederick Wilson, did not attend the lecture. I called him immediately. He's yet to contact me."

Ben leaned forward. "Did you notice anything unusual or out of place the evening of the lecture?"

"Not at all. I realize the message could simply be from a disgruntled employee—or perhaps could even be a prank—and really poses no danger as things stand now. However, in two days, Prince Alexander's daughter, Princess Ingrid, arrives in Washington from Liechtenstein."

Joe pulled up a calendar on his phone. "How long will she stay?"

"She's coming to Washington to study at Georgetown University this semester." A smile flickered across Margaret's face. "Our country is quite proud of her. She's a bright young woman—determined and insistent on living in a dormitory instead of here at the embassy."

"I assume she'll have a security detail around her?"

"Of course. However, the problems I mentioned earlier warrant Prince Alexander's attention regarding the safety of his daughter. The princess intends to explore this country, interacting with the public just as she does in Liechtenstein. The royal family refuses to allow threats to dictate their actions, but you can imagine the concern a father feels for his child."

Ben nodded. His brother-in-law, Rich, had deployed months earlier to an undisclosed location. The memory of Rich's goodbyes to his little girls darted through his thoughts. Rich almost seemed to know he wasn't coming back … Ben shook himself inwardly. *Focus.*

"My administrative assistant will give you the travel itinerary, class schedule, and housing arrangements of the princess," the ambassador continued. "My head of security will contact you this afternoon. He's anxious to determine the best course of action for the protection of the princess while she's in the United States." Ambassador Schrader hesitated. "I'm sure you'll need the note for analysis. What else would you suggest?"

"We'll contact Caldwell Research Institute. I think we need to speak with Mr. Wilson in person."

She handed Ben a business card. "This is my private line. Please call me if you discover anything."

As the ambassador said goodbye, her administrative assistant stepped into the office.

Two hours later, thoroughly briefed on the details of Princess Ingrid's stay in Washington, Ben and Joe nodded to the security guards on the way out.

Ben dug car keys from his pocket. "What do you think about the message the ambassador received?"

"Hopefully the note means nothing, but with a foreign country and an American institute involved, we can't afford to take chances."

"My thoughts exactly." Ben set his jaw. "An international incident is the last thing we need."

JANUARY 20
MONDAY, 10:17 A.M.
WASHINGTON, DC

Kate Peterson edged around slick patches of ice hopscotching the DC sidewalk. She angled a large umbrella over her camera equipment as freezing rain pelted her. Why hadn't she grabbed a hat on her mad dash out of the apartment? She shivered. The price she paid for those few extra minutes nestled in the warmth of her bed.

She strained to see names of the shops she passed, the cold air stinging her eyes. Stephanie's Dress Designs, Cards by Cynthia, O'Reilly's Antiques, Shane's Jewelers. She blew out a breath. Shane's Jewelers. At last.

A rush of heat enveloped her as she bumped open the door with her shoulder. She turned sideways to maneuver her equipment inside. She added her dripping umbrella to several others squashed into a blue-flowered container near the door.

"Make yourself at home—I'll be right out," a cheery voice called from the back.

Kate shifted her camera onto a large counter with racks of business cards. A moment to regroup was always a good thing.

She tugged off her coat and glanced around the shop. Polished hardwood floors gleamed. Rose-colored Oriental rugs in front of glass display cases added a touch of elegance. Smoothing her damp hair, Kate stepped toward the lighted display case closest to her.

Beautiful gold wedding bands interspersed with diamond engagement rings sparkled in the soft light. Uncertainty stung. She'd just celebrated her thirty-first birthday, and the relationship she thought would last forever had turned out to be nothing more than lies. She swallowed around the burning in her throat. Would Gavin's hatred reach her here?

Her gaze wandered to the window. The raw day matched her heart. She fingered the delicate cross dangling from the silver bracelet she clipped on every morning and breathed a wordless prayer.

Something furry slid across her ankle. Gasping, she jumped backward. A large black and white cat meowed.

Kate bent to stroke his sleek coat. "Sorry, buddy. You startled me."

"George, are you trying to chase away our customers?" A petite woman hurried from the back room. "He thinks he has to greet every person who comes through that door." She extended her hand. "I'm Nelda Shane, and this is our George."

"He must be a very sociable cat." Kate returned Nelda's handshake.

"My husband and I joke he's half dog. Now, how may I assist you?"

"I'm Kate Peterson from WOTN. I have an appointment to interview you and your husband."

"Oh, my goodness—my husband told me you were coming, but I thought he meant *next* week." Plainly distressed, she smoothed back strands of chestnut hair that had escaped from her neat bun. "I had a special dress picked out so I'd look nice on television."

"Nelda, you know you're always beautiful." A thin man with twinkling eyes limped over to them. He slipped an arm around Nelda's waist. "I'm Levi Shane, proprietor of this fine store, but more importantly, husband of this wonderful woman. You must be Kate Peterson, the illustrious reporter from television."

Kate grinned. Though she'd won several awards during her eight years in TV news, Levi was the first to describe her as *illustrious*. "A pleasure to meet you."

"I understand you've recently moved here from Ohio. I hope you enjoy DC. The city has been good to us."

"I'm looking forward to hearing your story. Thirty years in business is quite impressive."

"Let's make ourselves comfortable in the office." Nelda glanced out the window. "On a day like this, we'll probably be very slow."

Kate set up the camera and clipped on the Shanes' microphones. The two perched on a worn floral sofa, holding hands like school kids. Kate smiled. True love. No doubt.

"This is so exciting." Nelda beamed. "I've never been on television before."

"Before we talk about the jewelry store, I'd like to hear how the two of you met."

"Of course. We're our favorite subject." Levi settled back into the sofa cushions.

"Ready?" At their nods, Kate clicked on the camera. She introduced the Shanes, then turned to the couple. "I understand you've had many wonderful years together. When did the two of you meet?"

"We met at the ripe old age of eleven." Levi winked. "Nelda decided I would be her boyfriend the moment she laid eyes on me."

"I certainly did not." Nelda gave him a playful swat. "Levi was the most mischievous boy in school—"

The jingle of a bell interrupted Nelda's words. Kate clicked off the camera.

"Oh, dear, we have a customer. Will the interruption ruin the interview?"

"Not at all. I edit the film before the broadcast. We can start and stop as much as we need to."

"Good. I'll be right back." Nelda bustled out of the back room, George on her heels.

Levi pulled himself up from the couch. "How about a cup of hot cocoa?"

"Yes, thank you."

He shuffled around the small area of the office serving as their kitchen. Kate started to offer help when an odd gasping noise sounded behind her. She spun around and froze.

Nelda swayed in the doorway of the jewelry store's office. The barrel of a gun glinted against her temple. Her panicked eyes pleaded for help. A lanky teenager towered behind her.

Kate's stomach roiled. She sucked in a breath.

"Let her go!" Levi lunged toward Nelda.

A swift kick from the young man's booted foot caught Levi's side, spinning him backward into a large desk. "I'll kill her if you try anything stupid again."

Kate's pulse pounded. What would Joe do? Her brother was an FBI agent, and always said cool heads saved lives.

"You don't have to hurt her." Kate willed calm into her voice. "That way when you get caught, you'll receive a lighter prison sentence."

The intruder's eyes narrowed. "Are you a cop?"

"No." Would telling him her brother was a DC Special Agent help matters or make them worse? "What's your name?"

For an instant, a scared boy inside the hardened young man stared back. "Angelo."

Kate stepped forward. Confusion flickered on his face. He gripped Nelda tighter and glowered. "Shut up and get the jewelry case keys from the old man. Lock the front door, then switch off the lights. If you act like a hero, she dies."

Trembling, Kate hurried to Levi. *Why didn't I keep my mouth shut?*

Levi fumbled through a desk drawer and pulled out a ring of keys. He pressed them into her hand, agony twisting his features.

She stepped quickly to the front room. Shuffling sounded behind her, then Nelda's soft moan. Kate bit her lip. No chance to call for help. Angelo wasn't letting anyone out of his sight.

She switched off the lights. Before she reached the front door to turn the lock, the clang of the bell above the door jolted her senses. Kate stifled a cry. Her eyes darted to the gun against Nelda's head.

A young woman with wind-blown auburn hair breezed in, her attention on the packages she carried. When she looked up, her face contorted. "Levi? Nelda? Wh-what's going on?"

Angelo barked a command. "Lock the door behind you, then come over beside the old man."

Her chin lifted. "You can't hold me here. I'm Sophie O'Reilly, and I'm—"

"I don't care who you are. Do what I tell you, or you'll die."

The packages toppled to the floor. Sophie quickly locked the door. Fear radiated from her eyes. She hurried past Kate to Levi.

Angelo jerked a leather bag from underneath his coat. He flung the bag at Kate. "Fill it."

Kate glanced at Levi. He stood motionless. Her hand shook as she tried each key in the lock of the display case beside her.

"Hurry up or I'll—"

A key finally clicked. Kate swept an emerald necklace into the bag, along with other jewelry on display. She moved to the next case. Her mind rushed ahead. The crime had four witnesses. Angelo would certainly kill them when he got what he wanted.

A sudden flash of bright pink danced across Kate's peripheral vision. Her gaze flicked to the window. Outside, a wide-eyed little girl stared, pointing. A man bent over her and looked in. A split-second later he jerked the little girl away.

Kate glanced at Angelo. He was silhouetted in the office doorway, the weapon he held in plain view. *They saw the gun. Please, Lord, let them get help.*

She drew a sharp breath. They needed time. She relaxed her hand and the keys clattered to the floor. She slowly bent.

A gunshot cracked. The mirror near the door exploded. Kate covered her head and her ringing ears, bracing for whatever came next.

Silence stretched.

Inch by inch, Kate raised her eyes. She pivoted her gaze to Angelo, who had his weapon trained on her. Would the next bullet be hers?

"Do you think I'm kidding?" Angelo bellowed. "I'm two seconds away from killing all of you."

Her heart hammered as she stood.

He laughed, the abrupt tone glazing her insides. "Don't you see? I'm in charge. Not you. Not even my boss." He waved the gun. "Fill the bag."

Kate retrieved the keys and moved to the next display case. Fragments from the broken mirror dusted the top of the case. As she raked pearl necklaces into the bag, a sliver of glass sliced her finger. She clenched her teeth against the sharp sting while she eased the remaining jewelry into the bag. Drops of red pooled on the white velvet lining.

Angelo's swings between rage and laughter quieted. Nelda's labored breathing filled the void.

Kate reached the last case.

"This is Pete Sanders of the Metropolitan Police Department!"

Kate jerked. Her eyes shot to the window. Police officers crouched behind cruisers. One held a white megaphone.

"Answer the phone when it rings," the officer continued. "We'll work this out. Let's talk."

Angelo swore. "Into the back room."

When he released Nelda, Levi's arm whisked around her. The barrel of Angelo's gun jabbed into Kate's ribs. He shoved the four of them into the office and onto the sofa.

They huddled there while he leaned against a stool beside the desk, his gun pointed at them. The ring of the landline phone blasted Kate's consciousness.

Her nerves pulsated with each ring. Finally, Angelo answered the call.

"What?" He listened for a moment, then cursed and slammed the receiver back into place.

Kate watched him from the corner of her eye.

He settled onto the stool, mute, his gaze matching the steel of the gun he aimed at them.

CHAPTER 2

Ben steered the car away from the Liechtenstein embassy and merged into traffic. He passed a tow truck assisting a car on the road's shoulder. Driving promised to be dicey even though the sleet had tapered off.

Joe pulled out his cell phone. "I'll give Frederick Wilson a call."

The one-sided conversation left no doubt in Ben's mind. Joe was getting the runaround. At last, he connected with a person in authority and set up an appointment.

Joe blew out a breath as he pushed his phone back into his pocket. "I hope you're free tomorrow morning. I thought I'd better take whatever time Wilson's assistant offered us while I had the chance."

"Tomorrow morning sounds fine." Ben flicked the heat up a degree. "You know, I'm surprised Wilson never returned Margaret Schrader's call. You'd think connecting with her would be a priority with the research exchange in progress."

"Maybe he's been on vacation, but his lack of communication is something to pursue. By the way, the turn for the Chinese restaurant is coming up. Why don't you join Kate and me for lunch?"

Ben considered the invitation. He'd planned to drop Joe at the restaurant and use his lunch hour to run errands.

The car slid and Ben gripped the steering wheel. He jerked his foot from the gas pedal until the tires gained traction. Okay, maybe his plan was flawed. In this weather, the errands could wait.

Besides, he'd met all of Joe's seven brothers and sisters except Kate. "Thanks, Joe. You talked me into it. Speaking of Kate, what does she think of Washington?"

"She seems to like the city. Jenny's Aunt Martha was kind enough to offer her a place to live while she finds an apartment of her own."

Joe had proposed to Jenny Thomas a month ago. Ben had never seen him happier. He buried a sigh. He needed to meet the right woman and settle down. The memory of McKenzie cut through him.

He maneuvered into the left lane and turned at the next intersection. Police cars with flashing lights surrounded the streets ahead. His pulse quickened. "I'll bet there's been a major traffic accident because of the weather. I'll park on the next street over, then we can come back to see if anyone needs help."

Moments later, they ducked under the cordon with ID badges open. He recognized Pete Sanders of the Metropolitan Police Department and headed toward him.

"What happened, Pete?"

"A hostage situation in a jewelry store. Four civilians—we assume the two owners along with two shoppers—are inside." Pete worked his jaw. "A passerby saw a man holding a gun against a woman's head."

"Kate," Joe whispered.

Ben turned to Joe. "What?"

Joe jerked his arm toward the television station's SUV visible in the next block. "One of the civilians inside the store is Kate." He raised his voice with each word. "She had an interview scheduled with the Shanes. That's why we planned to meet at the restaurant down the street." He started to move. "She's in there. I'm going to get her out."

"Easy, buddy." Ben grabbed Joe's arm.

Pete stood squarely in front of them. "You're not going anywhere unless I tell you. You guys might be FBI, but this is my jurisdiction. Until I receive orders from higher up, I call the shots. A negotiator, John Wilkins, is in communication with the suspect. He'll try to get hostages out in exchange for food, transportation, whatever else we can bargain with. If the plan doesn't work, our SWAT team is ready."

Joe sucked in a breath and paced a few steps away, his fists clenched. Ben gave him space. While Pete turned to confer with another officer, Ben stepped back to survey the area.

He'd grown up in DC. His family had shopped in many of the stores along this street. The jewelry store had seemed larger years ago—things always appeared bigger when you were a kid.

He studied the antique shop housed in the same building. The antique shop hadn't always been there.

Had it? Regardless, maybe an inside door joined the two stores.

He walked over to Pete. "Any access between the two shops?"

Pete shook his head and motioned to Joe. "Come inside."

The antique shop teemed with police officers who'd turned the store into a makeshift command center.

"The jewelry shop originally took up this entire building until the Shanes scaled back about fifteen years ago," Pete continued. "As you can see, the owner of the building put up a dividing wall to separate the two shops. He left no adjoining doors."

An officer hurried over to them. Ben caught the urgency in his face. "Sorry to interrupt, sir. Wilkins is ready to make another call."

❧

Minutes had dragged into an hour, then two. Kate changed positions. Her shoulders ached and she longed to stand. She glanced sideways, past a rigid Sophie, to Levi and Nelda. Her heart ached for them. Thirty wonderful years in business shouldn't end this way.

A clock sat on the shelf behind Angelo. *A few minutes past one. Joe will wonder why I'm not at the restaurant.*

Her pulse quickened. He would know exactly where she was. Police surrounded the shop, and her station's vehicle sat on the street. She squeezed her eyes shut. Her brother wouldn't hesitate to storm through the door to rescue her.

The phone blasted.

Angelo jerked the receiver to his ear. "What do you want?" His foot tapped as he listened. "What kind of deal?" Distrust edged his tone.

Kate leaned forward. If only she could hear the voice on the other end of the conversation.

"Only one." Angelo ended the call.

Kate stilled as he stared at them. He pointed his gun first at Levi and Nelda, then Sophie, then her. He trained the weapon a second longer on her, then moved the gun back to Levi.

"You. Get up."

Levi didn't move.

"Can't you hear, old man? You're going out in exchange for food."

"No. My wife is going out instead."

"You do what I say." Angelo flung his stool toward the sofa. Kate raised her arms to shield the couple. She winced at the impact.

"Levi, please," Nelda pleaded.

Determination etched Levi's face. "No."

Kate sucked in a breath. "As long as someone goes out, you'll get food."

Angelo's gaze swept over them. He pointed his gun at Nelda. "If you try anything stupid, I'll kill your husband. Go."

Kate slowly exhaled. Nelda rose with a stifled sob, her agony palpable as she left Levi. Kate strained to see the door. Nelda stumbled on her way out, but arms swept her to safety. Two boxes were shoved inside before the door clicked shut.

"Get the food." Angelo pointed his gun at Kate.

She pulled herself up and eased to the front room, sidestepping broken glass. The smell of pizza wafted from the boxes. A wave of nausea rolled over her.

She almost dove for the door, but the thought of Levi and Sophie stopped her. When she reached the office, Angelo jerked the boxes from her.

Kate sank onto the sofa. While Angelo devoured the pizza, Sophie slowly turned to Kate. *"Hide this,"* she mouthed. She pressed something into Kate's hand.

Sophie turned back to a preoccupied Angelo, and Kate's hand closed over the object. A ring?

Kate glanced at Sophie's profile. Seriously? Couldn't she see there was more at stake than keeping her jewelry safe? Biting her lip, Kate slid the ring between the sofa cushions.

Angelo belched and swiped a sleeve across his mouth. He settled back onto the stool, his gaze fixed on the floor.

Kate swallowed hard. How much longer would this go on? Her thoughts muddled as she tried to think of an escape plan. Surely the police were formulating strategies. Would they rush in with guns and flash grenades? The chances of someone being hit would likely increase.

She licked her dry lips. Angelo had mentioned a boss. Had his boss hired him to rob the jewelry store or had Angelo acted on his own?

Gavin. The thought slammed her senses. Was he somehow behind this? Though Joe kept close watch on him through contacts at the Bureau, Gavin's threats to destroy her career, to destroy *her,* still haunted Kate. She squelched the panic. *Lord, help me think clearly.*

"Why are you stealing the jewelry?"

Kate started at Levi's question. Angelo scowled, silent.

"You don't know why?" Levi pressed.

"I need money." Hate laced Angelo's voice. "You can't understand, can you? You—with your fancy shop filled with gold and diamonds. You never went to bed with your gut hurting because you were hungry or had to listen to your baby sister cry because she was cold."

Levi's shoulders squared. "I did go to bed hungry as a young boy. My parents were immigrants. We had very little money."

"Then how'd you get all this?" Angelo gestured around the shop.

"When I came to this country, I swept floors and emptied garbage. I took whatever job I could find to earn money. Even today, I struggle when business is slow, but I work hard."

Angelo cursed. "Man, are you blind? Nobody wants you when you live on the streets." He fingered his weapon. "When somebody offers you the chance to make money, you take the job no matter what you have to do."

"Your boss is using you to do his dirty work. He'll sell the jewelry, then disappear while you go to prison. I have a friend who owns a construction company. He needs a worker. I'll help you get the job, because I do remember being hungry. I also remember how desperation feels."

Levi's compassion pierced Kate's heart. She glanced up at Angelo. Pain etched his features.

"Too late." Heaviness penetrated the young man's voice. "And I'm not going to prison. I'll die first."

His words chilled Kate to her very core. *Lord,* she breathed, *help us.*

❈

Ben rubbed his eyes. He needed aspirin. He glanced up from one of the command center computers. Though Nelda had given a description of the suspect, whom she'd referred to as Angelo, along with every bit of information she could recall, he'd found no matches from their database.

He checked his watch. Four o'clock. He hated this waiting game.

Nelda sat by the window, wrapped in a blanket the paramedics had left after they'd checked her. The older woman's help had been invaluable. She'd given details about the suspect, along with the position of the other hostages, the layout of the shop, and the location of the store's security cameras. She'd answered every question they asked with a poise Ben admired. Now she simply stared out of the window, anguish buckling her features.

He pushed back his chair and stepped over to a corner table laden with sandwiches and coffee. He poured the steaming liquid into a foam cup, snagged sugar packets and creamer.

"Coffee, Mrs. Shane?"

She seemed to gather herself. "Thank you." Smiling at him, she wrapped her hands around the cup. "Plain is fine. What did you say your name is?"

"Ben."

"I guess you're accustomed to this kind of thing, Ben, but I'm not." She sipped her coffee. "Do you think my husband and the others will get out of this alive?"

He hesitated an instant. How much assurance could he offer? "Our police department is one of the finest."

She nodded, as if accepting the words left unspoken.

"Ben, come over here." Joe motioned him to the other side of the shop. The look on his partner's face indicated the news wasn't good.

Ben nodded to Mrs. Shane. "Excuse me, ma'am." He strode over to Joe, Pete, and John Wilkins. "What's happened?"

"The suspect stopped communicating." John shook his head. "He has a short fuse, and we have nothing to work with."

Pete rubbed the bridge of his nose. "Then the SWAT team will go in. The time for negotiations is over."

Joe's eyes flashed. "The suspect is in the office. The back entrance is down a separate hall. With the security cameras, he has a clear line of sight to both the back and front doors. He'd have time to kill the hostages before the flash grenades ever reach him. One of those hostages is my sister." The last word ended with a finger jab at the man in charge.

Pete glared at Joe. "I'm sorry your sister is in there. We have no other options."

Ben turned toward the wall separating the two shops. If only there was a way through. An idea sparked.

Ben spun around to Pete. "Get the blueprints of the building. There might be another option after all."

❁

Pushing himself with his elbows and knees, Ben crawled through the overhead heating duct. Ugh. He hated tight spaces. The cumbersome Kevlar vest he wore didn't help. He paused by a vent and peered down. Almost over the jewelry store.

He strained to see ahead. A second duct should intersect in a few yards. He slid forward, thankful for the vents letting in light from below.

His nose burned and he buried his head against his arm to stifle the sneeze. The ducts had obviously not been cleaned for years, but they provided a way in. The blueprints had confirmed when the wall was built, the heating and air system had been left undisturbed and spanned both shops. He'd finally convinced Pete to give his plan a chance.

A moment later, Ben reached the second duct. He slid toward the next vent. At last. "Joe, I'm over the display cases," he whispered into his microphone.

"Roger that," Joe replied. "I'm starting in behind you. I should be able to crawl through the first duct to the office in about five minutes."

Ben pulled himself to the end of the duct and checked his position. He shifted over to the rectangular grid holding the filter. Bingo. He let out a long breath. The grid measured roughly two-and-a-half by three feet—enough space for him to squeeze through and drop into the corner of the jewelry shop's front room.

He eased the filter aside, then tugged a screwdriver and small flashlight from his pocket. Clenching the flashlight with his teeth, he turned the screwdriver to release the first screw holding the grid in place. After a few sharp twists, he removed the rusted screw. He moved to the next one.

He shifted his body. His muscles cramped with the tedious task. He flexed his fingers and continued.

Was Joe over the office yet? He'd be their eyes, with his gun trained on the suspect during the operation.

Ben placed the screwdriver against the last screw. The metal refused to budge.

Great. He fumbled in his pocket for the tiny canister of oil he'd brought. He squeezed a few drops over the screw and tried again. Nothing.

He emptied the remainder of the small canister, gripped the screwdriver, and turned. Still nothing. If he forced the grid off, he'd risk being heard. He drew a sharp breath. He'd come this far. One more try ...

He grasped the screwdriver and twisted with all his strength. The screw moved.

Thank you, Lord. After several more turns, he edged the grid aside and studied the shop below. The office door stood diagonally across from him. A solid wall separated the office from the display area, just as Nelda had described.

Seconds later, Pete's voice sounded in his earpiece. "Ben, are you in place?"

"Ready."

"Joe, are you above the office?"

"Roger," came Joe's muffled voice.

"Wilkins will call the suspect in one minute," Pete continued. "If the distraction doesn't work and you run into trouble, just say the word. The SWAT team will take over."

"Copy." Ben rehearsed his course of action while seconds blinked on the lighted face of his watch. Would the hostages still be seated on the sofa? As long as there was distance between them and the suspect, he and Joe would have a clear line of fire.

His muscles tightened. Fifty-seven seconds ... Fifty-eight, fifty-nine ...

The phone pealed. He dropped to the floor and gripped his weapon.

Seconds passed. Angelo didn't answer the call.

Plan B. Ben crawled toward the office door. Joe would give the signal.

"Ben, take cover."

Joe's urgent whisper registered. Ben dove behind the closest display case. Voices sounded.

"It will be dark soon. Then I'm leaving. The three of you are coming with me."

Ben moved slightly to see around the case. Angelo pointed a gun at the hostages.

"Angelo, you need to rethink your plan."

Ben glimpsed a profile. The resemblance was plain. Joe's sister Kate.

"Even if they give you a car," she continued, "they'll follow you and eventually catch you. Don't throw your whole life away. Things will go easier for you if you turn yourself in now."

"I'm not going to prison." The agitation in Angelo's voice resonated. "Get into the office."

Back to square one. If Angelo separated himself from the hostages, he and Joe could revert to the original plan. Ben lowered his head. "Joe, what are the positions?"

He strained to hear the barely audible response.

"Civilians on sofa. Suspect three yards away."

Ben's muscles tightened. "Pete, tell Wilkins to make another call," he whispered into his microphone.

An instant later, the phone rang.

"Suspect's turned away from the door." Joe's terse whisper filtered through Ben's earpiece. "Move."

Ben sprang into the room with his gun trained on Angelo's back. "FBI—drop your weapon."

Angelo's arm flinched.

"Don't, Angelo. Drop the gun or you're a dead man."

Ben locked his eyes on the suspect. His instincts screamed the warning that Angelo would spin around to face him at any instant.

A second passed. Then another.

Ben eased a step closer. "Drop the gun, Angelo."

Another step.

Suddenly a cry of pure agony spewed from Angelo, his back still toward Ben. "Kill me! What are you waiting for?"

"Nobody has to die, Angelo."

"Kill me. If you don't, they will."

"Drop the weapon."

Angelo pivoted. Ben closed his hand around Angelo's gun and ripped the weapon from his grasp.

Angelo fell to his knees. Sobs wracked his body.

"Suspect disarmed," Ben barked into his microphone.

A team of police officers jammed into the jewelry store and surrounded Angelo. Joe kicked the grid away above them and dropped to the floor. He flashed a thumbs-up to Ben as he sprinted to his sister.

Ben slumped against a desk and exhaled a long breath. Everyone alive. An act of God. The truth of the reality washed over him, and he whispered a prayer of thanks.

Joe wrapped Kate in a long hug. When she pulled away, she smiled at her brother, her dark eyes radiating warmth.

She turned to Ben. His breath hitched. Her smile could stop a guy's heart.

She rushed over and threw her arms around him. "Thank you so much for saving us." Her touch sizzled through him. She stepped back, color tinging her cheeks. "I'm sorry. I don't usually—"

Joe stepped up and draped an arm around her shoulders. "Ben, my sister Kate. She's right—she normally doesn't tackle someone until *after* she's been introduced."

Kate elbowed Joe. "I'm happy to meet you, Ben. Anyway, I just wanted to thank you." She sobered. "You and Joe risked your lives for us."

Ben met her gaze. "Your lives were worth the risk."

Something stirred in her eyes. Before he could say more, Pete Sanders wove his way through the maze of law enforcement personnel.

"Good job, guys. We couldn't have had a better outcome."

Ben frowned inwardly. *Go away, Pete.*

He handed papers to Ben. "I have reports for you and Joe to fill out." He turned to Kate. "The paramedics are here to check you and the other hostages, ma'am."

Kate nodded and moved away. Ben sighed. Since he worked with her brother, at least he could find her again.

He *needed* to find her again. Because for the first time in two years, the wall he'd built around his heart had just cracked.

❈

Kate sipped the sweetened tea Joe had bought for her. She'd been starved earlier. Now she couldn't eat. She rubbed her forehead to ease the throbbing in her head. Only a few more minutes before they reached WOTN.

"You'll be a celebrity at the station. Think you can handle your new-found fame?"

Worry simmered beneath Joe's lighthearted question. A crew from WOTN, along with every station in town, had camped out behind barricades during the crisis at the jewelry store. Thankfully, they'd given her space when she'd left the shop surrounded by police presence, but the interview requests would come.

"I'm fine, Joe. Really." *Not. But he doesn't need to know.*

"By the way, Kate, I decided I wouldn't take chances." Joe paused a beat. "I contacted my friend at the Cleveland office. He's tracking Gavin. Your ex has been flying under the radar lately, but there's no evidence he's anywhere in this area. My friend will let me know when he finds something."

"When Angelo mentioned having a boss, my thoughts went to Gavin." Kate exhaled a long breath. "Have I told you how glad I am you're my big brother?"

"Not since we pulled out of the fast-food drive-through—about three minutes ago."

Kate tried to laugh. Only a squeak sounded. "I'd better step things up, then." She swallowed hard. "I'm proud of you, Joe. You cope with danger every day … robberies, hostage situations, bullets—"

"I didn't have to worry about bullets today. Who needs a Kevlar vest when you have a heating duct around you?"

Kate swiped the moisture on her cheeks. "Good thing you're not claustrophobic. I never would have gotten more than a few feet inside."

"Didn't have time to think about the tight space. I had to get my sister out of trouble."

"You've always come to my rescue. Remember when you took all of us kids camping, and I got lost looking for chipmunks? I was terrified until you found me."

"So was I. I kept thinking about what Mom and Dad would do to me if I came back without you."

"Then years later, when Will dared me to drive before I had my license and I took the car on the dirt road behind our house—"

"Which would have been smart for an inexperienced driver such as yourself, except for the fact there had been a torrential downpour a few hours before." Joe laughed. "I thought I never would get the tires out of those ruts."

Kate strained to see his face in the dark. "Do you think Mom and Dad ever found out?"

"If they did, they didn't hear the story from me." He paused. "Speaking of Mom and Dad, would you like for me to call them?"

Kate caught her breath. "Do you think they've heard? They'll be frantic with worry. Maybe I haven't made the news in Kansas yet."

"Probably not," he replied, clearly trying to reassure her.

She groaned as another thought occurred to her. "What about Ann?" Their youngest sister had recently enrolled at George Mason University in nearby Fairfax, Virginia.

"Knowing Ann, I imagine she's too busy studying to catch the news, but I'll call her, too."

Joe pulled into the station's parking garage. Kate directed him to her parking spot. "Thanks for driving the station's vehicle back. If I hadn't ridden the Metro this morning, Jenny wouldn't have had to come out in this awful weather to take us home."

"She just completed her shift at the hospital, so everything worked out fine."

Kate heard the smile in his voice. "I'm so happy for you, Joe."

"Thanks. She's an amazing woman."

Moments later, they entered the newsroom. "I just need to turn in the keys——"

Before she could finish her sentence, someone called "Kate's here!" Heads popped up from cubicles. In a matter of seconds, members of her team not on location crowded around her.

"Are you okay?" Ellen Taylor, a photographer, hugged her. "I was so worried about you."

"If the FBI hadn't shown up, I'd have gotten you out." Mitch Bryant, a reporter, looked down at her as he flexed his muscles.

Kate almost laughed. Her brother stood behind her. If only she could see the look on Joe's face.

Even Alex White, a producer with an attitude problem, softened his "You're supposed to report the news, not make the news" with a genuine smile.

Their concern touched her. The news director, Vince Carson, joined them. Kate introduced Joe.

"You've had a long day, Kate." Vince reached out to hug her. "Actually, we've all had a long day. I'll bet our ratings are up—you were our breaking news." His tired grin faded, and his voice turned serious. "We're glad you're safe. You need time to recover, so I want you to take a couple of days off. Mitch will continue the story on Shanes' Jewelers. Be ready to work when you come back, though. We just got word a princess from Liechtenstein will arrive in a couple of days to study at Georgetown. Alex wants you to do a series on her visit here." He shrugged as he turned toward his office. "I guess an interview with a princess will be tame compared with today."

Kate swallowed hard. *Let's hope so.*

Joe's cell phone buzzed. He stepped away to answer the call. While the rest of the team scattered to their desks, Kate ambled over to an empty chair. Might as well check her messages while she and Joe waited for Jenny.

She scrolled down missed calls, texts, and emails. She noticed one voicemail which had been left only a few minutes ago. She touched the number to retrieve the message.

"Hi, Kate. This is Sophie."

Sophie? Kate leaned forward. Sophie had asked for Kate's number before they'd left the jewelry store this evening.

"I ... I need to talk to someone," the message continued. "I have no one I can—" A door slammed on the recording. Sophie's voice dropped to a whisper. "I'll call you later. Don't try to phone me."

Kate frowned. Sophie's voice contained a note of desperation. Why? They were safe now. Sophie even had her ring back. Leaning her head back against the wall, Kate closed her eyes. Maybe Sophie just needed someone to help her process what had happened today.

Still, something about the slam of the door and Sophie's whisper troubled Kate, and she couldn't push away the puzzling call.

CHAPTER 3

Frederick Wilson jogged on the treadmill, streams of perspiration dripping down his face. "I'll be with you in four minutes."

Ben loosened his tie and joined Joe on a wooden bench against the wall. The odor of sweat hung in the humid air. Too bad he hadn't worn workout clothes.

Joe shrugged off his jacket. "Wilson's assistant failed to mention we'd be conducting our meeting with the president of Caldwell Research Institute in the basement gym."

Ben studied the equipment, most of which was in use. "Looks like a state-of-the-art facility. Except for the ventilation system."

"No kidding. I guess we'll *smell* like we worked out." Joe leaned back against the cinder block wall. "Kate's apartment building—really, Aunt Martha's apartment building—has a gym. There aren't as many machines, so the gym is always crowded. Kate told me her prime workout time is ten at night."

Ben rubbed sweaty palms against his khakis. The perfect opening. "I enjoyed meeting Kate last night even though the circumstances left a lot to be desired." He'd just made the understatement of the year and managed to sound casual while he did. He glanced sideways at Joe and caught a look of amusement mixed with ... caution? Aggravation?

"I knew this was coming," Joe muttered. He sighed as he turned to Ben. "I saw the way you looked when I introduced you. You're my best friend, and I think you'd be good for Kate. She needs somebody like you. But she's my sister, so if you hurt her, I'll pound your head. Are we clear?"

"Crystal." Ben blew out a breath. He'd just jumped the first hurdle. Now, if only he could get Kate to agree to see him. He pulled out his phone and couldn't stop his grin. "By the way, what's her number?"

Joe shook his head. "I'll text her number to you. I have a feeling you're not going to waste any time."

"Got that right."

"Well, Romeo, try to get your head back in the game. Frederick Wilson just finished his workout."

Ben flicked his gaze to Wilson. The man mopped his face with a towel and tilted a black water bottle against his lips. He appeared to be in his forties, and struck Ben as someone who refused to be hurried. Or was he simply adept at stall tactics?

A moment later, Wilson snagged his gym bag and headed toward them. He sank onto the seat of a weight bench in front of them, a thin line etching his brow. "Sorry to keep you waiting. I've been in Europe on business—just arrived home last night. I'm afraid I can't give you much time. I need to shower and leave by eight to make my next meeting."

"We'll be brief," Ben said. "We'd like to ask you a few questions concerning your research exchange project with the country of Liechtenstein."

"Ah, yes." A smile spread across Wilson's face. "I'm excited about the exchange. We've worked for months to prepare for this program. We're close to the implementation." He gestured to a door behind them. "If you don't object, we can use the vacant office next to the gym."

Once they were seated inside the office, Joe flipped open a small notebook. "How many of your employees are involved in the project?"

Wilson clasped his fingers as he studied the ceiling. "CRI employs forty-five research analysts. The Liechtenstein program involves only twenty-six."

Ben leaned forward. "How would you describe the general feeling among the analysts concerning the exchange?"

Wilson thought for a moment. "Enthusiastic, with a true sense of accomplishment. They've worked long hours to see this project come to fruition."

"Can you think of anyone who might object to the project? Ever hear any negative comments?" Ben pressed.

"Never." Wilson's affable expression altered. "Maybe you should tell me what this is all about."

Joe shifted in his chair. "Are you aware the ambassador of Liechtenstein received a message—a threat, actually—discouraging the exchange?"

Wilson's eyes widened. "I was not."

"Ambassador Schrader found the message in her program after attending a lecture at the institute three days ago," Joe continued. "She told us she's been unable to reach you."

"As I said, I've been out of the country. The work required my full attention. I have a number of calls and emails to return."

Ben studied Wilson. "With the threat directed to a foreign dignitary who is a guest in our country, this issue is serious and sensitive. We'll need the files of all employees who've worked on this project."

"Of course." Wilson rummaged through his gym bag and pulled out a cell phone. "I'll inform my administrative assistant so she can access the files." After a brief conversation, he turned back to them. Uncertainty flickered over his face. "In light of what you've told me, I feel I should mention that one of our employees who worked on the project, Ethan Fitzgerald, is ... missing."

Ben frowned. "Missing?"

"He hasn't called or come to work for the past two weeks, which is highly unusual for Ethan. He's a very conscientious, if introverted, employee."

"Have you reported this to the authorities?"

"We contacted a cousin. As far as we know, she's his only relative. She said he'd told her he needed to sort things out and planned to take some time off. Though he does have a month of vacation, to take time without approval is highly irregular. If he does come back, I'm not sure his job will be waiting. You'll find his cousin's name and address in the file you'll receive."

As they stood, Wilson gestured toward the hallway. "My assistant's office is located on the third floor. If you'll give her your email information, she'll send the files to you shortly. Let me know if there's anything more I can do."

Ben nodded. "Thank you. We'll be in contact."

Ben and Joe left the office, bypassed the elevator, and climbed the stairs to the third floor.

"Twenty-six employees involved in the exchange," Joe mused. "Well, actually, twenty-five employees and one MIA. What do you think is going on in Ethan Fitzgerald's life?"

"Only one person can give us the answer." Ben blew out a breath. "I just hope we'll be able to find him to ask."

JANUARY 21
TUESDAY, 9:42 A.M.
N TROY STREET, ARLINGTON, VA

Kate rubbed her eyes and shoved a strand of hair out of her face. Why was the room so bright? She squinted to bring the numbers on the alarm clock into focus. When the time registered, panic erupted.

She threw back the covers. Her hand hit the bedside table and the lamp clattered to the floor. As she jumped out of bed to scoop up the lamp, Vince's words from last night played somewhere in the fog of her brain.

Take a couple of days off.

She groaned and sank back onto the bed. What a way to wake up. Especially since she'd tossed and turned most of the night, her sleep plagued by disturbing dreams.

Movement from the closet caught her eye. Three of Aunt Martha's five cats peered at her, tails swishing and eyes enormous. She couldn't help but chuckle. "Sorry, girls. I didn't mean to startle you."

She bent and held out her hand. Lucy, the eldest, padded over and seemed to weigh the offer of friendship before rubbing her face against Kate's hand. Cleopatra, a beautiful Persian, kept her distance and meowed. Emmy, the little orange tabby, yawned as if she hoped everyone would go back to sleep.

"Good kittens." Kate returned Emmy's yawn. "Go find Ginger and Snap. I have to get up now."

Kate pulled her robe on over her pajamas and peeked into the living room. She certainly didn't want to parade through in her pajamas if Aunt Martha had company. *Coast is clear.*

Moments later, she wandered into the kitchen to find her host seated at the table, her head bent over her Bible. When Aunt Martha spied Kate hovering in the doorway, she popped up and hurried over to envelope Kate in a hug.

"You had quite a day yesterday."

Kate nodded. "Not one I'd care to repeat anytime soon."

"I'm sure you wouldn't. Now, you sit down while I cook breakfast. How about a bacon and cheese omelet, and waffles with strawberries?"

"An omelet and waffles sound delicious," Kate began, "but you don't need to—"

Aunt Martha held up her hands. "No arguments—I love to cook." She tilted her head to one side and grinned. "Well, maybe I don't love to cook, but I love to feed people. Especially my family."

Kate's heart warmed. As Joe's sister, Aunt Martha included Kate in her circle of family. Aunt Martha had been wonderful to her over the past four weeks. Kate had stayed longer than she'd intended. Finding an affordable apartment had been a challenge.

They chatted while Aunt Martha cooked and Kate set the table. A short time later, Aunt Martha sipped tea while Kate piled strawberries on a golden waffle.

"I'm glad you came to DC. I've wanted to get acquainted with both you and your sister Ann. Joe's very proud of you, you know."

Kate spoke around a mouthful of berries. "He's the one who encouraged me to move here."

"Have you found your job to be everything you'd hoped?"

Kate reflected on the question. "To be honest, the answer depends on the day. DC is a larger market than Cleveland, so the pace is a little faster and the competition keener."

"A new job always requires a period of adjustment. I feel certain you've made a good move."

"I *hope* I've made the right move. I prayed for God's guidance. This job seemed perfect. I love living near Joe and Ann, and I'm excited to get to know you and Jenny better. Yet ..." Kate struggled to find the words.

"Something isn't quite right?"

"I've learned over this past month you don't leave your struggles behind when you move to a new location. The biggest reason I wanted to leave Cleveland wasn't my job. I left because the man I thought I would marry turned out to be someone I didn't really know. I felt betrayed, vulnerable—and incredibly stupid. I thought a move to a new place would change things. Unfortunately, those feelings followed."

Aunt Martha leaned across the table and squeezed her hand. "I'm sorry, Kate. The pain of a broken heart sometimes feels unbearable, but God wants to put the pieces back together."

"The process is hard."

"I have to agree. Even at my age—" She stopped, a grin spreading across her face. "which I *refuse* to tell—I still struggle. However, I see God's faithfulness in the fight."

"Thank you for your encouragement, and for everything you've done for me."

"I've enjoyed having you here, Kate." She poured another cup of tea. "I wanted to speak with you about an email I received last night. My dear friend from college, Frances Devereaux, had planned to move here with me after an extended visit with her children. According to the email she sent, she's decided to live with her daughter instead." The disappointment in Aunt Martha's voice was plain.

"I'm sorry. I know you were excited about her coming."

"Yes, I was, but I believe this is for the best. Frances has been through a very difficult time with the arrest of her husband. She was devastated to learn he was using her art gallery to cover his terrorist activities. She needs her children now. I'm glad she'll be with them." Aunt Martha brightened. "On the positive side, you can finally take a break from apartment-hunting."

Kate opened her mouth to protest, but Aunt Martha continued. "I'd love for you to stay here, Kate. There's plenty of room, and you can concentrate on your job without the stress of finding a place to live."

Kate contemplated Aunt Martha's generous offer. Though she'd spent every spare moment searching for an apartment, she'd found nothing even close to her budget. Moving in with her sister or brother wasn't feasible. Ann lived in a dorm, and Joe's small apartment had only one bedroom. Of course, she would insist on paying rent, and her furniture could be stored. Kate hopped up from the table to hug Aunt Martha. While they chatted over details, a weight lifted from Kate's shoulders.

The doorbell chime floated through the apartment. Aunt Martha hurried into the living room.

"Come in, Jenny." Aunt Martha's voice reached the kitchen. "I'm so glad to see you."

Kate looked down at her pajamas and cringed. What would her future sister-in-law think? Oh, well. Jenny would know what her new family was really like before the wedding. Kate put her dishes into the dishwasher and strolled into the living room to greet Jenny.

"Hi, Kate." Jenny flashed a radiant smile and held up her iPad. "I've picked out the bridesmaids' dresses. Come and see!"

Kate shooed Ginger and Snap off the sofa, then sat beside Jenny to study the pictures. "I love the color. Such a beautiful shade of blue."

"So stylish," Aunt Martha added.

Jenny enlarged the picture. "I think they'll look great on everyone."

Her happiness bubbled over. Kate smiled. Jenny deserved to be happy. Two months ago, terrorists had kidnapped her. Jenny had worked hard to put the ordeal behind her.

Aunt Martha tapped her forehead. "Let's see, who's in the wedding party again?"

"Joe's sisters—Kate, Ann, Christy, and Rachel, and my roommate Kelly. Kelly will be the maid-of-honor. Our brothers—Chase, Tom, Will, and Sam—will be the groomsmen."

"And the best man?"

"Ben."

Hearing his name, Kate's thoughts drifted again to the handsome man who had burst into the jewelry store office last night to rescue her. *Your lives were worth the risk.* His words echoed in welcome contrast to those Gavin had shouted when he'd ended their relationship. To Gavin, she was worth nothing at all because she refused to use her media contacts to cast false allegations on his business competitor. How had she not seen through him? She shoved away the frustration and turned her attention back to the conversation.

"April will be a beautiful time for a wedding." Aunt Martha beamed.

"Remember the Greens? They've offered their home on the lake for the wedding. We'll be married outside, just as I've always hoped."

"Perfect," Aunt Martha exclaimed. She turned to Kate. "Mary and Scott are landscape architects. The grounds of their home are immaculate. With the sparkling lake—what a wonderful setting."

Kate propped a pillow behind her back. Sharing in Jenny and Joe's happiness was just what she needed.

"I've always thought an outdoor wedding would be so romantic. After the ceremony, a light shower would float over, and all the couples would dance in the rain. I don't know where I got the idea—an old movie, maybe?"

Jenny shook her head. "I can't think of … wait, would *Singing in the Rain* work?"

Kate chuckled. "There would be nothing romantic about singing in the rain if I were the one singing."

While they talked over more wedding plans, the picture of a dance in the rain played across Kate's mind again. She wore a beautiful dress, and her partner was tall and handsome. She grinned inwardly. In his day job, he even rescued hostages from jewelry stores.

JANUARY 21
TUESDAY, 10:57 A.M.
ALEXANDRIA, VA

The brown lab dropped a worn tennis ball at Ben's feet and wagged his whole body. Ben hurled the soggy ball to a line of trees across the park. The dog stretched to his full length, powerful muscles propelling him forward. A wave of nostalgia hit. *I need a dog.*

Joe laughed. "Look at him go."

Charlotte Fitzgerald nodded. "Gibbs loves nothing better than chasing a ball."

Ben turned to her. "How long have you owned him, Ms. Fitzgerald?"

"Almost a year. Please, call me Charlotte. Ethan found Gibbs wandering around a grocery store parking lot." The dog trotted back, ball clenched between his teeth, his breath visible in the cold air.

They stopped beside a park bench. "When was the last time you spoke with your cousin?"

"A little over two weeks ago. Ethan told me he planned to take some time off from work to sort out some things. I didn't realize he meant immediately until his office called." She dropped to the bench and ruffled Gibbs's fur. "Why are you here? Surely a well-earned vacation is not a federal offense, even if the dates weren't approved."

"We need to ask your cousin some questions about a work-related matter." Ben kept his voice even.

"We plan to interview other CRI employees as well," Joe added. "Do you have any idea where we might find Ethan?"

"Unfortunately, no." She twisted Gibbs's leash around her fingers. "I don't know where he is."

Ben shifted his weight. "Does he normally leave without telling you where he's going?"

"Not usually. He did go camping several years ago without telling me. He was gone for almost a month—I have no idea where."

Ben pulled out a business card from his wallet. "If you think of anything or hear from him, please call us." He patted Gibbs. "By the way, any idea what he needed to sort out?"

She lowered her eyes. "No." She snapped on Gibbs's leash, waved goodbye, and broke into a jog.

Ben studied her. They'd learned at least one thing.

Charlotte Fitzgerald wasn't a good liar.

JANUARY 21
TUESDAY, 4:24 P.M.
STARBUCKS, DC

Kate unsnapped the lid from her Grande Americano and inhaled the rich aromas surrounding her. She could just sit at a Starbucks and breathe in the soothing smells even if she didn't drink coffee. After yesterday, soothing was a good thing.

Sophie O'Reilly had called earlier in the afternoon and asked to meet. Though her voice sounded calmer than last night, a note of urgency filtered through their conversation.

Kate glanced around at the customers filling every table. Had the clatter and conversation of the coffee shop drowned out her ringtone? Sophie had definitely said four o'clock. Kate checked her phone. No "Missed Call" glowed on the screen. Perhaps traffic delayed her. If anybody was sympathetic to running late, Kate was.

The chime of Kate's phone interrupted her thoughts. The number wasn't familiar. Maybe Sophie was calling from a different phone.

"Hello?" A rousing chorus of "Happy Birthday" from the table next to hers swallowed up the caller's words. She clapped her hand over her ear. "Hello? I'm sorry—could you hold for just a moment?"

After the applause died down, she tried again. "Sophie, is this you?"

"No," a deep voice replied. "This is Ben Anderson."

Kate gulped in a breath. *Ben.* "Yes, how are you?"

"Actually, I'm mad at Joe. He didn't tell me today was your birthday."

She chuckled. "Today isn't my birthday. I'm at a Starbucks, and people were singing to a lady at the table next to mine."

"Oh, well, I guess your brother is off the hook, then." His light tone turned serious. "Kate, I wanted to check on you, see if you're recovering from your ordeal yesterday."

Was she? "I'm … not sure. I didn't sleep well last night. My boss gave me a couple of days off, though, so I think a break from work will help."

"These things take time. You endured a lot yesterday, but you fought through like a champ."

His words settled over her heart. Did he really mean them? She gave herself a mental shake. Time to stop viewing every compliment through the lens of her failed relationship with Gavin. "Thank you, Ben." Hopefully, he hadn't noticed the slight tremor in her voice.

Another burst of laughter and scraping of chairs sounded as the party at the table next to hers rose to leave. She strained to hear Ben's words.

"I won't keep you, but I wondered … may I call you again?"

Her heartbeat quickened. "I'd like that."

"Great." The pleasure in his voice warmed her. "I'll talk to you in a few days."

As they said goodbye, Kate's thoughts whirled. Did a few days mean three or four? Or two? Regardless, she would keep her phone charged and close at all times.

"Hi. Sorry I'm late."

Kate looked up into the troubled eyes of Sophie O'Reilly and smiled. "Trust me, I'm the last person you need to apologize to for being late."

Sophie plunked down her purse and keys, carefully settling her beverage on the table. "I tried to catch your attention while I was ordering my coffee. You were in deep conversation."

Kate pushed down the little wave of excitement lingering from Ben's call and focused on Sophie. She appeared close to Kate's own age, maybe a few years younger. Her hair and face were striking, though her perfectly applied makeup couldn't conceal the dark circles beneath her eyes. Lines furrowed her forehead.

"Thank you for meeting me here," Sophie said. "When I heard you were a TV reporter, I knew you'd be the perfect one."

Kate raised an eyebrow. "Perfect one?"

"Yes." Sophie leaned forward. "My uncle is in trouble. He owns the antique shop next to Levi and Nelda."

Kate thought back to Sophie's entrance into the jewelry store yesterday. *That's how she knew the Shanes' names.*

"After the police finally left my uncle's shop last night, I helped him get everything back in order. I was in the office when a man came in. He told my uncle his payment for the shop had increased and tried to collect the money on the spot. They argued for a long time. I called you while the man was still there. Business has been slow, and I'd already been thinking about ways to help." Her lips formed a tight line. "Uncle Max raised me. I'm not going to stand by and watch him go under without a fight. When the Shanes told me about your interview with them, I thought maybe you could do a story on my uncle—showcase his business to bring in customers."

Kate's brain bounced between the pros and cons of Sophie's request. Would her producer at WOTN consider a story on an antique shop newsworthy?

"I would have to get my producer's approval. I'm not sure he would okay the story." She smiled at Sophie to soften her words. "I was covering the Shanes' thirty years in business because our station's general manager is a friend of theirs."

"How about if you covered my uncle's shop in conjunction with the attempted robbery?"

"I'm no longer assigned to the Shanes' interview. I'm now *part* of the story rather than the reporter. I'd much rather be the reporter, by the way."

Sophie's shoulders sagged. "There must be some way to help my uncle. His isn't the only business struggling. The Shanes, along with the dress shop and card shop in the next building, are all fighting to stay afloat. The situation is sad. All four of those shops have been in business for years. They're part of the history of this neighborhood."

"Small businesses have definitely taken a hit in today's economy." Kate sipped her coffee. "Maybe I could interest my producer in a series on the plight of local small businesses."

"If that doesn't work, I did have another idea for a story." Sophie reached into her purse and set a ring on the table in front of Kate. "This is the ring I asked you to hide yesterday at the jewelry store. I brought the ring to the shop to get an appraisal from Levi." She shuddered. "I was terrified Angelo would see."

Kate studied the gold ring. "How impressive. The etched band looks like something a man would wear. The design seems to be a crest of some sort, inlaid with … diamonds?"

"I need to check with Levi. I believe the stones are diamonds."

"My grandmother loved genealogies and family coats-of-arms. This design reminds me of some of her pictures. I wonder if this is someone's family history." Someone's past. The thought intrigued her. Grandma Peterson, with her own roots sunk deep into the rich soil of their Kansas family farm, had instilled a love of family lineage in Kate years ago. History meant something. Kate returned the ring to Sophie. "Is your uncle buying the piece for his shop?"

Sophie shook her head. "We found the ring on the floor one night when we closed. The ring was underneath a counter and rolled out when I was sweeping." She zipped the band into a compartment of her purse. "I told Uncle Max he should sell the ring and use the money for the rent. He thinks selling the ring without trying to find the owner would be dishonest. I guess he's right, but the money sure would help."

"No one has come back to the shop to claim the ring?"

"No. We believe the piece was lost over the last few days, though, because I clean the floors every week." Her green eyes warmed. "I thought this would make a good human-interest story—you know, how my uncle is honest and wants to find the owner. Obviously, we could give a general description. Whoever comes to claim the ring would have to describe specific details."

"I like your idea. Even if my producer wanted something on the struggles of the business, I could weave the ring into the story."

Sophie clasped her hands together. "Really? Thank you, Kate. I'm sure this will help the shop, if nothing more than getting our name in front of the public."

Kate couldn't help grinning at Sophie's burst of enthusiasm. Of course, getting her producer to see things their way might take some convincing.

They chatted while they finished their coffee. Later, they said goodbye and headed in opposite directions. Kate pondered her presentation to her producer on the way to the parking garage. She waited for the light at the corner to blink "walk," then stepped into the street.

A blur of color and the squeal of tires snapped through her senses. She whirled around. Headlights and a metal grill sped toward her.

She propelled backward, landing on pavement as a *whoosh* of air rushed past. She gasped for breath. Black dots danced before her eyes.

"Get her to the curb." A female voice floated over her.

Strong arms pulled her, and her hands scraped asphalt. The black dots faded. Anxious faces of a middle-aged couple peered at her.

"Are you okay? Look, your hands are bleeding."

The woman pushed several crumpled tissues into Kate's throbbing palms. The couple helped her stand.

"I'm just glad you're still alive, little lady. My wife and I are from west Texas. We don't have wild drivers like the maniac who almost mowed you over." A couple of swear words punctuated his observation. "I wish I'd caught the idiot's license plate number. I saw him look straight at you as he got closer. He'd be sitting in jail if I had anything to say."

Kate's head swirled. She gathered herself. "Thank you for stopping to help me. I had a close call."

"We'll be glad to walk with you to your car," the lady offered.

"You're very kind, but my car is less than a block away." She gave a shaky laugh. "I should be fine if I can navigate the traffic this time."

She thanked the couple again and crossed the street, aware of their watchful eyes. She reached her car and sank into the driver's side.

Held hostage yesterday. Almost hit by a car today. She blew out a breath. It wasn't even Wednesday yet.

She gingerly wrapped her fingers around the steering wheel. She'd simply been in the wrong place at the wrong time. Twice. She shook her head and started the engine. What were the odds?

Once the thought crossed her mind, the idea wouldn't let go. Were the two incidents somehow related?

They couldn't be.

Could they?

CHAPTER 4

Kate strolled across the campus of Georgetown University. The days off from work had ended yesterday. Thankfully. She needed to get back to her job, to put distance between herself and the events at the jewelry store.

When you're thrown from a horse, get right back in the saddle. Her dad's words echoed across the years. She squared her shoulders. She would. Despite the troubling images still peppering her thoughts.

She checked the map on her phone. The Leavey Center wasn't too far ahead. Kate quickened her pace and turned her thoughts to the assignment. Who would have thought years ago, a farm girl from Kansas would someday interview the Princess of Liechtenstein? She couldn't wait to hear the reactions of her family when she told them. They'd love the idea, especially her youngest sister. Ann had loved all things royal ever since she was a little girl. When their family visited Europe one summer, Ann's dream was to glimpse a king or queen. She'd never succeeded, though she'd spent hours outside Buckingham Palace. *Maybe I can introduce her to Princess Ingrid.*

She'd have to be careful if she started introducing the princess to her family, though. Will and Sam, her twin brothers who were enrolled in medical school, would hound her to arrange dates for them. She shook her head. As if they weren't already competitive enough.

Moments later, Kate entered the Leavey Center and headed to the university bookstore. She chose a chair near the bookstore's entrance to wait for Princess Ingrid. This was a popular gathering spot if the number of students in the hallway and stores was any indication.

The students looked so young, or was she just old? Nine years of hard work had passed since her own college days. The thought sobered her.

She glanced at the photo of the princess she'd downloaded to her phone. Princess Ingrid stood next to her father, her dark hair and eyes matching his. Her long dress flowed around her, and she wore a crown. Definitely royal.

Kate pulled a notebook and pen from her purse. Her purpose today was to decide times for her series of interviews. Once she had definite dates, she'd program them into her phone's calendar. Princess Ingrid's secretary had been vague regarding the schedule of the princess. Kate grinned inwardly. Maybe she was the one being interviewed today.

Kate looked up and spotted a tall, dark-haired woman strolling her way. She carried herself with grace, but in jeans and sweatshirt, her hair pulled loosely back into a ponytail, she blended in with all the other students. Kate noted two men in dark sports coats following a few feet behind. A twinge of sympathy whisked through her. Always surrounded by security must be hard.

"Kate Peterson?"

Kate rose to her feet. "Yes. You must be Princess Ingrid."

The princess extended her hand. "A pleasure to meet you. Please, call me Ingrid. My assistant tells me your television station would like to conduct a series of interviews."

"We'd like to give our viewers a glimpse of your life at an American university—your goals, impressions of our nation's capital, your studies at Georgetown."

"Of course. I'd be delighted to speak with you."

Kate couldn't help smiling as they settled in chairs. "You've participated in interviews a few times before, I'd guess."

The slightly guarded look in Ingrid's eyes lessened. "My first interview took place at age two. I tried to eat the microphone." She tilted her head. "Don't worry, though. Now I always eat a snack before I speak with reporters."

Kate laughed. The princess possessed a sense of humor. This assignment could be fun.

They chatted a moment longer and compared schedules. They decided on three definite dates, with an extra penciled in as a backup. When an alarm on Princess Ingrid's phone sounded, she said goodbye and hurried to her next class, security trailing a few steps behind. No one waved or spoke while she wound her way through the maze of students. Had she made any friends? Or was she accustomed to being alone?

✤

Kate gathered her things and headed to the exit. Someone held the door. When she looked up to say thank you, her heart flipped. Ben Anderson smiled down at her.

"This is an unexpected pleasure, Kate. I'd planned to call you tonight. Seeing you is even better."

"Ben. Are you taking classes here?" Brilliant. He was an FBI agent, not a college student.

"No, I had a meeting. Just headed back to my car. I wouldn't mind being a student though." He chuckled. "Once you graduate and dive into the real world, you realize how good life in school really is."

They left the Leavy building and headed along the sidewalk. "I couldn't wait to graduate because I thought college was stressful. I quickly realized I didn't know the meaning of the word until I landed a job as a reporter." She looked up at him and decided the blue of his eyes matched the sky. No, they were a deeper blue. Maybe the color of the Mediterranean.

"What brings you to Georgetown today?" he asked.

"I'm doing a story on Princess Ingrid from Lichtenstein. I'm looking forward to the interviews. She seems very nice."

"I haven't met the princess, but I did meet the head of her security team."

"Is your unit part of her security detail?"

"Only on a consulting basis at this point."

Kate thought back to the two men with Princess Ingrid. "I think having people follow you everywhere would be a difficult way to live."

Ben nodded. "I guess you get used to the company, especially as a member of a royal family."

"Now that I think back, being the middle in a family of eight kids meant I did have people following me everywhere I went. The little ones always wanted to tag along."

He laughed. "I had one younger sister. She stuck like glue."

The rich sound of his laughter warmed her. "Do you see your sister often?"

"Yes. Leah lives in Fairfax." His eyes softened. "Her two little girls have me wrapped around their fingers. Especially now their dad is gone."

"I'm so sorry."

"He was a Marine … killed on deployment."

Kate swallowed hard. "In my book, those serving in the military are heroes. I think we sometimes take for granted everything they do to protect our way of life."

"Believe me, I don't. I've seen the sacrifice first hand."

"How is your sister coping?"

"Not well. Since our parents are gone, I'm all she has." Ben slowed and moved slightly behind her to allow several students with bulging backpacks to pass. His shoulder brushed hers when he fell into step beside her. "I'd like to introduce you two," he added.

"I'd love to meet her. Did you and Leah grow up in DC?"

"Born and raised here. I think that's why I enjoy hearing Joe's stories about your family's farm. Does he really know how to lasso a llama?"

"He does—one of his many hidden talents. The talent comes with a price, though. Our llama spits at Joe whenever she sees a rope in his hands. We have good memories from living on the farm, as well as great stories for ammunition."

They walked in a comfortable silence for a few paces. A class of what appeared to be elementary school kids passed.

Ben waved to the kids. "I must say, college students are getting younger every year."

"I'll bet they're on a field trip. I used to love field trips because we didn't have homework afterward." Kate thought back to her childhood. "When our third-grade class visited the local television station, I decided then and there on my life's profession."

"Ever change your mind?"

She shook her head. "The interest stayed strong even as I got older. I bought *Time* and *Newsweek* when all my friends were reading magazines on hair and makeup."

They had almost reached Kate's car. Could she walk past so she wouldn't have to say goodbye? She dismissed the idea. The station's white SUV, with red, bold lettering on the side, sat in plain view. Still …

"Well, looks like this is your vehicle."

So much for trying to sneak something past the FBI. She fished her keys from her purse and pushed the button to unlock the car. Ben opened the door for her.

"You know, I have a very reliable source who tells me you enjoy hiking. I'd love to take you one day soon."

Kate's stomach somersaulted. "Wonderful! I haven't hiked since I moved here."

"I have to work this weekend, but how does next Saturday sound?"

"Perfect." Absolutely perfect.

"Great—I'll call you soon with the details. 'Bye, Kate."

Those blue eyes held hers an extra beat before he continued down the sidewalk.

A spark of hope ignited in her heart. After her breakup with Gavin, she'd decided her brothers were the only good guys left in the world.

Maybe she was wrong. She smiled. This time, being wrong wasn't a bad thing.

JANUARY 24
FRIDAY, 2:33 P.M.
N TROY STREET, ARLINGTON, VA

Martha clicked off the vacuum cleaner in time to hear her cell phone chime. She hurried to her bedroom and glanced at the caller ID. *Restricted.* Foreboding hit. "Hello?"

"Martha? Frank."

"Frank? Where *are* you?"

"I tried to—" The rest of his words garbled, and the call ended.

Martha moved the phone from her ear. Frank Edwards was alive.

She sank onto the sofa. Two months ago, his blood-stained car had turned up on a lonely road. Frank had disappeared.

She and Frank had worked together for the CIA years ago. He'd been a loyal friend. Frank was also the last person to see her husband Charles alive. She covered her ears to quiet the accusing words of the traitor George Merck, spoken one early morning this past November ...

"So happy to see you again, Ms. Thomas."

"You're happy to see me ... again?"

"Of course. Don't you recognize me?"

"No."

"The Eiffel Tower, thirty years ago. You photographed— shall we say—a business transaction of mine."

"I photographed George Merck selling US military secrets to the Russians."

"Precisely."

"But George Merck died in prison."

"My dear Ms. Thomas, has your agency yet to figure out what really happened after all this time?"

"Apparently. Why don't you set the record straight?"

He sighed, and his voice took on the tone of someone explaining a simple fact to a child. "How did George Merck die?"

"Accomplices smuggled weapons into the prison. He died in a gunfight with another prisoner. They were both killed that day."

"In reality, only one prisoner died that day, and it wasn't me." His laugh sent chills up Martha's spine. "One of your own CIA agents planned and carried out the whole cover-up. I was taken out on a stretcher with a sheet covering my face, just like the dead man. Then I was smuggled to Russia to work with their scientists to recreate the military information your agency, unfortunately, confiscated from me."

Martha's head pounded as she processed the information. If this were true, she'd made a grave error by not bringing agents to back her up. Merck must be taken to prison again.

As if reading her mind, he nodded, and three men, holding guns aimed straight at her, stepped from the shadows. "I told you to come alone, but I never said I would."

She wouldn't stand a chance if she went for her gun. "Professor Merck, this has been a very enlightening conversation, but you haven't answered the question of why you brought me here. You said you have information on someone I care for deeply. Where is my niece?"

"I have no idea where your niece is."

A puzzled look crossed his face, and with a sinking heart, she believed him.

He continued. "You're the one who keeps referring to your niece. The information I have is about your husband."

"My ... husband?" A sickening dizziness enveloped her. She willed herself to maintain control. "What do you mean?"

"I know who murdered him."

She stood very still, and fought the overwhelming urge to turn and run. "Yes?"

The strength of her voice surprised her.

"The man who killed him is the same man who got me out of prison. We worked closely together in Russia for several years. Then, at the end of the Cold War, we went our separate ways." He paused. "But, as the saying goes, once a spy, always a spy. We are both still in business, just with another of America's enemies."

"You're despicable."

"You're probably right. Which brings me to the reason I called you. This double agent has, you might say, double-crossed me. I won't bore you with details, but I'm determined to get my revenge."

"And what does your revenge have to do with me?"

He stared at her for a moment. "Even though we're on

opposite sides, Martha Thomas, I know you're a person of integrity. When I reveal this man's identity, you won't stop until he's brought to justice."

"Who is he?"

"Frank Edwards."

The squeal of brakes from the noisy street outside drew Martha to the present. She snatched up her phone to call Ted Bradley, the CIA agent heading up the search for Frank. He needed to know Frank was alive. Judging from the condition of Frank's car, CIA agents weren't the only ones searching for him.

While she waited for Ted's answer, her thoughts swirled. Was Frank's appearance in DC at the same time as Merck's simply bad timing, or was there more to his visit? She certainly didn't trust Merck, yet why had Frank left so suddenly during the crisis of Jenny's kidnapping?

And where was he now?

JANUARY 25
SATURDAY, 1:07 P.M.
ALEXANDRIA, VA

Ben reached into the bag, snagged a chip, and crunched down on the salty treat. Surveillance always made him hungry. At least, when nothing happened, and for the last four hours, nothing had happened. He peered into the binoculars. A half block away, Charlotte Fitzgerald's townhouse appeared deserted.

Joe popped a piece of gum into his mouth. "Think Fitzgerald will show?"

"Charlotte or Ethan?"

"At this point, I'd be happy with either."

Ben stretched. "According to Dave, there hasn't been much activity since we visited Charlotte on Tuesday. And no action at Ethan's apartment." Dave Spencer, a member of their team, had coordinated the surveillance of the Fitzgeralds.

"Ethan hasn't used his cell phone or credit cards since he dropped off the radar. Maybe he really is camping, and Charlotte was telling the truth," Joe mused.

"Maybe, but her body language said otherwise." Ben shifted positions. The seats of the repair van they were using for a cover slanted. "Interesting, though, that every employee at CRI has a squeaky-clean record—even Ethan, if you don't count taking unapproved vacation."

"Hopefully, the note received by the Liechtenstein ambassador won't amount to anything and we can wrap up this investigation."

"Sounds good to—" Ben stopped. A man, tall and muscular, lingered on the sidewalk in front of Charlotte's home. Ben studied his face through the binoculars.

Joe grabbed his camera. He snapped photos in rapid succession.

The man pivoted and walked up the steps to pound on the door of Charlotte's townhouse. When the door opened, he disappeared inside. "I say we tail him when he comes out, see where he takes us," Ben said. "This could have nothing to do with Ethan. Or, this could be the break we need."

Moments passed, and the man reappeared. He strode down the steps of the townhouse, heading in the direction he'd come from.

Ben clicked his seat belt around him. "I'll wait until he turns the corner."

"Hold up." Joe pointed to the townhouse. Charlotte stood by the door, plainly watching her visitor. Seconds later, she bounded down the steps and strode in the opposite direction, toward Ben and Joe's repair van.

Ben straightened. "She's definitely on a mission. Following her might be more productive than tailing her guest. I have a feeling she's going to meet her cousin."

Joe nodded. "Possibly to warn him about something. By the looks of the guy who just left, he wasn't from the neighborhood sunshine committee."

They waited. When Charlotte reached the next block, they got out of the van and followed. Her pace quickened.

Joe zipped his jacket. "Looks like we might be going for a jog."

Ben pulled his sweater over his shoulder holster. "Except she's not headed toward the park. We're moving in the direction of the shopping mall."

Ten minutes later, Ben and Joe sat inside an IMAX cinema eight rows behind Charlotte. The theater was semi-dark. The sparse crowd waited for the movie to start. Ben glanced around. Charlotte had chosen a seat in an empty row, with no one in front or behind her. She busied herself with a bag of popcorn.

Joe sighed. "I wish she'd picked a movie I hadn't already seen."

"Well, I haven't seen this one, so don't ruin the ending for me."

The lights dimmed and the previews began. A few more people hurried in. Surely Ethan Fitzgerald was here and would join his cousin. Ben trained his eyes on Charlotte.

No one came. Flashes of light from outdoor scenes on the screen illumined people settled in for a typical Saturday afternoon at the movies.

Charlotte rose from her seat and left. Ben tensed. Was Ethan in the lobby? They waited several seconds, then followed her.

Charlotte exited the cinema, walked the same route home, and disappeared into her house.

Moments later, Ben and Joe settled back in the van to wait for agents on the next shift to relieve them. "Well, that was fun." Ben uncapped a water bottle. "I wonder why Ethan didn't show."

"I'll bet his cousin is wondering the same thing." Joe frowned. "You'd think Charlotte would have waited for Ethan a little longer."

"Maybe they agreed on waiting a certain amount of time. If one of them doesn't show, the other leaves."

"You've got to admit, a dark theater is a good place to rendezvous when you want to hide."

Why—and what—did Ethan want to hide? Ben thought back to the note Margaret Schrader had received. *Stop the research exchange now—or someone will get hurt.*

Was Ethan planning something to jeopardize the future of CRI? Would his plans have international repercussions? Or, was he simply a man tired of his job and taking time off? As much as Ben wanted to believe the latter, Charlotte's surreptitious trip to the theater pointed to something more.

They needed answers. Ben tamped down a surge of frustration.

They needed to find Ethan.

JANUARY 26
SUNDAY, 3:45 P.M.
MEADOW DRIVE, FAIRFAX, VA

Wet, fluffy snowflakes swirled from gray skies. Ben veered off the sidewalk to the path that led behind his sister's house. His nieces would be thrilled with the winter weather.

Laughter floated through the air. The girls twirled around in the back yard—their tongues stuck out to catch snowflakes. Six-year-old Bekah caught sight of him and squealed with delight.

"Bonnie, Uncle Ben is here." She ran to him, her big smile revealing two missing front teeth.

"Come into the playhouse, Uncle Ben." Bonnie, two years older than her sister, grabbed his arm and tugged him inside the playhouse Rich had built just before he deployed.

Ben squeezed into the structure definitely not designed for his six-foot-two frame. When he sat down, his knees pushed against his chin.

Bekah surveyed him with one eye hidden beneath an adult-sized orange hat. "Did you bring us a surprise?"

He reached over and pulled the hat down over both eyes. "What do you think, short-stuff?"

Bekah doubled over into a fit of giggles as Bonnie dove into his jacket pocket. "I think you did." She grinned and whisked out a white bakery bag. "I knew you wouldn't forget."

The girls munched contentedly on the gingerbread men that had become a tradition ever since they'd visited the bakery near his apartment. Red sugar crystals stuck to their lips. His heart stirred with affection. *Why, Lord? Why did Rich have to die?* Grief swept over him. *They're just little girls.*

"Uncle Ben, are you coming to my school play?" Bekah licked her fingers and looked up, her blue eyes wide. "I'm Little Bo Peep."

He paused a beat to steady his voice. "You know I'd never miss seeing you round up a bunch of lost sheep. You have a big job."

She grinned. "I get to carry a big stick."

Ben's feet tingled, and he shifted positions. "What's your mom up to?"

"Crying." Bonnie's expression sobered. "Some days she won't stop for a long time."

"I told her not to cry because Daddy is with Jesus, but she cries anyway," Bekah added.

He gazed into their troubled faces. "I'm sorry." The inadequacy of his words stabbed. He glanced at the house. No lights shone in the windows despite the gray afternoon. "While I talk to your mom, you girls see how many snowflakes you can catch."

He struggled to rise, and shuffled toward the house. His gut clenched. His sister's tears broke his heart.

Ben crunched across the snowy deck. He entered the dark kitchen and switched on the lamp beside the door. "Leah?"

A muffled noise sounded from the den. She sat on the sofa, her head buried in her hands, sobbing. He strode over and gently turned her into his shoulder.

"I can't do this. It's not fair," she moaned.

His eyes burned. Rich had been like a brother to him. The loss cut through him. Again. If only he could fix things. Nothing he could do would bring Rich back. He steadied his sister's shakes.

God would take them through this. Ben looked out at the dismal day. God *had* to take them through this.

Because his strength would be the only way they'd come out on the other side.

CHAPTER 5

"Thank you for telling our story, Kate." Max O'Reilly's round face beamed. "Sophie believes this will cause our business to boom."

"Well ..." Kate began.

"Oh, I know," Max interrupted "I told her not to expect miracles, but your story will remind people we're here."

"Miracles happen every day, Uncle Max. We're not going under." Sophie turned to Kate. "When will you interview Cynthia and Stephanie?"

"I go to the card shop tomorrow evening and the dress shop on Wednesday." Kate's producer, Alex, had not been in favor of this idea. As a last resort, she'd offered to do the work on her own time. Finally, he'd agreed. But squeezing in interviews around other assignments wasn't easy.

She zipped her camera into the case. "I spoke with Nelda and Levi earlier today. They looked exhausted."

"They're waiting for the landlord to assess the damage to their shop. The wall hit by the bullet needs repair. An electrical panel was apparently struck as well because a section of lights doesn't work. The Shanes are too old to have to deal with this," Max snorted.

Sophie linked her arm through his. "Uncle Max, you're the same age as Nelda and Levi."

A startled look darted across his face. "Okay, we're *all* too old for this."

Kate suppressed a grin. Both the Shanes and Uncle Max had spunk. No question. If only her series *could* help their businesses. What had Sophie said earlier? *They're part of the history of this neighborhood.* The shops were plainly more than a means of support. They were a way of life.

"I'm going to head to the station and edit our interview." Kate gathered her things. "The story should air tomorrow evening. I'll call you if I have any questions."

The front door swung open. A man ambled in and leaned against the counter.

He clenched his hands, one finger at a time, into fists. "Here late today, huh, Max?"

Kate's gaze darted to Max. His features froze.

Quiet hung.

Sophie stepped to the door. "Yeah, Ian, we're here late, and now we're ready to close."

The man's gaze swept over the three of them and settled on Kate. "Well, well, Kate Peterson from channel ten. Doing a story?"

She stiffened. "Yes."

He surveyed her camera equipment and grunted. "News must be slow if you can't find anything better than Max to report on."

Warmth rose to her face. "I'll let the two million viewers of WOTN be the judges."

His eyes hardened. "I'll be watching for your report. After all, I need to keep my friend here in line. See ya around, Max." He sauntered out.

The door swung shut behind him. Sophie's breath blew out in a tiny sob. "Why doesn't he leave us alone?"

"I'm a little behind on my payments, that's all." Max turned to Kate. "You stood right up to him. I like your spirit. You must have Irish blood in you."

"Actually, I just might." She worked to keep her voice light. "My family is originally from Scotland, but some of the Petersons settled in Ireland." She hesitated. "I should go now. Can I do anything for you?"

"You've done more than enough. Thank you, Katie."

No one had called her Katie since Grandma Peterson. She missed her grandmother.

She trudged the darkened sidewalks, thankful she'd found a parking space close by. Her thoughts turned to the man in the antique shop. Sophie had called him "Ian." He possessed a personality she could live without. The look on Max's face said she wasn't alone in her feelings.

As Kate moved closer to her vehicle, the streetlight beside her car illumined something on the windshield. She squinted. The object almost looked like … a long-stemmed rose?

Her heartbeat quickened. Ben? They hadn't even had their first date, and, somehow, he didn't strike her as a rose-on-the-windshield type of guy.

She closed the distance to her car and froze.

The rose was black, a shredded, soiled ribbon tied around the stem. An open box of candy, every piece smashed, lay propped beside the rose. Words in white letters scrawled over the windshield pulsed through her senses. *What Will I Do Next?*

Her heart pounded as she struggled for air. Her eyes swept across the shadows along the shops. Something moved.

She clutched her camera equipment, her legs leaden. The shape loomed larger, then separated.

Out of the darkness trotted a golden retriever, his master close behind. The dog ran over and sniffed her boots. She shuddered. The man quickly reined in the dog.

"Sorry he startled you."

She nodded, the "that's okay" she intended to say lodged in her throat. The pair moved on, and her knees wobbled beneath her.

She willed herself to walk, to load her equipment, to get into the car. She clicked the doors locked.

A sudden heat surged through her veins and dissolved the fear. She could take a practical joke as well as the next person, but this displayed sick humor. Who had left a dead flower, smashed candy, and the eerie message? And why? *Maybe I should call Joe. Or Ben.*

She gave herself an inward shake. They'd already rescued her from being held hostage. How would they have time to do their jobs at the FBI if they had to babysit her? Joe already spent time surveilling Gavin. She wouldn't mention this. At least, not yet.

She snapped the windshield wipers to their highest speed. The disgusting rose and candy hurtled into the darkness. She shoved the button to wash the windshield, the *swish* of the wipers slowly erasing the hateful words.

This probably wasn't even intended for her. No doubt someone wanted to send a message to WOTN.

She hadn't driven the station's vehicle. She swallowed the acid rising in her throat.

What if this wasn't just a sick joke?

JANUARY 29
WEDNESDAY, 9:38 A.M.
HOOVER BUILDING, DC

Ben leaned back in his chair as he scanned the last of the twenty-six Caldwell Research Institute's employee files. Again. On the surface, everything appeared in order. Background checks were clean. Highly respected men and women dedicated to economics. Nothing in the files to raise red flags.

Margaret Schrader had assured him the Liechtenstein economists had passed stringent background checks as well. Susan Strickland, a member of his unit, had analyzed every detail of the note received by the ambassador, down to the type of paper. No fingerprints other than the ambassador's were lifted from the message, and Susan had found nothing on which they could move forward.

Joe strolled toward his desk. "Coffee? I'm headed that way."

"No, thanks." Ben shifted to relieve the cramp in his neck. "Any new ideas on the CRI investigation?"

"None. If Charlotte hadn't made the trip to the IMAX cinema, I'd think there was nothing to this."

"Ethan Fitzgerald is the big question mark." Ben clicked his computer to the calendar. "According to Wilson's assistant, Ethan's vacation officially ends next Tuesday evening, February fourth."

"So, I guess I know what we'll be doing on February fifth. If Ethan's planning to return to CRI, he should show up that morning. We'd better get to him first, because he'll have some explaining to do once Wilson sees him."

Joe's cell phone buzzed, and Ben turned back to his work. Ben's interest piqued when Margaret Schrader's name filtered into his consciousness.

The conversation was brief. Joe shot Ben a troubled look as he ended the call. "A Liechtenstein citizen was arrested yesterday in Switzerland on charges related to tampering with Prince Alexander's vehicle. This person was also one of the economists scheduled to fly to the US during the exchange."

Ben blew out a breath. "Ms. Schrader said her principality had uncovered bribery along with threats regarding government appointments to offices. Maybe the threat she received concerning the economic exchange is part of political unrest in Liechtenstein and has nothing to do with Caldwell Research Institute."

"Makes sense. The note could have been written by an employee within the embassy. By the way, has the head of Princess Ingrid's security touched base with you this week?"

"Yesterday. Things are progressing smoothly. No concerns have surfaced for her safety."

"I hope Ethan Fitzgerald shows up for work next week, so we can close the investigation on our end."

"You and me, both, buddy."

Joe headed to the coffeepot and Ben turned to his computer. He needed to update case notes on a drug ring his unit was surveilling.

He was deep in thought when he heard his name called across the open office. Janet Hanson, an administrative assistant, motioned to him.

"Charlotte Fitzgerald is downstairs. She says it's urgent she speak with you. I can bring her up if you'd like."

Moments later, Charlotte Fitzgerald sat across from Ben and Joe at the conference table.

"I'm worried about Ethan. I believe something has happened to him."

"Why would you think so?" Joe leaned back in his chair. "We understand his vacation isn't officially over until next week."

She drew a deep breath. "I lied to you."

Ben studied her. "You've heard from him?"

"Yes, I have—did, I mean, until he stopped communication. We were supposed to meet at a movie theater near my house last Saturday. He didn't come." She clasped her hands together. "I know I was wrong to lie to you and Ethan's college roommate … but Ethan is like a brother to me. He's all the family I have. I wanted to protect him."

Ben straightened. "Ethan's college roommate?"

"He came to my house right before I was supposed to meet Ethan. I was afraid I'd be late."

"Why did he stop by?"

"He said he was visiting the area and wanted to see Ethan. I'm not sure how he got my address. I'd never heard Ethan mention him before."

Joe opened his laptop. "His name?"

Confusion wavered in her face. "He never told me, just introduced himself as Ethan's roommate at Princeton. He asked if I'd spoken with Ethan lately, if he ever talked to me about his work, that sort of thing."

"And you said …?"

She shrugged. "I told him I hadn't seen Ethan."

"Ms. Fitzgerald, the time for truth is long overdue." Ben paused. "What did Ethan tell you about his work?"

"Only that he needed to sort things out. He never said anything more—I'm not lying to you now. He checked into a hotel on the other side of town. He wouldn't tell me which one. He said he used an assumed name and planned to pay for everything with cash. He laughed when I asked him why. He said he didn't want his employer tracking him down. Even though he laughed, his voice sounded … panicked."

"How often did you speak with him before he stopped communication?"

"He called every few days from a hotel phone. We talked about the books he was reading, and he always asked about my dog. We also met at the movie theater twice. Like I said, we were supposed to meet last Saturday …"

Joe's phone buzzed. He silenced the device. "Who are Ethan's friends?"

"I'm not sure he has any friends. Like I said earlier, I'd never heard him mention his college roommate." Charlotte squared her shoulders. "There's nothing wrong with my cousin. He's a great guy and he's super intelligent. He just enjoys books and his computer more than people. An introvert, you know?"

Ben swallowed a sigh. They needed solid leads. "Did he ever mention any of his co-workers' names?"

She furrowed her brow. "A couple of months ago, he mentioned a woman who worked in his office. Cindy, or maybe Mindy. I remember I perked up because I wondered if he might be interested in her. He told me the office was planning a Christmas party, and she'd asked him if he were going. He decided not to attend the party. He didn't mention her again."

Cindy or Mindy. Ben mentally scrolled through the list of CRI employees they'd investigated. If this woman did indeed work for CRI, she was not one of the twenty-six employees involved in the research exchange. "Can you think of any other information?"

Charlotte bit her lip. "The real reason I came in this morning, and the thing worrying me the most, is the ring."

A blank look crossed Joe's face. "The ring?"

She nodded. "Last night, on channel ten news, a reporter did a story about O'Reilly's Antiques."

Kate's story. In the past, Ben had rarely watched the evening news. Now he caught the broadcasts as often as possible. "I saw the interview." He turned to Joe. "Kate is doing a series on the struggle of local small businesses."

"I remember, but I missed her interview." Joe looked at Charlotte. "What does a ring at an antique store have to do with Ethan?"

"From the general description given on the news, the ring might possibly be the one his father gave Ethan before he died. The ring had our family crest. Ethan was only twelve and he's never taken off the ring since.

He would have retraced every step if he'd somehow lost the ring."

Ben frowned. "If your cousin didn't want to be seen, why do you think he'd go shopping at an antique store?"

"I have no idea. I think something has happened to him."

Was she grasping at straws thinking the ring belonged to Ethan? Ben looked at Joe and caught his slight nod. There was only one way to find out.

❋

A short while later, they stood inside O'Reilly's Antiques. Charlotte Fitzgerald described the ring to Max O'Reilly down to the last detail.

Max nodded. "I'll get the ring from the safe in my office." He disappeared into the back room. He returned with a small velvet bag.

Charlotte opened the bag. She peered inside and sighed. "This is his ring."

Joe showed Max a photo of Ethan. "Does this man look familiar? Ever come into your shop?"

Max studied the picture. "No, I don't think so. Of course, I can't remember all my customers. His face doesn't ring a bell."

Ben pushed his business card across the counter. "Mr. O'Reilly, we'd like to leave the ring with you for a while longer. If someone comes in to claim the piece, call this number immediately."

Max's eyes widened. "Is this some kind of trap?"

"Just looking for information."

Ben's gut told him this was a long shot.

But one certainly worth a try.

JANUARY 31
FRIDAY, 12:10 P.M.
NATIONAL MALL, WASHINGTON, DC

"In summary, I believe a knowledge of history is imperative to our success in the future." Princess Ingrid spoke confidently into the microphone Kate held.

Kate looked toward the camera. "For Princess Ingrid, her love of history is a driving force as she explores life in our nation's capital. Live from the Washington Monument, Kate Peterson, WOTN."

"That's a wrap." Ellen Taylor flashed a thumbs-up and took Kate's microphone.

Ingrid turned to Ellen. "Do you and Kate work together often?"

"Depends on the day and number of assignments." Ellen lifted the camera from the tripod. "Kate shot on her previous job, so she's an old pro."

Kate laughed. "Let's not go that far." She helped pack up the equipment. "Having Ellen film is a treat."

"Well, off to my next assignment." Ellen smiled at Ingrid. "I enjoyed meeting you. I'll probably see you again if we do another live shot."

Kate turned to Ingrid. "We'll plan on the university for our next interview. I'll call ahead to make sure your schedule hasn't changed."

Ingrid nodded. She glanced around the National Mall, filled with people. A shadow passed over her face. "How wonderful to enjoy a whole day with no responsibilities."

Kate's heart went out to her. "I have some time before I need to leave. Would you like to walk for a few minutes?"

"Yes! Thank you."

They strolled along the walkway, one of Ingrid's security guards ahead, the other a few paces behind.

"Do you and your family get away from the palace for vacations often?"

"My mother died when I was a little girl, so there's just me and my father." Ingrid shrugged. "We travel quite a bit, but we're always in the public eye. Our only real holidays are visits to our country estate. We own horses, so my father and I go on long rides. I love those times. My father is a wonderful man and fun to be with. When we're in the country, our time is our own." She paused. "You know, even though my life has been completely mapped out, I struggle to find purpose. Sometimes I feel I'll be nothing more than a royal figurehead. Life lacks meaning."

Kate considered Ingrid's words. "I think we all battle at times to find purpose. I was ready to change the world when I graduated from college and began my career. I thought I could do everything on my own, but I ran into one wall after another. I felt as if I'd never get life right. A friend reminded me of a Bible verse that says God fashioned the days for me before I was even born. I love the picture. God shaped each of my days to fit me. I realized I have a unique purpose." She smiled at Ingrid. "You do, too. We just have to look to God."

Ingrid plainly grappled with the idea. "Something to think about."

Kate's stomach rumbled. "Would you like to get lunch? I don't have time for a restaurant, but we can grab something from a food truck. I'm starved."

"Of course. I hope we find hot dogs."

A short while later, they settled on a bench with sodas and hot dogs loaded with chili and slaw.

"Delicious," Kate murmured around a mouthful of food. She spread another napkin over her lap. "I just hope I'm not wearing this lunch the rest of the day." She nodded toward the security guards. "Do they ever eat?"

"Not on duty. We'll go directly to the university after we leave here, then a new shift will take over."

"Have you had a chance to get to know other students yet?"

"I have a private room. I haven't really talked to the girls on my hall yet." A smile masked her face.

Ingrid needed a friend. "You mentioned riding with your father. I love horses, too, and there are lots of stables in the area. Maybe we could go for a ride sometime."

"Marvelous. I've missed my horses."

"Do your security guys ride?"

"They're all expert riders, but some enjoy the sport more than others." Ingrid's eyes twinkled. "I'll let them decide who gets the pleasure of our company."

They finished lunch and headed back to their vehicles. A vendor on the street sold paintings of flowers. The image of the black rose darted through Kate's mind. She shuddered.

As she waved goodbye to Ingrid, Kate's thoughts turned to the message left on her windshield. *What Will I Do Next?*

Gripping her car keys tighter, she scanned the surrounding area. People were everywhere. Tourists, businessmen and women, students with backpacks … She was perfectly safe. Besides, whoever left the message was probably miles away.

She bit her lip. Was he?

Kate reached the parking garage and pushed away the unsettling thoughts. Stairs or elevator? Stairs. Even though she'd parked on the top floor. Her workouts should be good for something. The *clang* of the metal door closing reverberated through the deserted stairwell. Strange how quiet things seemed for midday.

When she reached the second floor, the slam of the door echoed again. Footsteps sounded beneath her. Kate leaned over the railing and glimpsed a man sprinting up the steps. His head was down, but something about his build reminded her of someone she'd seen recently. Her thoughts skimmed across the past few days. Her breath hitched. The man at O'Reilly's Antiques—Ian.

Kate darted up the next flight of stairs. Would he catch up with her? She really didn't want to face him again after their uncomfortable exchange in the antique shop.

On the next floor, she glanced backward in time to see a flash of sunlight. A woman stepped through the second-floor doorway.

Loud voices from the floor below replaced the pounding of Ian's footsteps. Was he threatening the woman? Kate flattened herself against the cold cinder block of the stairwell wall. Inch by inch, she moved closer to the railing.

A group of teenagers wearing school uniforms streamed through the doorway from the parking area past Ian and the woman. A moment later, the pair exited the stairwell.

Kate gulped a breath as she raced up the remaining stairs to the top floor. No need to stick around. The two plainly knew each other and apparently had settled their argument.

Seconds later, Kate merged her car into the stream of traffic. While she drove to her next assignment, her thoughts turned to her encounter with Ian at O'Reilly's Antiques. He'd recognized her from television, but she had no memory of ever meeting him.

Sudden alarm strobed her senses. *Did he follow me while I was with Ingrid and then into the parking garage? Could he have written the words on my windshield?*

She focused her scattered thoughts. Ian left the shop only moments before her the night she found the dead rose. He wouldn't have had time to get to her car. Could he have gone there while she was interviewing the O'Reillys? But why? And how would he have known which vehicle she drove?

She exhaled a long breath. She was jumping to conclusions about Ian and the night at O'Reilly's Antiques. Seeing him at the parking garage was coincidence, too. He probably came to meet the woman. What reason would he have to follow her?

Her fingers stiffened around the steering wheel. Then again, what reason prompted someone to leave a dead rose, smashed candy, and a sick message on her windshield?

FEBRUARY 1
SATURDAY, 1:07 P.M.
VA

Ben stuck his hiking boot between two rocks and pulled himself up the steep incline. He turned to Kate. "Need a hand?" When she smiled up at him, his heart rate spiked.

Her fingers curled in his, Kate scrambled up the path. He sighed inwardly. Too bad the trail leveled out for a while. He held her hand an instant longer than necessary. "We have about a mile left before we get to the top. How about a break?"

"Sounds good." Kate surveyed a large rock and sat down. "What a great trail." She pointed to the river winding below them. "I love the sound of water rushing over rocks."

Ben slid off his backpack and joined her. "I come here every chance I get. The drive's a bit long, but the view at the top is worth every mile." He offered the snacks he'd brought.

Kate peered inside the bag. "You were right when you said you came prepared." She chose a package of trail mix and a bottle of water. "How did you find this spot?"

Ben unwrapped a protein bar. "Trying out new trails is sort of a hobby of mine—like taking a mini vacation." He pointed to the trees towering over them. Sunlight filtered through the branches. "I see things in my job I wish I didn't. Getting out in the middle of God's creation gives perspective. I realize he's still in control even when life isn't always the way I'd like."

Concern glimmered in Kate's dark eyes. "You have a difficult job. You face things on a daily basis some people are never even aware of."

"I'm sure you've seen your share of difficulties as a television reporter."

Kate nodded. "I think the hardest stories involve children. My first assignment was on a little girl hit by a stray bullet during a drug deal. She was playing in the park with her grandmother at the time. The little girl died an hour later." She was silent for a moment. "I constantly pray God will keep my heart soft, and I won't become cynical. He definitely used that first assignment to give me a passion for seeing justice and giving a voice to those who don't have one."

Ben's heart stirred. Her passion mirrored his own. "I remember how I felt when my parents died. A drunk driver traveling on the wrong side of the interstate crashed into their car. I was eight years old." He absorbed the pain of the memory. "My world shattered."

Kate touched his arm. "What a tragedy for a young boy to deal with."

"Leah and I were fortunate, though. Our aunt and uncle took us in. They raised us like we were their own. Their unwavering faith in God became the anchor I needed."

"Were your parents' deaths the reason you decided on law enforcement?" Kate asked softly.

"Yes. My uncle's belief that God would bring good out of our tragedy became mine. He encouraged me to forgive, to turn my hurt into the positive of helping others. Best advice I ever received."

A sudden rustle sounded.

Kate started. "The weather *is* too cold for snakes to be crawling around, right?"

"The noise came from behind us. See?"

"What?"

"By the fallen tree trunk. A chipmunk."

"I love chipmunks. Maybe I can get a photo."

The chipmunk posed while Kate fumbled for her phone, then scurried away when she snapped the picture. She surveyed her screen. "I got a great photo of the tree trunk."

"Maybe we'll see another one." Ben stretched and stood. "Ready to go? A surprise is waiting at the top of the trail."

She hopped up. "Absolutely."

A small leaf floated down, lodging in her hair. Ben moved closer. He brushed away the leaf and looked deep into those brown eyes. *You're a beautiful woman, Kate Peterson—inside and out.* He almost spoke his thought but settled for smoothing a strand of blonde hair.

Near the top of the trail, the climb became steeper. "Almost there. You go first." Ben steered Kate in front of him.

When they reached the trail's end, she gasped. "How beautiful."

The waterfall cascading in front of them never failed to awe Ben. They settled on a bench beside the trail. This time, instead of watching the waterfall, he watched Kate.

"I expected to look out over a valley," she breathed. "The waterfall is such a beautiful surprise."

Spray from the cascading water misted over them. Kate zipped up her jacket, and Ben slipped his arm across her shoulders.

A sense of loss had gripped a corner of his soul for as long as he could remember. Loss of parents, aunt and uncle, brother-in-law. The end of his engagement to McKenzie two years ago. But now, God had brought Kate into his life. Contentment worked through his heart at the hope of the blessing.

A breeze blew, and Kate shivered beneath his arm. He slowly stood. "I guess we should head down before our jackets turn to ice."

"Thank you for bringing me here, Ben. What a special spot." She held up her phone. "Let's get a photo of ourselves with the waterfall in the background to remember our first hike."

His shoulder brushed hers, and he breathed in the sweetness of her perfume. He smiled down at her. He wouldn't need a picture to remember this day. His heart had captured every moment.

CHAPTER 6

"He's here to claim the ring."

The breathlessness in Max O'Reilly's hushed voice pulsated through the phone. Ben signaled to Joe to head to O'Reilly's Antiques. "We'll be there in five minutes, Max."

Joe switched on the flashing dashboard light and accelerated into traffic.

"I'm positive he's the man in your picture." Max's voice shook. "He's wearing a blue baseball cap and a red jacket."

O'Reilly needed to calm down before things went south. "Take a deep breath, Max. Everything's okay. All you need to do is get his description of the ring."

"Yeah. Yeah, okay."

Ben sucked in a breath. Great. While they sat outside Caldwell Research Institute, Fitzgerald showed up at O'Reilly's. Thankfully, they were only moments away. But why did he choose this morning—the morning he should have returned to work?

Joe slowed the car a block from O'Reilly's. "You take the front entrance. I'll park in the alley behind the store."

Ben nodded and dashed from the car while drivers blasted their horns. A flash of movement near O'Reilly's Antiques caught his eye. A man ran down the crowded sidewalk, shoving pedestrians out of his way. The man darted left, then crossed the street. A few yards ahead, someone in the middle of the intersection broke into a run. The clothes of the person chased matched Max's description. *Ethan.*

Ben bolted to the corner and across the street, seconds before a wall of cars accelerated through the intersection.

Ethan dashed toward the Metro, the man chasing him gaining ground. Ben lost sight of them for an instant. Panic surged through him. He reached the escalators leading to the trains.

"FBI!" he bellowed to people blocking his path. They jumped to one side. He lunged past, taking two moving steps at a time.

He sprinted through the wide corridors. He glimpsed Ethan running toward the trains, still ahead of the man chasing him. Ben whisked out his Metro card and pushed through the barrier.

People filled the platform. He spotted Ethan's pursuer and scanned the area around him. Ethan had vanished in the crowd.

Red against gray drew Ben's eye. He turned in time to see a maintenance worker pick up a red jacket from the floor. No doubt a baseball cap was tucked inside.

Ben pivoted to Ethan's pursuer, who stood searching the crowd. If he couldn't find Ethan, this guy was the next best thing. Ben ran through the maze of people toward him. The man turned and locked eyes with Ben.

The face from the photos Joe shot at Charlotte Fitzgerald's townhouse registered. *The man claiming to be Ethan's college roommate.* Ben clenched his jaw. Ethan's college roommate had died three years ago.

The imposter darted around the crowd and jumped through the doors of the nearest train. Red lights along the platform flashed. The doors snapped shut.

Ben skidded to a halt as the train pulled away. He flicked a glance to the screen above. Eleven minutes until the next train.

He turned back to the sea of faces around him. Ethan could be anywhere. He might have even left the station by now.

Ben continued to search, but reality hammered. Fitzgerald was nowhere in sight. Ben squelched frustration and headed to the escalators. He hated to lose.

He stepped out into the bright sunlight. Why had Ethan gone to O'Reilly's when he was supposedly in hiding? How had the imposter known Ethan's whereabouts?

Moments later, Ben pushed open the door to O'Reilly's Antiques. Max sat in a chair behind the counter, rubbing his elbow. He talked to Joe while Levi Shane hovered behind.

"The guy seemed fidgety the whole time he was here. He kept looking out the window while he described the ring. I tried to stall him until you came. The moment I placed the thing in his hand, he took off in such a hurry he knocked me to the floor." Max's eyes blazed.

"Never even helped me." He slowly rose. "I need a couple of aspirins."

Ben's phone buzzed. He snagged the device from his pocket. "Ben Anderson."

"Frederick Wilson here."

Ben pressed the phone closer to his ear.

"Just wanted to touch base with you regarding Ethan Fitzgerald," Wilson continued. "His vacation ended today, but he hasn't come back to work. If he were coming, he should have been here by now. I thought you'd like to know."

Ben blew out a breath. "Thank you for staying in contact, Mr. Wilson." Before he could say goodbye, Wilson interrupted.

"Actually, I have more information for you. Something disturbing has come to our attention. We have reason to believe Ethan has been embezzling funds from grants for the research exchange program. Some of the economists who worked with Ethan discovered the discrepancies."

Ben processed the information. If Ethan had been embezzling funds, would he try to sabotage the project to keep from being discovered?

The events of the morning had raised a whole new set of questions.

And the man with the answers was on the run.

FEBRUARY 5
WEDNESDAY, 5:17 P.M.
ARLINGTON, VA

Ben stood outside Ethan Fitzgerald's apartment, his hand on his Glock. Joe pounded on the front door. An hour earlier, they'd obtained a warrant to search his apartment. Though they hadn't had probable cause before, with the beginning of an investigation into alleged embezzlement, they had probable cause now.

Moments later, after making a sweep of the inside, Ben returned his gun to his holster. He scanned the combination den, dining area, and kitchen. Piles of clothes dotted the floor, almost as if Ethan had left them exactly where he'd taken them off. Scattered papers and books covered the furniture. Duct tape held together a broken windowpane. Two open pizza boxes sat empty beside dozens of soda cans lining the dining room table.

Joe tossed Ben a pair of gloves. "I'd say Ethan is one of the more … *relaxed* housekeepers we've investigated." He wound his way through the den. "Isn't clutter a sign of genius?"

Ben laughed. "Only if the clutter is yours." He poked his head into a kitchen overflowing with dirty dishes. "If clutter *is* a sign of genius, Ethan's IQ must be off the charts."

"Guess we'd better get going or we'll be here all night." Joe gestured toward the den. "I'll start here if you want to take the bedroom."

"I'll bet the bedroom is immaculate. All his clothes are in the den." When Ben moved down the tiny hall, he shook his head. Just as bad.

He moved systematically around the bedroom. Judging from the subject matter of open books, Ethan appeared intelligent and interested in a wide range of topics.

The lack of personal items struck Ben. No photos of his cousin, no sports memorabilia, nothing to indicate a life apart from books. *And no electronic devices. Ethan must have taken his computer, phone, and whatever else he owns with him.*

Ben started his search with a desk in the room's corner. Textbooks and class schedules from Ethan's college days filled the larger, lower drawers. A collection of paper clips, pens, staples, and rubber bands rattled around the drawers above. A roll of orange and black duct tape caught Ben's eye. The tape matched the strip on the broken window in the den. He picked up the roll. Orange and black—the color of a tiger. Of course. Princeton's mascot was a tiger.

He returned the tape and papers to the drawers. Other than a love for academics, nothing in the room indicated who Ethan Fitzgerald really was. Nothing pointed to involvement in anything illegal. Not yet, anyway, but the person chasing him at the Metro certainly wanted something from Ethan. If only they could trace the man's identity.

Ben stumbled over a full trashcan beside the desk. When he scanned the room for something to spread the trash on, he noticed an empty plastic bag from a dry cleaner. He spread the plastic over the desk and shook out gum wrappers, receipts for fast-food restaurants, and circulars advertising men's clothing. He gathered the receipts in a pile and stuffed the remaining trash back into the wastebasket.

He searched the closet, bureau, and nightstand. A few more receipts and an overdue notice for a library book lay in the drawers. He lifted the mattress of the unmade bed, then dropped to his knees. Dust balls the size of tumbleweeds covered the floor. His sister would go nuts if she saw this. He'd never worry about his own housekeeping abilities again.

When he pulled himself up, color caught his eye—something was wedged between the bed and the nightstand. He leaned over and picked up a folded, glossy paper. Probably another clothing flier. He scanned the words.

"How are things going in here?" Joe stood in the doorway.

"I just found something. Seems Ethan attended a lecture at the Caldwell Research Institute on January eighteenth—the evening Margaret Schrader received the message regarding the research exchange project." He held up the program in a gloved hand.

Joe leaned over and studied the flier. "The plot thickens. Especially since Ethan started his unapproved vacation over a week earlier. Even if he knew Frederick Wilson wouldn't be in attendance, I'd think he wouldn't want to be seen by other employees who might attend the lecture."

"Let's call Frederick Wilson's assistant. We need a list of those in attendance that night. We also need to check the security cameras in the facility." Ben straightened. "Maybe we'll finally get answers."

FEBRUARY 7
FRIDAY, 10:38 A.M.
PENNSYLVANIA AVENUE, DC

"Your office is beautiful, Liza." Martha turned to the windows overlooking the Potomac. "The view is magnificent."

Liza Tyler shrugged. "I guess I've come a long way since we met at Tanglewood Elementary."

Martha's friend from eons ago had changed from a gangly tomboy with a mass of unruly curls to a self-assured woman with every hair in place. "What I remember most about you were the scrapes always covering your knees and elbows."

Liza drummed her fingers on her desk. "Good thing I learned how to fight back then, because I had my share of battles entering the business world when I did. Being a businesswoman in today's world isn't easy. Back then things were—" She bit her lip. "I almost forgot—you're more religious than me. I'll try to watch my language."

Martha's heart went out to her friend. A certain wariness in Liza's eyes hinted at a life of struggle. "Your work has certainly paid off. Tyler Wealth Management—your own investment company."

"The company has done well over the years. I don't take our success lightly." She swiveled her chair to face Martha. "We do quite a bit of charity work for different organizations. The one that means the most to me is Brannen Children's Hospital. You know, I never married and had a family. When I visit the children at the hospital, I almost feel like they're my own."

"I understand completely. Charles and I had no children, but God blessed us with many special nieces and nephews."

"Our annual benefit is coming up. I wondered if you'd be willing to donate some of your art. I've seen your work featured in several magazines—absolutely beautiful."

Martha smiled. "Thank you. I'd be honored to be a part of the benefit. I have paintings as well as photographs. Just tell me what you—"

A light tap at the door interrupted Martha.

"Hi, Liza." A man wearing a dark suit hovered in the doorway. "Got a minute?"

"Actually, no, Brandon, I don't." Liza's eyebrows morphed together. "If you'd like to make an appointment—"

"I would have, but your assistant is away from her desk." A definite whine laced his words.

A flash of impatience shot across Liza's face. Martha braced. Unless her old friend's temperament had changed, she'd bet sparks were about to fly. Brandon appeared undaunted.

He strolled over to Martha and extended his hand. "Brandon Lancaster. I'm Liza's brother-in-law." He flashed a wicked grin in her direction. "Her favorite brother-in-law."

Liza snorted. "My *only* brother-in-law." She turned to Martha. "My sister Vivien's husband." Her voice softened. "We lost Vivien last April."

Martha reached through childhood memories for Vivien's likeness. She pictured Liza's younger sister, as dainty as Liza was daring. "I'm so sorry, Liza."

Brandon straightened his tie and moved closer to Liza's desk. "Vivien would have wanted me in the position of your Chief Financial Officer. She would have taken great comfort knowing I was here to look after you."

Disgust etched Liza's features. "Don't try to worm your way into this company with platitudes about my sister. You want to discuss the position of CFO? Make. An. Appointment."

"Sure, Liza." He turned outstretched palms toward her and backed out of the office. "No harm, no foul.

I'll make an appointment right now." He shut the door behind him.

Martha studied her friend. "Not a nice guy?"

"He's a weasel," she muttered, her eyes dark. "If you ask me, he never cared about Vivien. He married her so he could spend her money. What he said is true, though. Vivien *would* have wanted him in the business. She loved him."

"What profession is he in now?"

"Real estate. He owns office buildings and leases them. Though he's done quite well, this position would be substantially more profitable."

Martha smiled at her friend. "I'm sure you'll make the right decision."

Liza shrugged and returned Martha's smile. "Now, where were we before we were so rudely interrupted?"

They talked about the benefit, and Liza seemed to forget about Brandon. Yet Martha couldn't help thinking her friend wasn't telling her the whole story.

FEBRUARY 8
SATURDAY, 12:47 P.M.
PENTAGON CITY MALL, ARLINGTON, VA

Jenny promenaded out of the dressing room in a cloud of white, and Kate swiped at the sudden moisture clouding her vision. "Your wedding dress is the most beautiful one I've ever seen."

"You're not crying, are you? I thought you liked me," Jenny teased.

"Can't help myself. I always cry in bridal shops. These are happy tears." Kate truly couldn't be more thrilled for Joe and Jenny. When her brother lost his first wife to cancer, he had been devastated. Kate was ecstatic at his newfound happiness.

She hopped up from her chair to inspect the gown. Lace and pearls adorned the satin bodice. The fitted waist gave way to a softly pleated skirt. Jenny slowly turned to reveal tiny, satin-covered buttons along the back.

Kate smiled. "I wouldn't change a thing."

Jenny surveyed herself in the mirror. "Do you really think Joe will like the dress?"

"He'll love the dress. Trust me."

The salesclerk came over to discuss shortening the hem. Kate wandered around racks filled with tulle, lace, and satin.

The memory of standing in the sewing room of Gavin's mother ambushed her. Mrs. Morton had pulled out her wedding dress, insisting Kate try on the gown. Gavin's family had assumed they'd marry within the year. She had, too. But a month later, when she'd refused to go along with his crooked scheme to destroy his business competitor, he'd blindsided her with a hatred she never could have imagined.

She exhaled a long breath. She had to move forward. After all, she didn't want to miss what God was doing *now*. He had dropped Ben Anderson into her life. Literally. How many men would come through a ceiling to rescue someone? If their relationship continued, they would have a great story when people asked how they met.

"Ready to find Ann?" Jenny had changed out of her wedding dress and joined Kate. "What are you grinning about?"

"Just thinking about ... someone."

"I'm pretty sure I know who." They headed to the center of the mall. "It helps when your fiancé is best friends with ... someone," she added, her eyes twinkling.

A short while later, they spotted Kate's youngest sister Ann waiting for them at an ice cream shop.

"Perfect timing. I just arrived two seconds ago." After wrapping them both in big hugs, Ann turned wide eyes to Kate. "I'm so glad you're safe after the jewelry store robbery. I thought Joe was joking when he first told me."

"I'm okay, Annie." Ann worried about all her brothers and sisters even though she was the youngest.

"Between you being held hostage and Jenny being kidnapped by terrorists, I guess I lead a pretty dull life."

Kate laughed. "Believe me, dull is good."

Once they placed their orders, they settled at a table. Kate dipped a spoon into her ice cream sundae. "Jenny's dress is gorgeous, Ann."

She and Jenny described the gown and they chatted about the wedding. During a lull in the conversation, Kate caught a knowing look pass between Jenny and her sister.

Ann cleared her throat. "So, how did things go?"

Kate furrowed her brow. "How did what things go?"

"Your date with Ben."

No privacy in the Peterson clan. She took a huge bite of ice cream to prolong the suspense.

She had no trouble warming to her subject as she told them about the hike and their conversation. "I really admire Ben. The heartache he's lived through has strengthened his faith. So many people turn bitter after tragedy, but he's letting God use the pain in his life for good."

She stopped, the words she'd spoken settling over her. Though her relationship with Gavin held nothing of the agony Ben had endured in losing his parents, her pain had been real. She was bitter.

The sudden truth resonated through her soul. Ben had forgiven the drunk driver for killing his parents. He refused to let bitterness take root in his heart.

What about her? Had she forgiven Gavin? How could she move forward in a relationship with Ben until she did?

Ann talked about her classes at George Mason, and Kate struggled to focus on the conversation. Later, they strolled through the mall, Jenny and Ann making several purchases. Kate tried to show interest, but weariness penetrated her soul.

Forgiveness was hard. Unforgiveness was a crushing weight.

A weight she still carried.

CHAPTER 7

"Yes, I saw Ethan at the lecture on January eighteenth." Mindy West, Ethan Fitzgerald's colleague, spoke in a soft voice.

Ben glanced at Joe. The first CRI employee they'd interviewed to see Ethan at the lecture. Or was she simply the first employee to admit seeing him? "What did the two of you talk about?"

"Just chit-chat, really. I asked him about his Christmas holiday."

"Were you with Ethan the entire time of the lecture?"

"No, we didn't sit together. We talked for a few minutes in the lobby before the lecture began, then he went into the auditorium ahead of me." She glanced down. "I assumed he must be with someone else."

Mindy looked so disappointed Ben couldn't help feeling sorry for her. *Forget Ethan, Mindy. Unless you love cleaning and laundry.*

Joe sipped the bottled water she'd offered. "Were you aware when you talked to Ethan that he hadn't been at work for over a week?"

She shook her head. "We work on different floors, so I don't see him every day."

Ben studied her. "Have you seen or heard from him since the lecture?"

Mindy stood and paced over to the window, her agitation palpable. "Yes. He called me a week ago. Said he had stumbled onto things in the office that were ... crazy. He wanted my help to access files from the Liechtenstein exchange program."

"Why would he need you to access files from a project he worked on?"

"Each researcher has a specific area concerning the project. I told him no." Her voice shook. "I won't risk my job. I have a daughter to support."

If Ethan had embezzled funds from CRI, was he planning to use Mindy to cover up his crimes? Or, had he truly found something wrong and people within CRI were setting him up? Ben pulled out his phone. "We need the number Ethan used to call you."

"I can do better than that. He called me from his hotel to give me the address in case I changed my mind about wanting to help him." Her voice faltered. "He checked in under the name Jerry Atkins. He told me not to tell anyone. He sounded ... afraid." She unlocked a desk drawer and pulled out a sheet of paper. She hesitated a second before handing the paper to Ben.

"Thank you for your help, Mindy. If he's innocent, he has nothing to fear."

Thirty minutes later, Ben and Joe arrived at a small hotel set back off the interstate.

Ben scanned the area. The hotel rooms opened to the outside walkway. A neon sign with the word *Office* glowed at one end of the building, a small diner stood at the other. "Think he'll talk?"

Joe shrugged. "I think he'd better. The longer he hides, the worse things look."

They got out of the car and followed the sidewalk around the building to room fourteen. The door stood ajar.

Ben sucked in a breath. "FBI! Mr. Fitzgerald?"

"Nobody here but me." A teenaged girl with spiked purple hair holding an armful of folded towels edged to the door. A frown creased her brow. "Check-in time isn't for another three hours."

Joe pulled out a photo of Ethan. "We're looking for this man. We were told he occupied this room."

"Well, if he *was* in this room, he's not here now. He must have checked out." She chomped her gum. "I've got more rooms to clean."

Ben glanced past the girl into the room. Beds made, everything in order. She'd plainly finished here. "Did you ever run into him?"

"No. Just started this job today." She flicked an irritated look in their direction. "I'd like to keep the job, so if you want more answers, go to the office."

They headed to the neon sign. A man with a long gray ponytail sat behind a counter cluttered with newspapers. A cigarette hung from his mouth.

"May I help you?" Ashes drifted onto the counter.

Joe stepped forward with the photo of Ethan. "We'd like to ask you some questions regarding this man. He checked in under the name Jerry Atkins."

"Sorry, can't give information about our guests. Privacy issues, you know?"

His eyes widened when Ben and Joe flipped open their badges. He ground his cigarette into a plastic ashtray and answered questions through tight lips. Yes, a Jerry Atkins occupied room fourteen since January eighth. He'd checked out six days ago and paid cash. No, he hadn't given any indication where he was headed.

Disappointment coursed through Ben as he thanked the clerk for his help. The clerk nodded. With a shaking hand, he reached for the pack of cigarettes stuffed in his front shirt pocket.

Ben and Joe left the office and walked back to the car.

"Mindy said Ethan gave her the name of this hotel a week ago." Ben slid into the driver's side of his vehicle. "Why check out a day later if he hoped she'd change her mind about helping him?"

"Maybe he decided waiting around wasn't worth the risk of someone finding him." Joe reached for his seatbelt. "I think we need to pay another visit to Ethan's cousin."

"My thoughts exactly."

Ethan Fitzgerald always managed to stay a step ahead of them.

Ben's gut told him Charlotte had a hand in helping him.

FEBRUARY 11
TUESDAY, 10:10 A.M.
SHANE'S JEWELERS, DC

Kate held the opal necklace to the light. Delicate pinks and blues radiated from the stone. She handed

Levi Shane her credit card. "This is just what I had in mind for my mom's birthday. She'll be thrilled— the necklace is a perfect match for a ring she always wears."

"This is a particularly nice piece. Nelda can wrap your gift real pretty." Levi carefully returned the necklace to the small box. "I'll be right back."

He moved slower than he had when she'd first met him three weeks ago. No doubt the robbery attempt had taken a toll on him. She shivered. The day certainly had taken a toll on her.

A few minutes later, Nelda hurried from the office, the beautifully wrapped gift in hand. "Kate, I'm so happy to see you."

Kate reached out to hug her. "How are you, Nelda? And where's George?"

She smiled and shrugged. "George stays under the couch in the office most days. As for Levi and me, we're doing pretty well. We're trying to get back into a normal routine and not dwell too much on the robbery attempt. I must admit, though, I still find myself a little startled every time the front door opens."

"I'm really sorry for all you and Levi have gone through. Is there anything I can do for you?"

"We're fine. The only thing we're waiting on is the owner of this building." She pointed to the wall behind Kate. "You can see the damage where the bullet hit. We're also having electrical issues. The landlord said he's still waiting to hear from the insurance company—"

Levi joined them. "There have been other times he said the same thing, yet he never made repairs even though we found out the insurance company paid. I think he just keeps the money and doesn't care if the building falls apart."

The Shanes plainly didn't trust their landlord. And their landlord was the O'Reillys' landlord.

Levi returned Kate's credit card, the twinkle back in his eyes. "I owe you a cup of hot cocoa. Maybe this time I can get the cocoa ready before we're robbed again."

Kate grinned. "Let's give it a try."

Levi led the way to the office and filled three mugs. Kate joined the Shanes around a small table.

"Marshmallows?"

"Absolutely." Kate plopped the soft confection into her mug and pushed the bag to Nelda. "By the way, a man came in the antique store when I was there a couple of weeks ago. Sophie called him 'Ian.' I got the impression he'd been harassing the O'Reillys about money. Later, Max mentioned he was late on his payments." Her pulse quickened. Her family said she had a protective streak a mile wide. They were right. "Does anyone bother you about your rent?"

"I know who you're talking about. Ian works for our landlord. Thinks he's a tough guy." Levi's face reddened. "He better not come in here. I wouldn't give him the time of day."

"Easy, Levi," Nelda soothed. "To answer your question, Kate, no. He doesn't come in. I think he tries to intimidate Max because of the loan."

Kate blinked. "The loan?"

"When Max was going through a rough time last year, the landlord offered him a loan."

"I told him not to sign the paper." Levi glowered. "I tried to give Max some money myself. Told him he didn't need to pay me back. But he wouldn't hear of such a thing—too proud."

"I think Max is having trouble paying off the debt." Nelda shook her head. "The interest is exorbitant."

Kate sipped her cocoa. "Sophie told me once he was having problems because the rent had increased."

"The rent has increased, but the loan is the real problem. Max never told Sophie about the loan, though. He didn't want her to worry." Levi added another marshmallow to his cocoa. "He raised her since she was just a little thing. She means the world to him."

Kate sighed. "I wish I could help."

"You have." Nelda beamed. "You did the wonderful series on our businesses. I saw your interviews with Cynthia and Stephanie next door. You did a marvelous job."

"I was hoping the series might bring you a little more business. Have you noticed an increase in the number of customers?"

"We've had several customers who mentioned seeing the series on channel ten. They were very complimentary."

Kate twirled her half empty cup. *A tactful way of saying no.*

Nelda seemed to read her mind. "The months after the holidays are always slower. Business will pick back up. We'll be fine."

Admiration swept through Kate. What a wonderful couple. They chatted a moment longer, then said goodbye.

Kate stepped outside and glanced at her watch. She really didn't have time. Still ... She hurried into O'Reilly's Antiques. No one stood behind the counter.

"Max? Sophie?"

"Coming!" Max appeared from the back room.

Kate caught her breath. A purple bruise dappled the skin beneath his puffy eye. "Max—what happened?" She rushed over to him.

"Hi, Katie. I'm okay. I slipped and fell, that's all."

Kate searched his face. He looked away. "Max, has someone hit you?"

"Like I said, I fell."

She bit back a protest. Maybe he was telling the truth, but the way he refused to meet her eyes said otherwise.

She touched his arm. "Do you need help? I can call the FBI, because—"

He swung a panicked gaze back to her. "No, Katie, don't. Please."

"Okay, Max." She smiled at him. "You have a refrigerator, don't you? Let's get you some ice." She guided him into the back office and wrapped a dishtowel around some ice cubes. She gently placed the towel over his bruise.

"Ah, much better. Thank you, Katie."

"I have to go now. But remember, if you *should* need help—"

He playfully waved her off. She turned to go.

He was a stubborn Irishman, but Kate was stubborn, too. He'd looked so frightened—she wouldn't tell Joe or Ben, but would keep an eye on him. Along with the Shanes.

God had brought them into her life. She considered them friends and would be there to help them

FEBRUARY 11
TUESDAY, 11:10 A.M.
ALEXANDRIA, VA

"Why are you doing this to my cousin?" Charlotte Fitzgerald screamed through the narrow space between her chained front door and the doorjamb. "Are you crazy? He needs your help."

Ben edged a step closer. She was coming unglued. "Calm down, Ms. Fitzgerald. If you'll open the door, we can talk." Did she have a gun? He placed a hand over his weapon.

Joe stepped to one side, clearly ready to react as she continued to rant.

Ben's mind raced through her rambling accusations. He finally caught the words "You shot at him."

"We did not shoot at your cousin," he shouted. She stilled, her mouth hanging open.

"Ethan said—" Her hand flew to her mouth.

"When did you speak with him?"

"I ... he ..." she stammered.

"Ben—Fitzgerald's here."

Joe's words registered. Ben spun around in time to see Ethan Fitzgerald run across the street and dart down a tree-lined sidewalk.

Ben raced after him, his stride matching Joe's. Ethan lunged through a manicured lawn and jumped across children's bicycles lying in a driveway. Ben sucked in air, pushing ahead. Ethan Fitzgerald would not get away this time.

Ethan zigzagged through the neighborhood. An elderly man shook his fist while a woman swooped up her child when they hurtled past.

He and Joe inched closer to Ethan. Ben's left calf muscle cramped. He clenched his teeth through the pain.

Ethan flung a glance behind him. He leaped from the sidewalk into the street. A shout stuck in Ben's throat.

Brakes squealed as a vehicle skidded. Ethan propelled himself headfirst out of the car's path. His body slammed against pavement and crumpled.

Ben reached him at the same time the driver jumped from her vehicle. "He ran out in front of me." The woman's voice shook. "I didn't hit him, did I? Oh, tell me he's alive …"

Ben knelt and leaned over Ethan. His pulse was steady, his breathing shallow. Blood pooled beneath the left side of Ethan's face. Was there any skin left? He'd slid across the pavement like a baseball player reaching home plate. Burns from the asphalt covered his hands, and his jacket was ripped apart. Had he sustained internal injuries? Ben continued to monitor Ethan's pulse.

"An ambulance is on the way." Joe stuffed his phone back into his pocket and stooped beside them.

Sweat stung Ben's eyes. If only he'd run a little faster, maybe Ethan wouldn't be lying here unconscious. Some days he hated this job.

The driver of the car sat beside them, weeping. "Please, God, oh, please—"

A shrill cry sliced Ben's senses. Joe jumped up to shield Charlotte Fitzgerald from the sight of her cousin.

Sirens cut through the air as an ambulance arrived, two police cars close behind. The paramedics sprang into action. Moments later, the ambulance whisked Ethan away.

Statements were given and reports completed. Afterward, Charlotte was taken to St. Michael's Hospital to be with her cousin.

Ben glanced around. Clusters of neighbors were turning to go back inside their houses. He hadn't noticed they'd come out.

"Ready to head to the hospital?"

Ben nodded. Joe looked as miserable as he felt. "This didn't turn out like I'd hoped."

"No kidding."

They walked slowly back to their car. According to Charlotte Fitzgerald, someone had shot at her cousin. Was Ethan working with another person who'd decided Ethan was a liability? Or, was Ethan innocent and about to expose a crime?

Ben's gut clenched. Whether Ethan was innocent or guilty, someone wanted him dead.

FEBRUARY 11
TUESDAY, 7:58 P.M.
ST. MICHAEL'S HOSPITAL, DC

"I'm afraid I can't disclose the condition of any patient transported to St. Michael's. As a physician, I must respect the right to privacy." The gray-haired ER doctor studied Ben and Joe.

Ben exhaled a long breath. If needed, they would subpoena Ethan Fitzgerald's medical records. Sometimes listening to what the attending physician said—and didn't say—could answer the most pressing questions. "We understand. Is Mr. Fitzgerald allowed visitors?"

"His family is with him now." The doctor consulted his laptop. "You're welcome to check back tomorrow during regular visiting hours."

A good sign—visitors allowed. "We appreciate your time, sir."

The doctor shook hands and moved on. Ben turned to Joe. "I'll leave our names at the nurses' station and brief them about the guard who will be posted at Fitzgerald's door."

Joe nodded. "The head of hospital security is sending someone right up. I'll wait here for him."

The nurse behind the desk took Ben's information. As he turned to leave, he glanced past her. Through the glass partition, he saw Charlotte Fitzgerald. *Ethan's room.*

Charlotte stood beside the bed. A woman in a chair next to her looked up.

Mindy West. The realization hit full force. How did Mindy know Ethan was in the hospital? Had Charlotte called her after the accident? Or, had they been in contact all along?

Ben slammed the button to open the doors leading back into the hall. His hand pulsated. Being lied to didn't agree with him.

But Ethan Fitzgerald wasn't going anywhere. Separating the truth from lies was only a matter of time.

FEBRUARY 14
FRIDAY, 6:40 P.M.
LAKEWOOD PARK ELEMENTARY SCHOOL, VA

Kate followed Ben into his nieces' elementary school. A few things in life seemed constant. Elementary school was one. Colorful artwork spilled from bulletin boards along the wide hallway. A large banner announced an upcoming spelling bee, and fire safety posters hung along the walls.

Ben reached for her hand. "You know what my favorite thing about elementary school was?"

She grinned. "Recess?"

"Fish sticks."

"Fish sticks?"

"Yeah. They were always on the menu for Fridays. I still remember asking my teacher what part of the fish was inside. She never did give me an answer."

Kate chuckled. "I always loved music class. At my school, we had music once a week. Come to think of it, the class was always on Friday. I guess Fridays are good days no matter what age you are."

Children's voices sounded nearby. When Kate peeked down a hallway, smiling little faces poked out of classrooms. "Looks like the kids are lining up. Are your nieces excited about the play?"

"Bouncing-off-the-ceiling excited. Thank you for coming with me, Kate." He squeezed her hand. "I know grabbing a quick dinner and heading to a school play is an unusual way to spend Valentine's Day. I hope the flowers made up for this evening a little."

Her heart skipped a beat at the thought of the extravagant, gorgeous arrangement he'd sent to her office. "Ben, this is a perfect way to spend Valentine's Day. I mean that." The depth of his eyes made looking any place else impossible. "Will we sit with Leah?"

"No, she's helping backstage." He pointed to the small bag slung over his shoulder. "I have strict instructions to catch everything on film."

Seats in the auditorium were filling up. Ben scanned the rows and pointed to two empty seats close to the front.

"Those seats look like a good spot for filming, but there are a lot of knees to squeeze past. What do you think?"

"I've been to so many sporting events with my brothers, I can battle my way past a row of people while I hold a soda, burger, and fries. And not lose a single fry."

"Hmm, a great idea for the next school play—selling ballpark food in the aisles."

When they reached the front of the auditorium, Kate ducked her head and led the way to their seats, her "excuse me" met with tolerant smiles. Once settled, she had little room, but she didn't mind. She leaned against Ben's arm, her insides fluttering.

She opened the program she'd received at the door to study the names. "Little Bo Peep—Bekah Morris. Bonnie is Mother Goose. Wow—they have starring roles."

"They get their acting abilities from their uncle." Ben's eyes twinkled. "I brought the house down in my second-grade school play."

"Who were you?"

"More like *what*. I was a mushroom."

Kate laughed. "Well, bringing the house down as a mushroom is definitely a testament to your acting ability." She reached over to squeeze his hand. He laced his fingers through hers.

The lights blinked and an expectant murmur rippled through the crowd.

"There's my cue." Ben reached for the video camera. A program from the seat in front fluttered onto the floor. A woman turned.

"I'm sorry. Could you please … Ben?"

"McKenzie?"

Kate glanced from one to the other. Surprise swept across Ben's features. Something she couldn't read reflected in his eyes.

Ben handed the program to her. "Are you in DC for a visit?"

"No. I'm back to stay."

The muscles in Ben's strong jaw twitched as beats of silence passed. Kate stilled. The delight she'd felt earlier evaporated, caution flooding its place.

Ben broke the silence. "McKenzie, this is Kate Peterson." He turned to Kate. "Kate, McKenzie Lewis."

"A pleasure." Kate nodded and extended her hand.

The auditorium descended into blackness. Mercifully. A spotlight cut through the darkness, lighting the stage, and the play began. Though Kate tried to concentrate as the children danced across the stage, the exchange between Ben and McKenzie fluttered through her mind. The two had history. From the look on their faces, the history might well have another chapter.

She slumped in the darkness. Had she only imagined the spark between Ben and herself? Was she so blinded by a relationship gone bad she couldn't see clearly any longer?

The curtain fell when Act One concluded. Kate clapped with an enthusiasm not quite reaching her heart. She glanced sideways at Ben. Was she jumping to conclusions? He'd smiled at McKenzie. Period. And what about the beautiful flowers that had arrived at her office this morning?

She sighed inwardly. Relationships were confusing. Hard. Maybe not worth the heartache they consistently seemed to slam her with. She needed to rein in her emotions. She would not be hurt again.

Later, the play ended with the children marching across the stage for a final bow. After the audience gave a standing ovation, everyone began to gather their belongings. McKenzie looked at Ben, whose attention was focused on his camera. She filed out of her row.

Ben zipped his camera into the case, then turned to Kate. "Since people are heading to both sides of the aisle, I don't think we're blocking anyone. Would you like to wait here a minute until the crowd thins out?"

She nodded. His voice sounded strained. He faced her and gently held her hand. The look in his eyes squeezed her heart.

"The woman I introduced you to—McKenzie—" He paused a beat. "McKenzie and I were engaged two years ago. Three months into the engagement, she broke things off. Said she needed to find who she was. She moved away, and I haven't seen or spoken with her until now. Running into her again was quite a surprise."

For both of us. Why hadn't he told her about McKenzie? Yet they hadn't discussed Gavin. Kate swallowed hard. "Do you still have things to talk about?"

He shifted in his seat. "Kate, I won't lie. I loved McKenzie. Losing her hurt deeply. But that part of my life is over. After she broke our engagement, I thought long and hard about the relationship. I realized we'd been headed in different directions. God has someone else for McKenzie." His voice softened. "And I know he has someone else for me."

His blue eyes melted her. She wanted to believe him. He clearly believed what he said. As she thought about the look McKenzie had tossed his way, she couldn't help wondering.

Did *McKenzie* know their relationship was over?

CHAPTER 8

Ethan Fitzgerald stared out of his hospital window. The pounding in his head had lessened to a dull ache. He finally saw only one of everything, and he could sit in the recliner without becoming nauseous.

He shut his eyes to block out all the faces. Doctors in white lab coats. Nurses hovering over him. FBI agents. Charlotte … and Mindy. Why had Mindy come? Did she think of him as anything other than a co-worker? At times she appeared interested in him, only to slam an emotional door in his face if he got too close.

Opening his eyes, he reached for the cup of ginger ale. The fizz trickled down his dry throat. He might not be able to figure out relationships, but he knew his job. Those few hours he couldn't remember anything about his work had been terrifying. Gradually memories had glimmered through the fuzz of his brain, and finally his thoughts focused. Alarmingly so.

His cup almost slipped through hands slick with sweat. How much longer could he go on with this charade? *Retrograde amnesia*, the doctor had concluded. *The concussion was obviously more severe than they'd first thought for the memory loss to have lasted for several days.*

Ethan sighed. He hated to lie to Charlotte, to let her go on thinking he couldn't remember. Fatigue seeped through him. He leaned against the cushioned headrest. Maybe if he slept, he could form a plan when he woke up.

A bullet whizzed past his head. He cried out and lurched from the chair. His heart hammered.

He searched the room for the gunman. Sweat dripped from his brow. Finally, he sank again into the recliner and drew a shaky breath. *Only a dream.*

Someone *had* shot at him only days ago. Who?

Ethan shuddered. What had he gotten himself into? He should leave soon. If only he could think of a way to slip past the guard outside his door. Staying here wasn't an option. He needed to find someplace safe.

FEBRUARY 15
SATURDAY, 6:45 P.M.
MEADOW DRIVE, FAIRFAX, VA

"Thanks for the tacos, Uncle Ben." Bekah scrambled from her chair to hug him.

"The least I can do for the stars of last night's school play." Pride beat through Ben's heart.

Bonnie planted a kiss on his cheek. "Do you want to watch a princess movie with us?"

Ben ruffled her brown curls. "Sure. Just let me finish my enchilada. You girls start the movie. You can catch me and your mom up on the action."

He glanced at his sister. The light in Leah's smile faded as the girls bounced upstairs. He reached for her hand. "I know yesterday was hard for you. Rich would have loved seeing the girls in the play."

"I guess so." Bitterness punctuated her tone.

Ben searched her face. "Leah, I—"

She shook his hand off hers and scraped her chair away from the table. "Will you stop trying to make me feel better? You have no idea what I'm going through." Her voice rose with each word. She picked up her plate and started toward the sink. She whirled to face him. "Did you hear me? No idea." She slammed the dish against the counter. Glass splintered.

Fear surged through Ben's veins. "Leah—" He wrapped his arms around her. She struggled to break free.

"I'm going to break everything in this kitchen! I want to tear this house apart until nothing is standing." Her body heaved with sobs. "I hate him."

Ice glazed Ben's fear. *Help us, Lord.* He held her as she writhed. She punched his arms and begged him to leave.

"Leah, I'm not leaving you. We'll get through this together. I promise."

Slowly, her fight lessened. When the struggle stopped, she wilted against him. She was silent for a long time. When she spoke, her voice trembled. "Oh, Ben, I'm sorry, so sorry."

The sobs began again, softer. Ben led her to the small sofa by the kitchen window. She trembled, and he wrapped her in the afghan tossed across the sofa's arm.

She looked up at him, tears running down her cheeks. "Please, can you ever forgive me? I can't believe what I just did."

"Leah, there's nothing to forgive. I meant what I said. I'm not leaving you. We'll get through this."

She wiped her tears with the backs of her hands. "I'm not sure I want to get through this." Her breath came out in gasps. "There's something I haven't told you—or anybody else. Rich was planning to file for divorce when he came home."

Ben gaped. Leah must be mistaken. Rich loved her and the girls so much.

"He wanted the divorce, not me." She twirled the fringes of the afghan around her fingers. "He said we'd grown apart, that he was ready to move on. I couldn't believe what I was hearing. Sure, we had our problems like every couple, but nothing we couldn't have worked through." Her bottom lip quivered. "I meant my wedding vows. I would have stayed. Apparently, the vows meant nothing to Rich."

Ben tried to process Leah's words. His sister and brother-in-law had seemed so happy. On a hiking trip the three of them had taken last year, Rich's words hung in his memory. *You need to find someone and settle down, buddy. You won't regret the decision.* Ben hadn't spent much time with Rich before the deployment because of work schedules, but surely his feelings couldn't have changed so drastically. Could they?

He looked at Leah. She seemed so fragile. How could he have missed this? He went to the sink and poured a glass of water for her. His pulse throbbed in his temples. He was ready to break a few dishes himself.

She sipped the water he brought. "We had a terrible argument before he left. We said things I never would have believed either of us could say. Afterward, I almost drowned in anger. Little by little, God worked on my heart. I struggled, but I finally decided I would fight for him. I scheduled counseling sessions at our church. I signed up for golf lessons because he loves the game so much. I couldn't wait until he came home. I wrote a letter asking for his forgiveness, letting him know I wasn't giving up on us. I dreamed of him taking me into his arms and hearing him say the same. Now we'll never get the chance, will we?" Tears spilled again. "Oh, Ben, how can I deal with these feelings? I thought I'd gotten past the anger." She looked at the shards of glass on the floor. "I guess I haven't."

"Mommy! Where are you and Uncle Ben?" Bekah's voice floated down the stairs.

"Coming, sweetheart!" Ben called.

Leah jumped up and hurried to the pantry. She returned with a broom and dustpan. "I've got to sweep up the glass before the girls see."

Ben took the broom from her. "You go on up. I'll take care of this and join you in a minute."

Leah wiped her eyes. "Ben, thank you for everything."

She left, and he slowly pushed the shards into the dustpan. Exhaustion settled over his body. He had no answers.

FEBRUARY 16
SUNDAY, 3:45 P.M.
REINHART STABLES, DC

Kate breathed in the rich smell of leather mixed with the pungent scent of horse stalls. "I love the smell of a stable."

Ingrid laughed. "I do, too. Now I understand why we're becoming good friends. We're both crazy."

Kate removed the halter from her horse's head and slipped on a bridle. "Good boy, Dakota." She rubbed his nose, and he gave a low whinny. "Growing up, my sisters and I loved our horses so much we sometimes brought their blankets into our rooms. We pretended like the horses were inside with us." After checking the saddle's cinch again, she led her mount out into the bright sunshine. "I miss our farm," she called over her shoulder.

A moment later, Kate noted the owner of the stables walking out with Ingrid. His face beaming, he led her horse. A little royalty could brighten anyone's day.

They mounted and nudged their horses toward the waiting security guards. A wooded trail stretched before them. Kate relished the chance to relax and leave the bustle of the city behind. She missed riding. Maybe someday she'd buy a horse of her own, but the cost of boarding one pushed into the daydream. Maybe not.

Ingrid reined her horse in beside Kate. "So, your family owns a farm? We do as well, but the property is rather small. We only have about fifty horses. How many do you have?"

"Three." Kate chuckled at the look on Ingrid's face. "Actually, our farm isn't a horse farm. We do have other animals—sheep, cows, even a llama. Primarily, though, we grow wheat and corn. What crops are grown in Liechtenstein?"

"Potatoes, corn, wheat, barley. We also grow a variety of grapes and orchard fruits."

"I'd love to visit Liechtenstein someday." Kate patted Dakota's sleek neck. "I toured Switzerland, along with several other countries, when our family visited Europe one summer. The Alps were absolutely beautiful."

"Our country has magnificent scenery. Tourism is a major part of our economy. Speaking of economy, our country is partnering with the United States in a research exchange program."

Kate nodded. "I read about the program several months ago. The idea is fascinating."

"Our economists will fly to the United States this week. There will be a ceremony for them at Caldwell Research Institute."

"Could we do an interview there, maybe film the ceremony?"

"I'm sure we could. I'll speak with Ambassador Schrader and ask her to make the necessary arrangements."

The trail curved beside a sparkling stream. The only sounds were the rush of water running over rocks and the click of the horses' hooves.

The horses moved to the water's edge. Kate loosened Dakota's reins so he could drink from the stream. "I feel like I'm a hundred miles away from the city."

"What a perfect day." Ingrid turned in her saddle to face Kate. "I've been thinking about our conversation a couple of weeks ago—how God shapes our days to fit us. I've always thought of God as being distant, but if he has a unique purpose for everyone, he must care about each individual."

Kate brushed her fingers through her horse's mane. "The Bible says he gives names to all of the stars, yet he knows each of our names. He is both powerful and personal."

Ingrid's eyes widened. "I can't imagine naming all the stars when they can't even be counted. I read just the other day astronomers believe there are even more galaxies than previously thought."

"Think of how many people are in the world, yet God knows each one." Kate zipped her jacket as the sun slipped behind a cloud. "I love how Jesus sought out individuals to heal or comfort them. One person had—and still has—as much value to him as millions of people."

Once the horses finished drinking from the stream, the group continued along the trail, one security guard leading, the other following behind.

"You speak of God like he's your friend." Wistfulness touched Ingrid's words.

"He is, Ingrid. He wants to be your friend, too. That's why he sent his Son. I grew up attending church, so I knew facts about Jesus. I just couldn't understand how his death on a cross and his resurrection related to me. After all, those things happened two thousand years ago. My sister Rachel helped me understand Jesus took my place on that cross. Salvation is a gift I needed to accept for myself—not just in my head but in my heart."

Ingrid grew silent. Kate cast a sidelong glance at her. *I hope I said the right words.* She looked up at fluffy clouds floating across a blue sky. *Please, Lord, help her understand. Only you can change a heart.*

A moment later, Ingrid pointed ahead. "Look how straight and level the trail is. Why don't we let the horses stretch their legs?"

"Sure." Kate straightened. "Dakota was just telling me how fast he can run."

They nudged their horses into a canter, the guards following Ingrid's lead. Kate closed her eyes for a second, the cold wind against her skin and the speed of her horse exhilarating.

"Race you," Ingrid yelled to one of the guards.

He obliged, keeping his horse slightly in check. Finally, the trail began to narrow and the group slowed again.

"You won," the guard called, flashing a good-natured smile.

Kate grinned. Was never showing up royalty part of his job description?

The hour passed quickly. Kate sighed at the sight of the stable. She'd definitely come here again. Joe and Ann would love the trail. And Ben … The tingle of delight at the prospect faded at the thought of McKenzie. Would he see McKenzie again? He'd told Kate the relationship was over. She had no reason to doubt him. Ben wasn't Gavin.

She dismounted and handed the reins to the waiting groom. "Dakota is a wonderful horse."

He nodded. "One of our finest." His eyes flicked to Ingrid, still mounted. "I hope you and the princess enjoyed the ride."

"We did." Kate started to say more, but he was staring at Ingrid, awestruck.

Later, they headed to the parking area. Ingrid gave Kate a quick hug. "Thank you so much for today." She hesitated. "Thanks for being a friend."

Kate waved goodbye and waited as a chauffeur helped Ingrid, alone again except for the guards, into her car. Kate glanced back at the stable. A little throng of people had gathered to watch the princess depart. Ingrid's words at the National Mall replayed in her mind. *Sometimes I feel I'll be nothing more than a royal figurehead. Life lacks meaning.*

Kate turned to her car. Everyone knew Ingrid's title. How many people knew the person? *Lord, help her to know she has value to you, not because she's royal, but because you created her.*

Kate slid behind the wheel of her vehicle and switched on the ignition. Nothing. She tried again. Still dead.

She peered out of her windshield. Ingrid's black BMW was almost out of sight. Great. She clicked the latch to open the hood and got out to inspect the engine. If only she'd listened to her dad and brothers discuss the fine points of mechanics during their Saturday morning pancake breakfasts. She'd been more interested in buying a car than worrying about what was under the hood. Now she had no idea what she was looking for.

"Car trouble?"

The groom who had taken Dakota strolled up behind her and surveyed the engine. "I have a part-time job in a garage. Maybe I can help."

She studied him. "You must stay busy with two jobs."

He shrugged. "The work's not so bad." He leaned in for a closer look.

"Weird."

"What's wrong?"

"Battery cable. The thing has been cut completely in half."

Kate blinked. "How could the cable have been cut? Maybe the part was old and pulled apart."

He shook his head. "Look—no fraying. The edges are clean."

She shoved a strand of hair behind her ear. "If that's true, the cable would have been cut while I was riding. How could someone open the hood? My car was locked."

"Like I said—weird. We've never had a problem with anyone bothering vehicles in the parking area before." He stuffed his hands into his pockets. "I think I can help. My brother owns the garage where I work. He's coming to pick me up in about an hour. I could have him bring a cable and we could get you fixed up on the spot."

Kate blew out a breath. "Any idea what the cost will be?"

"I'll just charge you for the cable. My brother is coming out here anyway." He grinned. "If you could get me a date with the princess, I won't even charge for the part."

She laughed. "I don't know if I can arrange a date, but I'll definitely mention how helpful you were."

"Good enough." He touched the brim of his cap. "I'd better get back to the stable."

"I'll wait in my car until your brother comes. Thanks again."

She sank into the driver's seat and clicked the door locks. The groom headed back to the stable. Funny how he'd shown up the minute she opened the hood of her car. Had he waited in the parking area hoping to talk with Ingrid?

Her mind swirled. She was certain her car was locked while she and Ingrid rode. Still, to someone who knew what he was doing, a locked car probably wasn't an obstacle. Her eyes darted around the parking area. The vehicles appeared empty, the owners still enjoying an afternoon ride. Would they find their engines dead when they came back? Or, had she been singled out?

Thoughts of the past weeks churned through her brain. The attempted robbery at Shane's Jewelers had taken place a month ago. A car almost hit her the following day. The man from Texas who'd helped her said the driver looked straight at her. One week later, the black rose and smashed candy landed on her car. Five days after she found the flower, Ian showed up behind her in the parking garage. Following her? Probably not. Still …

Kate breathed a ragged sigh. Things had been quiet for two weeks. Until now. *What Will I Do Next?* She shivered. Someone wanted her attention.

Slowly, her chin lifted. Someone *had* her attention. She'd never backed down from a fight before. She refused to start now. As a reporter, she dug for facts. Chased truth. She had no idea what she'd been pulled into.

She was going to find out.

FEBRUARY 17
MONDAY, 10:17 A.M.
N QUINCY STREET, ARLINGTON, VA

Martha wandered down the rows of books at Arlington Central Library. She veered off course on her way to the photography section to scan titles of biographies. A book about Winston Churchill caught her eye. She opened the heavy volume, and after thumbing through pages, tucked the book under her arm. She'd curl up in front of the gas logs tonight and spend a cozy evening with a new book. Perfect.

"Martha—hello."

The voice behind her jarred her very core. She spun around. A gaunt Frank Edwards smiled at her. The book she held slipped from her grasp and thudded to the floor.

"Frank." The urge to throw her arms around the friend she'd worried about for months vied with one to punch him in the gut. She chose neither, opting for the only other thing she could think of. "We need to talk." The detachment in her voice surprised her, reminded her of the days in the CIA when she'd questioned suspects.

A hint of amusement glinted in Frank's eyes. She quashed her anger. The punch in the gut looked better all the time.

"The exact reason I followed you here—so we could talk. I went to a lot of trouble to make sure *I* wasn't followed." He kept his voice low and was all business. "I know I've left you with a lot of unanswered questions."

Years' worth. "Where do you want to go? The library isn't very busy this morning. We can find a spot where no one is around."

"Sounds good."

They located a table in a deserted area on the second floor, far back in the stacks. Frank settled in his chair. "Where should I begin?"

Martha studied him. He looked different from the last time she'd seen him. He'd lost weight, and his hair seemed grayer, but the change ran deeper than his physical appearance. The energy normally radiating from him wasn't there. He appeared worn. She pushed down the sympathy threatening to run through her. She needed answers. "For starters, your car was found on a deserted road almost three months ago. The windows were shattered and blood stained the driver's side. How did you manage to come out alive?"

"By the skin of my teeth, thank you. The only thing that saved me was my pursuer's vehicle skidding into a ditch. He lost consciousness long enough for me to drag myself to an old warehouse about two hundred yards away." Frank shifted in his chair. "I could barely keep from passing out myself. I managed to get inside the building and hide behind some equipment. I kept watch through a crack in the wall. When the shooter came to finish the job, the sun was setting. Everything was dark by the time he searched the warehouse. He must have come within two feet of me, yet never saw me."

Martha drew a breath. "You were bleeding. How did you get medical help?"

"I called in a favor from a buddy. When he finally found me, I'd lost a lot of blood. He got me to a hospital with little time to spare. I'm still not at the top of my game, but I'm better than I was a couple of months ago."

Martha processed the information. George Merck, the traitor she'd met with during Jenny's kidnapping, wanted Frank dead. The accusations Merck had leveled against Frank regarding the murder of her husband washed over her. She gripped the edge of the table. "When I met with Merck in November, he said you'd betrayed him, that he wanted revenge. Did he shoot you?"

"Though I'm sure Merck would have loved nothing better, someone higher on the food chain was after me."

"Who?"

He hesitated. "Martha, let's leave your question for later. There's something I need to tell you. When I was in the warehouse waiting for my buddy, I thought I might bleed to death. My biggest regret was not setting the record straight with you."

He looked at her with an emotion she couldn't read. She bit her lip. Could she handle what he was about to say?

"I'm sorry, very sorry I dropped out of your life after Charles died. I know you needed support during those weeks and months. The decision to break off all contact with you was one of the most difficult ones I've ever made. But I had to. I had a crucial reason for doing so."

Lord, please don't let him tell me he murdered my husband. She drew a sharp breath. *If he does, let the police get here before I tear him apart with my bare hands.* She gathered herself. "Okay … what was the reason?"

"I had begun working as a double agent about six months before Clarissa and I met with you and Charles in Switzerland."

Martha's thoughts rushed back years ago to the Swiss village of Zermatt. She and Charles had planned a relaxing week of skiing with Frank and his wife Clarissa. Yet during the tragic events which unfolded, she'd never guessed her old partner was a double agent. "Not long ago, I came across a note scribbled in a Bible belonging to Charles. He had written he needed to talk with you in Switzerland because something was wrong. He didn't know you were a double agent, did he?"

"Actually, he did. He was aware from the beginning. I think what he meant by his comment was simple. He knew my cover was about to be blown." Frank's eyes suddenly misted. "I wish he hadn't known. He might still be alive."

"What do you mean?" Had she shouted those words or whispered them?

"He always tried to watch my back. With his connections as a war correspondent, he knew before I did a Russian intelligence agent suspected I was double-crossing them. The day on the mountain, when Charles was killed—" Frank paused a moment. "We were almost at the bottom of the slope. I was a few yards ahead of Charles. A shot sounded, and the bullet kicked up wood from a tree to the right of us. A splinter lodged near my temple. Like a fool, I slowed. Charles caught up with me. He put himself between me and the sniper. He took the bullet—" Frank's voice cracked. "The bullet meant for me. I heard the sniper's gun click over and over, but the next bullet never came. The gun must have jammed, and he fled. I didn't go after him because I thought if I got help for Charles, he might live. Instead, I lost both Charles and the sniper." Bitterness coated Frank's words. "I never told you Charles died saving my life because the guilt almost consumed me. I set out to do everything I could to earn the Russians' trust. I was determined to find the person who killed Charles. When George Merck was arrested for selling military secrets to the Russians, I smuggled weapons into his prison. We set up his supposed death to get him out of jail and back to Russia. I was able to work for the US government while I was right under the Russians' noses. Though I thwarted most of Merck's work, I couldn't find the killer. Years later, when I stumbled across his identity, he had already died in a car crash." Frank's eyes met hers. "His name was Oleg Petrovich."

Heat surged through Martha. "Why wasn't I notified—if not by you, by the agency?"

"To keep from compromising the safety of another CIA operative," he answered simply.

Pain registered in Martha's brain. When she relaxed her clenched fists, she noticed a trickle of blood where her nails had dug into flesh. She opened her mouth to speak, but no words came. *Charles ...*

He had died trying to protect his friend. Tears flowed. After all these years, she still missed her husband—his strength, his gentleness, his laughter, his love. She missed his smelly socks on the bedroom floor, his whiskers in the bathroom, the dishes he could somehow stack in the kitchen sink but never get into the dishwasher ... If only he were here.

She stood, her breath tiny gasps. "I need to ... walk."

Frank nodded and rose to follow. She hurried down the stairs and shoved open the glass front door. She turned toward a park with a playground and baseball field. She pushed her hands deep into the pockets of her down jacket as she walked. Every time she reached a place of peace regarding the death of her husband, some new accusation or revelation plunged her again into turmoil.

"Martha."

She'd almost forgotten he was beside her. "What?"

"Maybe the time has come to let go."

She bit her lip. They walked in silence twice around the baseball field. They came to a picnic table and she sank onto the damp wooden bench.

Maybe the time has come to let go. Frank's words settled over her. Finally, she had the name of her husband's murderer. Yet she could do nothing. A deep sigh worked its way from the depths of her being. Justice was in God's hands. *And the death of Charles had nothing to do with my work in the CIA.*

The thought struck her with force. She'd never voiced her fear, even to herself. Relief slowly spread through her. Charles had died as he lived, a man ready to do anything for those he loved. God had allowed her a precious farewell memory. Frank was right. The past would cripple her if she continued to hold on.

She slowly lifted her eyes. "What you said is true, Frank. I need to let go of everything except the good memories."

He reached across the table and covered her hand with his. "You're cold. Let's find someplace warm and get something to eat." He hesitated a moment. "I'm afraid there's more to the story."

Martha gaped. "I can't take any more."

"Not about Charles," he added quickly. "About someone else who died in the line of duty. I need to find his killer, and time is running out."

CHAPTER 9

Martha swirled a chip, still warm to the touch, into the bowl of salsa. She loved this restaurant, but today she wasn't sure she could manage the entrée she'd ordered. What else did Frank have to tell her? She shot a look at him. He'd requested a booth in a corner of the restaurant near an exit. He sat with his back against the wall. The perfect spot to see whoever entered.

She could wait no longer. "You said there's more."

Frank pulled his gaze toward her and nodded. "You already know part of the story. Six months ago, a CIA operative named T. J. Moore was shot and killed."

"His name sounds familiar." Martha closed her eyes for a moment. "Of course … my niece Jenny stopped to help T. J. on the highway. A car rammed his off the road. Jenny and her friend called 9-1-1. He was hit in a drive-by shooting while they waited for an ambulance."

Frank clenched his hand into a fist. "Believe me, the hit was not random."

"Jenny was devastated to learn he died later. She showed me a newspaper article with the story. You were in the photo."

"A costly mistake on my part. A buddy of mine on the police force called me when he got to the scene. T. J. was like a son to me. He came to the agency toward the end of my career. We worked together for three years before I retired."

"That explains why I never met him—I would have already left the agency by then."

Frank's eyes darkened. "T. J. had a flash drive with him. He'd switched vehicles twice on the day of his murder to lose anyone following him. After his van was forced off the road, he hid the flash drive in Jenny's car. I retrieved the device from her later."

"She told me. What was on the flash drive?"

"Evidence pointing to criminal activity by a CIA operative."

Martha's muscles tightened. "Who?"

"Ted Bradley."

She sucked in a breath. "I called Ted Bradley to tell him you were alive. Did he shoot you? Frank, I'm so sorry."

He shrugged. "The fault is mine for waiting too long to talk with you. I believe he was the one behind T. J.'s death. I also believe the meeting between you and Merck during Jenny's kidnapping was set up by Bradley to find me. He knew I had information. He probably figured I'd try to contact you since I couldn't risk trusting anyone currently at the agency. Just in case I didn't, he knew you would lead him to me."

Martha raised an eyebrow. "Why would he think I'd try to find you?"

"If he could frame me for killing Charles, your coming after me would only be a matter of time." Frank smiled at her. "Your reputation lives on, you know."

She'd been dubbed "Bulldog" in one of her first cases at the agency because she refused to give up. The name stuck throughout her career. "When I spoke with Bradley a few weeks ago to tell him I'd heard from you, he set up a meeting with me. Said he had new information. He told me he had to leave the country for two weeks, so he set the time for March third."

"You're going, I hope?"

"Unless he's in jail by then." She searched his face. "You have the evidence, right?"

"We need more. A few pieces to the puzzle are still missing. We need solid proof Bradley ordered the death of one of his own CIA operatives." The old spark of determination flickered in Frank's eyes. "If you meet with him, maybe you can uncover who he's working with."

Martha shook her head. "You don't ask much, do you?"

The server came with huge plates of sizzling chicken, rice, and warm tortillas. As Martha took a few bites, her appetite slowly returned. While she ate, she pondered the information Frank had given her.

She had gained answers today. Were they true? She wanted to believe Frank, more than anything.

But she needed to hear Ted Bradley's side of the story.

FEBRUARY 18
TUESDAY, 1:10 P.M.
DC

The crowded Metro car lurched to a stop. Kate tightened her grip on the metal pole and shuffled her feet to keep her balance. A backpack belonging to someone behind her pressed into her shoulder. She shifted positions. The doors opened, people exited, and more passengers streamed in. She grinned. Life in the big city. She loved DC.

Kate glanced at her watch. She'd worked the night shift last evening and had this afternoon off. The Metro braked again. She pushed her way past people to the open door. Time to start a little investigative work of her own.

She walked the two blocks to Shane's Jewelers. Might as well start at the beginning. She quickened her pace. Even though the robbery had nothing to do with her, things started happening the following day.

She entered the jewelry store and followed the sound of laughter to the office. Maybe life was getting back to normal for her friends.

"Look who's here!" Levi Shane's face beamed. "Kate, you're just in time to watch me mop the floor with O'Reilly." He pointed to a checkerboard positioned on the table between the two men.

"Don't listen to him, Katie." Max shook his finger in Levi's direction. "He always talks a big game but never can deliver."

Nelda hugged Kate. "Just like two kids."

Kate pulled up a chair beside them. "Who's minding the store, Max?"

"Sophie's over there today. You'll have to stop in to see her after you watch me annihilate Levi."

"I'll do that." Kate studied Max's face. A week had passed since she'd seen him. The purple bruise around his eye had turned to a yellowish-brown. The swelling had lessened considerably.

Nelda passed a plate of fudge brownies in Kate's direction. She helped herself to two, then turned to watch the game. She savored moist layers of dark chocolate as she listened to the banter over the checkerboard. A sense of belonging warmed her. Family surrounded her on every side, not only with Joe, Ann, and now Jenny and Aunt Martha, but with these friends. DC was becoming home more quickly than any place she'd lived since her childhood in Kansas.

Her gaze wandered to the front room. From her vantage point, she could see the wall damaged by Angelo's bullet. Would the Shane's landlord fix the damage, or keep the insurance money for himself? Of course, choosing not to use the funds to repair his building wasn't illegal. Was it? Unless …

Levi clapped his checker across the board and took Max's last piece with a flourish. "I told you I'd win." He raised his arms and clasped his hands over his head. "Still the champ."

"I let you win because I felt sorry for you, you old goat. If you keep up the gloating, I'll have to beat you next time to show you who's boss."

"Now, now, boys." Nelda replaced the checkerboard with the plate of brownies. "Have some dessert."

Levi reached over and slapped Max on the back. "Looks like we're both winners, buddy. Nelda's brownies can't be beat."

"Best I ever ate," Kate agreed.

Nelda smiled at her. "How are you, Kate? Out on an assignment today?"

"No, I have the afternoon off. I wanted to come by for a visit." She glanced around the circle of faces. How much should she tell them? "I did have a question, though. I was thinking about the man who comes in your shops sometimes—Ian."

Max shrugged. "He's not worth worrying about, Katie."

"I think I saw him a couple of weeks ago. I wondered how long he's worked for your landlord."

"Ever since the current landlord bought the building two years ago."

"Who *is* your landlord?"

"Lancaster. Brandon Lancaster. Owns Lancaster Realty."

Kate gestured toward the front room. "Any word on repairs?"

Levi snorted. "When pigs fly. He'll do the same thing he did the last two times."

"The last two times?"

Nelda nodded. "Vandals damaged our shop, and Max's, twice over the last year and a half. Even though the insurance company paid, Lancaster never made repairs."

The nagging idea crystalized. "Does Lancaster own other buildings on this street?"

"He owns Cynthia and Stephanie's building next door." Max licked the last of a brownie off his fingers. "Their shops were broken into about the same time as ours last year. Unfortunately, the criminals were never apprehended."

Kate scanned the faces of her friends. Were they thinking the same thing about Lancaster she was? She squelched a sigh of disappointment when the conversation turned to Cynthia's gall bladder surgery. She might have wandered completely off track, but the vandalism sounded suspicious. And what about the robbery attempt a month ago? Was Lancaster behind the damage and robberies of his own buildings to collect money from insurance companies?

Her thoughts pivoted to Max's loan. Nelda had said the landlord arranged the loan and the interest was exorbitant. If Lancaster hired Ian to threaten Max, wouldn't Lancaster be guilty of extortion?

"Right, Katie?"

Kate snapped back to the present. Her friends smiled at her, plainly expecting her agreement. "Oh, what? Sorry, I was thinking about ... something else."

Max shifted to face her. "I just said the Washington Nationals baseball team is going to have a great season."

Kate nodded. "Can't argue with you there. I'm looking forward to the start of the season. I love baseball."

She chatted for a few more minutes and rose to leave. She wouldn't say anything about her suspicions just yet. She needed to dig a little deeper.

Once outside, Kate pulled out her phone. She punched "Lancaster Realty" into her GPS. The location was only a few blocks north. She wavered, then headed north. She'd talk with Sophie later.

While she walked, she pressed Joe's number.

"Hi, Kate. What's up? Only got a second."

"Remember when Angelo held us hostage?"

"Indelibly."

"Just before Ben took Angelo's gun, Angelo told Ben to kill him, because if he didn't, they would. Who are *they*?"

"Good question, Sis. One Pete Sanders isn't getting an answer to." Obvious frustration filtered through Joe's voice. "Angelo refuses to talk. I have a feeling someone is threatening to kill his sister and grandmother if he gives up his boss."

Kate's stomach clenched. "No wonder he doesn't want to talk."

"Yeah." Joe's voice muffled. "Sorry, Kate, I have to go now. Talk to you soon."

She slipped her phone into her purse. She'd prayed for Angelo, hoped he'd turn things around. Sadly, now other lives might be lost because of his choices.

Moments later, she stood in front of Lancaster Realty. The building appeared older yet well maintained. Huge planters of yellow pansies flanked the front entrance. The door opened, and an elderly couple ambled down the sidewalk in her direction. She lowered her eyes and continued walking.

She'd hoped to find leads on the troubling events swirling in her own life this past month. Instead, she'd stumbled on information concerning her friends. Information she couldn't ignore. She pulled the collar of her jacket higher. Was she drawing a conclusion without the basis of fact?

Max's face penetrated her thoughts. His bruises were real.

If her suspicions were true, Lancaster had to be stopped.

FEBRUARY 18
TUESDAY, 2:15 P.M.
HOOVER BUILDING, DC

Ben sprinted up the stairs to his unit's fifth floor office. A busy afternoon stretched ahead. Ethan Fitzgerald would be escorted here immediately after his release from the hospital. Though Ethan had claimed amnesia every time they'd questioned him, Ben had his doubts. His thoughts turned to Mindy West. What part did she play in this? How had she known Ethan was in the hospital? When they questioned Ethan's cousin, Charlotte claimed Mindy had just shown up. Ben sighed. A lot to untangle. Maybe Ethan would talk in the setting of the FBI headquarters.

Ben's phone pinged a text message. He glanced at the screen. *Hi, Ben. Good 2 see U at the play. Could we talk soon? McKenzie.* He stopped mid-step. Hadn't they already said everything?

The memories hit. The way her eyes crinkled the first time they met. Jogging together in the park. Laughing hysterically while she taught him to waltz.

He slowly resumed his climb. Things weren't all good. The desperation of watching their relationship splinter apart filtered the movie playing across his brain. She wanted a life filled with wealth and travel. She couldn't understand his choice of a career focused on something other than financial gain.

The pain of her dropping the engagement ring in his hand punched his gut. He mentally shook himself. No need to go back there. He'd finally moved forward.

He reached the office and headed to his desk.

"Ready to question Fitzgerald?" Joe swiveled his chair to face Ben.

"I told you earlier today I'm ready."

"What's eating you?"

"Nothing. Just a lot on my mind." Ben inhaled sharply. No point in trying to hide his feelings. Joe could always read him. "McKenzie moved back to DC. To stay."

Joe raised an eyebrow. "How do you know?"

"I ran into her—actually, Kate and I ran into her at my nieces' school play." He met Joe's questioning eyes. "Yes, I told Kate about her. What I told her is true. I loved McKenzie deeply, but we were headed in different directions. I believe God has someone else for me." He ran his hands through his hair. "Seeing McKenzie again kicked up unanswered questions."

"Like what?"

"Like, maybe if I'd done a better job of making her happy, she would have tried to work through the problems." Ben's thoughts moved to his sister. "I wonder if I'll make the same mistakes in my next relationship … and ultimately, in my marriage."

Joe steepled his fingers. "Yeah, I guess fear of failure hits everybody at some point. I definitely battle those feelings."

"How do you get past them?"

"By remembering God is the only one who can meet all of Jenny's needs—and mine. My responsibility is to love her unconditionally. In those times when I fail her, or she fails me, we have to decide to rely on God's love and forgiveness. I think happiness becomes a choice."

Joe's words resonated through Ben's soul. He had tried to make his relationship with McKenzie work by his own ability. And failed. Relying on God removed the weight of trying to do the impossible.

"Hey, guys. Got some information on Fitzgerald." Susan Strickland, the team's computer genius, handed them each a file folder. Ben turned his thoughts from the conversation with Joe to the task at hand.

"Ethan seems to be two-hundred-fifty thousand dollars richer than he was a couple of months ago," she added.

Ben sounded a low whistle. "A quarter of a million—nothing to sneeze at."

Joe opened the folder and thumbed through the papers. "Where did he deposit the money?"

"The money turned up in a Swiss bank account under Fitzgerald's name. The transfer of funds was made on Tuesday, February eleventh."

Ben tapped the calendar on his phone. "The day he landed in the hospital." Ben turned to Susan. "Got a time for the transaction?"

She checked her laptop. "Five-thirty p.m. Of course, Geneva is six hours ahead of us, so the transfer was made at eleven-thirty a.m. our time."

Ben shot a look at Joe. "What time did you call 9-1-1 that morning?"

Joe grabbed his phone and studied the screen. "Exactly eleven twenty-three. Fitzgerald was lying unconscious in the street when the money was transferred."

Either Fitzgerald was working with someone or he was being set up. "This should make for an interesting line of questioning once Dave gets here with Ethan. Thanks, Susan. Great work."

Joe and Susan returned to their desks. Ben studied the information on the bank account.

"Are you kidding me?" Joe's raised voice penetrated Ben's thoughts. "We're on our way." Joe motioned to Ben.

Ben headed after Joe, who already moved toward the door. They sped down the stairs. "What's happened?"

"Shots came from a parking garage across the street from St. Michael's Hospital. Ethan Fitzgerald is dead."

Frustration surged through Ben. Ever since Charlotte Fitzgerald told them someone shot at Ethan, security guarded him twenty-four seven. But security had been breached, plainly by an expert.

They raced to the scene. DC police, hospital security, and FBI agents swarmed the premises. Moments later, Dave briefed them while they pulled on Kevlar vests. They joined other agents in the cordoned-off garage and fanned out in pairs to search their assigned areas.

Cars filled nearly every space. Ben grasped his Glock. Every noise reverberated across his heightened senses. He searched under and around each vehicle. Joe swept the beam of his flashlight through the windows.

They moved from space to space. Sweat trickled down Ben's back. Being target practice for a sniper wasn't high on his priority list.

Finally, they reached the last vehicle in their area. Joe flicked the light across the inside. A man slumped in the back seat.

Ben trained his gun at the figure. Possibilities flashed through his brain. *Alive. Dead. Sniper. Victim.*

Joe crept to the other side of the car. He signaled, then swung the bright light into the man's face. Ben pounded on the door. "FBI! Get out with your hands up. Now."

The man jerked. He fumbled to open the door and tumbled out headfirst. He landed in a heap at Ben's feet.

"Please—" He turned open hands to Ben. "My wife just had a baby. I was only sleeping."

Ben sucked in a breath. The panicked man certainly *sounded* like a new dad. "Sir, stand up. We need information."

While Ben questioned him, Joe checked his identity. The story confirmed, they escorted the new father through a maze of law enforcement back to the hospital.

Ben stuck out his hand. "Sorry for the rude awakening, Mr. McMillan. Congratulations on your new daughter."

He returned Ben's handshake, his unshaven face relaxing into a grin. "Have I got a story to tell my wife." He turned toward the elevator. "I hope she believes me."

Ben smiled. He could help with that. He scribbled the couple's names and hospital room number on the palm of his hand. He'd call a florist when he could spare a moment.

He and Joe headed to join the other agents. Ben turned his thoughts back to the murder. The face of the man posing as Ethan's college roommate darted across his mind. Was he the one who'd shot at Ethan earlier? Had he waited for Ethan this afternoon to finish what he'd started?

They needed answers to the questions surrounding CRI, the Liechtenstein embassy, and the research exchange program. Proving Fitzgerald's guilt or innocence was crucial to the task.

A task that had swerved onto a deadly path.

FEBRUARY 20
THURSDAY, 12:50 P.M.
PENTAGON CITY MALL, ARLINGTON, VA

"I love this design. Simple, yet elegant." Jenny held up a package of napkins. "Look, the diamond shape in the center would be perfect for our monogram of *J&J*."

Kate grinned. Only a bride could get this excited about a paper napkin. "The color of the design matches the blue you've chosen. Don't you think so, Aunt Martha?"

Jenny's aunt nodded. "I also saw clear plates which would coordinate beautifully." She rummaged through a display on the next shelf. "Here they are."

"Shopping for the reception is so much fun. I'm glad Joe and I decided on something outdoors and informal." Jenny consulted a shopping list. "Let's see, we're planning to use wildflowers for the centerpieces, so we need vases. We also need small clear candleholders with white votive candles to place around the flowers."

"I saw candles on the way in." Kate grabbed a shopping cart. "How many?

"Let's see, fifteen tables, four on each table—sixty."

Kate headed to the aisle and began to carefully add boxes of candles and candleholders to her cart. She spotted a wedding cake topper with a little boy and girl dressed in wedding attire. Kate paused. She and her sisters had dressed up countless times as children and trudged across the yard for weddings under the huge oak tree by the pasture. They usually lacked the groom unless they could corner one of their brothers to fill in. Tom and Joe always managed to outrun their sisters, but sometimes Sam and Will could be coerced with promises of wedding cake.

She touched the small figures of the cake topper. Joe would be married in April. Their sister Christy's wedding was planned for October. Childhood dreams were becoming reality. *Is Ben the one you have for me, Lord?* Excitement rippled through her. She looked forward to finding out.

She joined Jenny and Aunt Martha. They wandered down aisles filled with displays of decorations, crafts, and supplies.

"I'd like to have little gifts for the guests." Jenny scanned the shelves. "Maybe we'll get ideas here."

A moment later, Kate spotted woven white baskets, small enough to surround the centerpieces. A shelf above the baskets held a display of garden supplies.

"Jenny, look at these packets of wildflower seeds." The front of the packets showed lovely bouquets of flowers. "We could give each guest one of these white baskets with a packet of wildflower seeds inside. Maybe we could attach a little card with something like 'Love Grows,' with your names and the date."

Jenny beamed. "What a great idea. This fits perfectly with our theme."

They added baskets, ribbon, and packets of seeds to the carts. After browsing a little longer, they headed to pay for their purchases. Once the last bag was loaded into Jenny's car, she turned to Kate and Aunt Martha. "Would you like to come back to my apartment for hot tea and ginger cookies?"

"Thank you, dear," Aunt Martha replied, "but Kate and I have an errand to run. I promised my friend Liza Tyler I'd donate some paintings and photographs for a benefit she's heading up. Kate offered to help me unload them. We'll definitely take a rain check."

After chatting a few moments longer, Kate and Aunt Martha headed to their vehicle. A short drive later, they turned onto a curved road flanked by a manicured golf course. Ahead, a sprawling country club stood on an immaculate green lawn.

"Nice," Kate murmured. "Very nice."

Aunt Martha nodded. "Just what I expected from Liza. She knows how to make a statement."

Inside, dozens of staff members readied place settings on round tables. Others arranged huge containers of gorgeous flowers on a stage at the front of the room. Empty easels skirted both sides of the stage.

"There's Liza." Aunt Martha pointed to a woman in earnest conversation with someone arranging flowers. "She looks busy. Let's start unloading."

Kate helped unpack Aunt Martha's work, marveling again at her talent. Her paintings included landscapes and portraits, some with vibrant color, others with subtle hues. Photographs laid among the paintings—a hummingbird in flight, a deer poised in a clearing, a little boy with wide blue eyes eating a huge cupcake, chocolate frosting smeared across his face.

Once the art was unloaded, they arranged the pieces on easels. "Which do you enjoy most, Aunt Martha, painting or photography?"

"Photography is my first love, but painting is wonderful for those snowy days you're stuck inside." She stepped back from an easel and straightened a framed photograph. "Art is a way to capture the memories of my travel over the years."

"Martha, dear, your work is amazing," a voice called from across the room. Liza Tyler strode over. She introduced herself to Kate. The picture of a general organizing troops for battle flashed across Kate's mind. "Every seat will be occupied this evening. We're expecting generous donations. Your art will be a major contributor, Martha. We're having an auction for each piece. Believe me, I will start the bidding high. Those children at the hospital are precious. They deserve the best care."

Liza's enthusiasm was contagious. "What will the money raised tonight be used for?" Kate asked.

A triumphant smile lit up Liza's face. "To further research on childhood cancer, as well as fund some much needed state-of-the-art equipment."

Aunt Martha beamed. "Just think of how many lives you'll touch. Not only the children's, but their families."

A young woman wearing a shirt with the country club's logo joined them. "Pardon me, Ms. Tyler. We need to go over the names of those being introduced this evening."

"Sorry to run off," Liza said across her shoulder as she hurried away. "So many details to check."

Kate turned to Aunt Martha. "I've never met someone with such energy. Not someone without a large cup of coffee in hand, that is."

"Liza has always displayed passion for whatever she does. Which is why she succeeded in building her own investment company from the ground up."

They continued to arrange the art. A short time later, the paintings and photographs were in place.

"Beautiful." Kate hugged Aunt Martha. "Liza isn't the only one with passion."

A raised voice from the podium echoed across the room. Kate glanced over. A man in a dark suit, gesturing furiously with his arms, stood with Liza. Her contorted features showed disgust.

"Oh, my," Aunt Martha murmured. "Probably not who Liza needs around today of all days."

Their voices rose and fell. Finally, the man headed for the door. He spotted them and veered over, instantly oozing charm.

"Hello again. I met you a few weeks ago. Madge?"

"Martha. This is my friend Kate Peterson."

"Brandon Lancaster." His eyes swept over her. "You look familiar. Have we met?"

"I don't think so."

"You've probably seen her on TV. She's WOTN's star reporter."

Kate stifled a chuckle. "I do work for WOTN, but I'm afraid I'm not quite their star reporter."

"Nonsense." Aunt Martha refused to be deterred. "You're the best I've seen."

"Now that I think back, I remember why you look familiar. You were one of the hostages in the jewelry store robbery back in January." Lancaster's smile faded. "Good thing the robber was apprehended. Too bad he won't tell the police anything."

Realization dawned. Brandon Lancaster. Levi and Max's landlord. She pivoted her attention back to him.

"I'm glad no one was hurt," Lancaster said. "The Shanes and O'Reillys are such nice people."

"They're wonderful," Kate agreed. "We've become good friends. I'll do anything I can to help them."

Hardness sliced his smile. "Well, ladies, nice to see you. I'm sure the benefit will be quite successful. Enjoy your day."

He left, and Kate turned to Aunt Martha. "Is Brandon Lancaster somehow related to the children's hospital?"

"He's related to Liza. He's her brother-in-law."

Clearly, Liza and Lancaster didn't get along. Kate pondered Lancaster's words. *Good thing the robber was apprehended. Too bad he won't tell the police anything.*

How did Lancaster know Angelo wouldn't talk? Had the police told him?

Kate's breath hitched. Or was Lancaster the one who'd threatened to kill Angelo's family?

CHAPTER 10

Kate peered through the viewfinder of her camera, stepped back, and adjusted the tripod. The conference room of the Caldwell Research Institute was large and elegant, with huge windows framing a beautiful view of the city. Rows of cushioned chairs faced a mahogany podium. Princess Ingrid and her entourage should arrive shortly for the ceremony welcoming eight Liechtenstein economists to the US. This spot would be perfect to capture everything on film.

After the ceremony, a tour of the Institute would be given to the princess. The festivities would conclude with a luncheon. Kate's stomach growled. A luncheon to which she had not been invited. Too bad she hadn't made time for breakfast this morning. She glanced at her purse. Wasn't a protein bar still stuffed in the bottom?

Before she could find out, a man and woman entered the room, plainly in serious conversation. When the man noticed Kate, a wide smile with perfect teeth replaced his intense expression.

"Frederick Wilson." He extended his hand. "I'm president of Caldwell Research Institute. Welcome. You must be from WOTN."

"Yes. Kate Peterson. We're excited about bringing the research exchange program to our viewers."

"We've certainly worked hard for this day." He gestured toward the woman. "This is Mindy West, one of our most valued researchers."

The woman at the parking garage. Kate quickly offered her hand. "Are you part of the exchange program?"

Mindy shook her head. "I work in a different area of the Institute. However, I'm very interested in this project. I'm looking forward to the ceremony."

Other people began filing in. The couple nodded to Kate and moved away. Kate studied Mindy's profile. How was she involved with Ian?

"I'm sorry, ma'am, I need to escort you out. The press isn't allowed at this event."

Kate turned to confront the person behind her, indignation bubbling up. "I've been issued clearance—" Mischief danced in Joe's brown eyes. Kate shook her head. "I should have known. Doesn't the FBI have anything better to do today than harass a hardworking citizen?"

Ben joined them, and Kate caught her breath. She'd spoken to him once since their date last week, the date when Ben introduced her to McKenzie. Their phone conversation seemed strained, or was her imagination kicking in?

"Hi, Kate." A broad smile spread across Ben's face. "I didn't know you were covering the ceremony."

His look warmed her. Maybe she *was* only imagining things. "Hi, Ben."

Kate felt Joe's eyes on her. "Well, I'll go grab some seats. See you later, Sis."

Ben stepped closer. Kate breathed in the clean scent of his cologne.

"I'm glad to see you, Kate. I was hoping we could get together soon. I have to work this weekend, but I do have an idea for next Saturday." He hesitated a beat. "I'm volunteering at a soup kitchen downtown. I wondered ... would you like to join me? We could go out for dinner afterward."

Kate gazed into his face, the hum of other conversations fading. "I'd love to, Ben."

"I'll call later with the details." He squeezed her hand and headed to join Joe.

She let out the breath she hadn't realized she was holding. Someone's phone pinged, and she checked to make sure she'd turned off the sound on her own.

She glanced around the room. All the seats were now taken except one row at the front. *I wonder why Ben and Joe are here today.* Ben had mentioned once his unit worked with the security detail for the princess. Maybe they were part of security for the ceremony.

Frederick Wilson strode to the podium. He paused a moment, then gestured for the audience to rise. A hush fell over the room. "May I present Her Royal Highness Princess Ingrid of Liechtenstein."

Princess Ingrid stepped through the doorway, followed by a woman Kate recognized as Margaret Schrader, the Liechtenstein ambassador. The eight Liechtenstein economists brought up the rear of the procession.

Pride welled up in Kate. Her friend looked every inch a royal. The ponytail was replaced by a sophisticated upswept hairstyle, jeans and sweatshirt by a classic white suit. She carried herself with dignity and poise.

Once the guests of honor were seated, Wilson began his opening remarks. The ceremony included speeches by Wilson, the ambassador, the princess, and several CRI economists.

At the conclusion of the ceremony, Kate followed Ingrid and her entourage to film their tour of Caldwell Research Institute. Her brain churned with ideas for future stories. She had already been assigned to follow up the series on the princess with one on the research project.

After conducting several interviews with the Liechtenstein economists, Kate began to pack up her equipment. Since the luncheon was scheduled to start soon, she could head to the station to edit.

"Hello, Kate."

Kate glanced up. "Ingrid, hi." She smiled at the princess. "You did a wonderful job today."

"Thank you."

Kate studied her friend. The guarded look Ingrid had worn the first day they met hovered over her features. Thin lines etched her forehead. "Is everything okay?"

Ingrid's eyes misted. She blinked rapidly, plainly working to gain control. "I'm ... I need to tell you something. We'll talk later."

The ambassador joined them. Ingrid masked her emotions while introductions were made. Ms. Schrader turned to Ingrid. "Your Highness, Mr. Wilson is waiting."

They nodded goodbye to Kate. Indignation pricked. The pressure of Ingrid's responsibilities must be enormous. She couldn't even have two minutes to herself if something were bothering her. They needed to go horseback riding again. Soon.

Kate noticed Mindy West staring at the princess, eyes narrowed. A moment later, she strolled over to Kate.

"I understand you're doing a series on the princess for your TV station."

"Yes. We're giving our viewers a glimpse of Princess Ingrid's life here in the US."

"How nice. I would imagine the two of you are becoming friends."

"We are. She's a wonderful person."

"If there's anything she needs or if she encounters any problems, please tell her to let us know." Mindy's tight smile pulled tighter. "I do hope she doesn't feel the need to concern herself with our research project. We can handle things on our own," she added, turning away.

Kate considered Mindy's words. The woman appeared to have something important to gain from this project.

Or lose.

FEBRUARY 21
FRIDAY, 2:37 P.M.
NEW YORK AVENUE, DC

Ben stared out the window of Frederick Wilson's office at Caldwell Research Institute. Leaden skies threatened snow. Again. He couldn't remember a winter with this much *weather.* If the snow did come, maybe enough would fall to give some decent sledding down the hill by his apartment.

He'd ask Kate the next time they talked if she enjoyed sledding. The pleasure of seeing her earlier today lingered. When they were together, the cloud of another potential failed relationship lifted. Joe was right. He needed to rely on God to navigate the ups and downs inherent in any relationship. Certainty settled over him. He was ready to open his heart again.

"What's so great outside?" Joe stood beside him, staring quizzically.

Ben shrugged. "What are you talking about?"

"Your grin is a mile wide." Joe shook his head. "Never mind. I don't want to know." He glanced at his watch. "I wonder what's keeping Wilson."

"He left the luncheon the same time we did. Guess he got sidetracked." Ben voiced the question nagging him. "Did you notice Wilson didn't mention Fitzgerald's death today?"

Joe nodded. "Since Ethan worked on this project, I'm surprised nothing was said."

"I never heard anyone bring up his name."

Moments later, the door opened. Wilson strolled into his office. "Gentlemen, sorry to keep you waiting. What a great day—one we've all anticipated for some time. Please, sit." He sank into the chair behind his desk and shuffled papers into a stack. "I'm sure you're as busy as I am. What can I do for you?"

Joe cleared his throat. "With the murder of Ethan Fitzgerald—"

"Ah, yes, what a tragedy," Wilson interrupted. "I've already extended my sympathies to Ethan's cousin. I almost spoke about Ethan today. However, with the discrepancies in our funds pointing to him, I decided against the idea."

Ben studied Wilson. Did he know more than he let on? "We need the names of those who reported the discrepancies. We'd like to speak with them further."

Wilson leaned forward. "I certainly hope you don't think anyone at CRI had anything to do with Ethan's murder."

"We simply have to explore every possibility. We may also need to expand our investigation beyond the group who worked on the Liechtenstein project."

Wilson started to speak, but apparently changed his mind. He jotted something on a notepad and handed the sheet to Ben. "Here are the names of those who reported the missing funds to me. Let me know if you need anything further."

Wilson stood, clearly done with their meeting. As Ben and Joe left the office, Ben glanced at the names. None raised red flags. They had already been checked and come up clean. But someone other than Ethan had transferred the money.

Joe paused at the elevator doors. "Let's stop by Mindy West's office. I'd like to hear her version of how she knew Ethan was in the hospital."

"Good idea."

When they reached Mindy's office, Ben knocked on the closed door. No answer.

"Looking for Mindy?"

A man filling a cup at the water cooler smiled. "You just missed her. Said she had to leave some information with Wilson's assistant. She should return shortly. I'm sure she wouldn't mind if you waited in her office."

"Thanks." Ben tried the door and found it unlocked.

Her office was much smaller than Wilson's. He hadn't noticed when they were here a week ago that she had a view of a brick wall instead of the city. A wilted plant by the window showed the effects of the lack of sunlight. A laptop sat closed on a desk devoid of paperwork.

Ben wandered over to several framed photographs hanging on the wall. A smiling little girl, younger than his nieces, held a trophy in one arm and a soccer ball in the other. He looked closer. The same little girl, wearing a ballerina costume, pirouetted in another photo and hugged a huge teddy bear in a third. He thought back to Mindy's words when they questioned her about the CRI lecture. *I won't risk my job. I have a daughter to support.*

The phone on her desk rang, and finally switched to voicemail. "Sunburst is on schedule," the caller said. "Your insurance is adequate." *Click.*

Joe paced to the window, clearly restless. "I wonder what Sunburst is. Sounds like a good name for sunscreen."

Before Ben could reply, Mindy West appeared in the doorway. "What are you doing here?"

"Hello, Ms. West. We have a couple of questions we'd like to ask you."

"I told you everything I know when you came here the last time. Now Ethan's dead—" Her voice faltered.

"I'm sure this is a difficult time," Ben responded. "We need to ask you about February eleventh, the day Ethan was admitted to the hospital. How did you know he was there?"

"His cousin Charlotte called me. She was terribly upset. I dropped everything and hurried over."

Not the story Charlotte had given. Which one was lying? "When you were with Ethan in the hospital, did he ever mention the files he asked you to access earlier?"

Surprise registered in her eyes. "No, of course not. He couldn't remember anything about his work."

Ben analyzed Mindy's reaction. Her confusion seemed genuine. Could Ethan really not remember? Had he simply convinced her he couldn't? Or, were he and Mindy working together?

If the latter were true, she was giving a performance worthy of an Oscar.

FEBRUARY 21
FRIDAY, 5:30 P.M.
WOTN, DC

Robbery. Almost hit by a car. Dead rose, smashed candy, weird message. Ian following me? Battery cable cut. Kate twirled a pen between her fingers and scanned the list. She added a timeframe. *January twenty-first—February sixteenth.*

She glanced at the calendar on her phone. The first incident happened a month earlier. The latest, five days ago. She studied each entry. Only one happened at night. Her muscles tensed at the memory of discovering the dead rose. She drew a line connecting the robbery and rose. *Same area.* The other incidents took place at random locations. She rubbed her eyes to ease the start of a headache. What about Ian? Was he really following her, or had they both simply been at the same place?

She scribbled "Possible Coincidence" beside *Robbery, Almost hit by a car,* and *Ian following me.* The other two entries stared back at her. If only she could explain them away. Of course, someone could have left the dead rose on her car but intended the sick message for another vehicle. Same with the battery cable? No, too much of a stretch.

She stuffed the list into her purse. She should call this a day. Her assignment was finished. She'd completed the edit of the CRI ceremony an hour ago, and the story was in the lineup for the six o'clock broadcast. If she headed to the gym for a workout, maybe her brain would stop replaying the disturbing events of the past month.

"Kate, you have a visitor."

She snapped back to the present. The receptionist stood at the entry to her cubicle. "Is this a good time?"

Before she could answer, a smiling Sophie O'Reilly appeared. "Hi, Kate."

"Sophie. I'm so glad to see you. Come in." Kate slid to one side as she gestured toward the other chair in her cubicle. When anyone came in, the space shrank considerably.

"Before I sit down, could you take me on a tour of the station? I'd love to see how everything works behind the scenes."

Kate pushed aside her weariness. "Sure, let's go."

She showed Sophie the studio where broadcasts aired, introduced her to some of the news team, and explained the process of filming and editing a story. Sophie took everything in with enthusiasm.

Back in her cubicle, Kate turned the conversation to Max. "I saw your uncle earlier this week. His eye looks better." She paused. "He told me he fell."

A shadow passed over Sophie's face. "He gave me the same story. I don't believe him. I think he and Ian got into an argument and Ian hit him."

"That was my first thought as well." Kate straightened. "Ian would be stopped if Max would contact the authorities."

"Don't think I haven't tried to convince Uncle Max. He believes he needs to handle everything on his own. Asking for help is a sign of weakness as far as he's concerned."

"Sophie, how much do you know about Brandon Lancaster?"

She blinked. "Only that he bought our building and the one next to us a couple of years ago. He's a terrible landlord. Even though he increases the rent, he doesn't make repairs on the building."

Kate almost asked about Max's loan, but bit back the question as Levi's words darted through her memory. *Max never told Sophie about the loan. He didn't want her to worry.*

"Why do you ask about Lancaster?"

"I think it's odd the shops in both buildings have been vandalized twice over the time Lancaster has owned them. I'm not even counting the attempted robbery a month ago."

Sophie's green eyes widened. "You mean you think Lancaster is somehow responsible? Why would he want to damage his own buildings?"

"To illegally collect money from his insurance companies. He could probably make quite a profit between collecting rent and insurance fraud ..." *And extortion*, she added silently.

"Then we need to tell Uncle Max and the Shanes."

Kate hesitated. "I might be totally off base. I don't want to upset everyone if I'm wrong. But we need to find out. I have a brother and a good friend who are FBI agents. I think I should talk with them." She thought about the list she'd made earlier. Maybe her suspicion about Lancaster wasn't the only thing she needed to bring up.

"I don't know how Uncle Max would react if Lancaster is responsible for everything. I certainly don't want him to get into any more fights."

"Things will be fine." She hoped.

Sophie stood. "I didn't mean to keep you. I just wanted to say hello since I was in the area."

After her friend left, Kate checked her assignments for the following week, organized her schedule, and packed up her computer. She headed out of the building and down the front steps to the sidewalk, her mind turning to Ben. Though she wouldn't see him this weekend, her heart fluttered at the thought of their date next Saturday.

Her ringtone sounded. She dug her phone from her purse. "Hello?"

"What will I do next?" a muffled voice responded.

Kate froze. "Who … is this?"

"I know where your family lives. Who your friends are. If you tell anyone about me, you'll regret it."

Fear ignited fire. "How dare you threaten me!"

Silence. She jerked the phone from her ear to check the number. *Restricted.*

A wave of nausea collided with her wrath. She grabbed the stair rail to steady herself. What had she walked into? Being the target of threats was bad.

Causing her family and friends to be targeted was unthinkable.

Streetlights clicked on. She peered into the dusk. Was he nearby? Could he see her? Urgency welled up inside. She needed to get someplace safe. Was she safe anywhere? Certainly not here in the dark. She hurried to her car.

If she chose a different route to the apartment, maybe she could see if someone followed. She flicked her eyes to the rearview mirror. After a few blocks, she blew out a shaky breath. Trying to figure out if you were being followed in a dark city was impossible. Almost all headlights looked alike.

Finally, she reached her neighborhood. The familiar streets calmed her. Nothing seemed sinister or out of the ordinary. She pulled into a space in front of her apartment building and switched off the engine.

What will I do next? The words throbbed through her being. The call confirmed her suspicions. The earlier message on the windshield was aimed at her. No question. She could probably strike off "possible coincidence" on everything else in the past weeks except the robbery. She was being stalked. Now, her family and friends had been sucked into this. She shoved a strand of hair behind her ear. Into what?

She opened her purse, pulled out the crumpled paper, and studied the words. A sudden connection ordered her swirling thoughts. The first three incidents happened when she interviewed the Shanes and O'Reillys. The last two, when she was with Ingrid. Her mind reached back to the advice a news director at her first job had given her. *"Keep your eyes open, Kate.*

News reporters are visible and vulnerable." Was she a target because of a story for WOTN?

Her stories were general interest, not investigative. Her series on the princess touched only briefly on politics. Everything else focused on goals, impressions, studies. Yet security surrounded Ingrid for a reason. No doubt the royal family dealt with threats all the time. The CRI ceremony spun through her brain. Ingrid had appeared upset, said she needed to talk. Could the problem be connected to the stalker?

Her thoughts shifted to the Shanes and O'Reillys. She witnessed the robbery, reported on their businesses ... Max's bruised face floated before her eyes. Maybe the stalker *was* Ian.

She glanced up to the second floor of her apartment building. A soft glow radiating from Aunt Martha's Tiffany lamp framed a window. Leaves of a hanging plant cascaded down, and Lucy sat curled up on the windowsill.

The stalker had threatened her friends and family. Was he bluffing to scare her? If so, he'd done a good job. But he might have nothing more than information available to anyone on the internet.

She needed to figure this out. He warned her not to tell anyone about him.

She bit her lip. She could handle things alone.

She had no choice.

FEBRUARY 24
MONDAY, 10:15 A.M.
ALEXANDRIA, VA

Ben eyed the front of Charlotte Fitzgerald's townhouse. Potted plants adorned the steps. Most likely ones from her cousin's funeral last week. Though the number of people at the service was small, plants and floral arrangements had been sent. He glanced at Joe. "This isn't going to be pleasant, especially after the search of her home earlier. Dave said she was furious."

Joe straightened his tie. "I'm sure she was, but since Ethan spent time here before his death, we have no choice. Especially since his computer and phone are still missing."

"I was certain they would be located in her house." Tiredness seeped through Ben's muscles despite two cups of strong coffee. "We need a break. Soon."

Six days of working around the clock since Ethan's death, his team had nothing. They came up empty in the search of the parking garage. Video from the garage's surveillance cameras showed only blurred images of a shadowy figure dressed in black, his faced covered. The gunman plainly was aware of camera angles. The hit had been well planned. License plates checks of cars leaving the garage in the seconds, minutes, and hours after the shooting had yielded nothing. Witnesses in the surrounding area during the time of Ethan's death had given no useful information, and the gunman's weapon had not yet been traced.

Ben rang the doorbell. A dog's ferocious bark sounded. "Gibbs is on the job today."

The door opened a crack. Displeasure glazed Charlotte Fitzgerald's features. "What do you want?"

"Ms. Fitzgerald, we need to speak with you."

"This is ridiculous. Can't you let me grieve in peace?"

"I'm very sorry. We'll be as brief as possible."

She jerked open the door. Though she was plainly

not pleased, her dog's tail wagged nonstop as he grabbed a toy bone and escorted them into the living room. Once they were seated, Gibbs flopped down. He rested his head on Ben's shoe.

"Again, we're truly sorry for your loss, Ms. Fitzgerald," Joe began.

"I'll just bet you are." Charlotte sank into a chair opposite them. "If you hadn't chased Ethan, he never would have ended up in the hospital and been shot. I plan to consult my lawyers about this."

Ben shifted on the sofa. "I assure you, finding Ethan's killer is our top priority."

She crossed her arms tightly around a pillow. "I would think you'd be busy questioning everyone at CRI instead of hounding me. I've already told you everything I know. Why can't you do your job and leave me alone?"

Gibbs clawed at the fur around his neck. Ben reached down. Maybe the collar was too tight. His fingers touched something smooth on its underside. While Charlotte continued her tirade regarding the FBI's ineptitude, Ben turned over the collar. He glanced down. A piece of duct tape stuck to the material. The word "Sunburst" was printed in black letters. Ben straightened the collar and patted Gibbs.

Sunburst. Where had he heard the word? The memory hit. The message on Mindy West's answering machine. *Sunburst is on schedule. Your insurance is adequate.*

Questions swirled. What was Sunburst? Why had the word been written on Gibbs's collar? Did Charlotte know about the duct tape, or had Ethan put the tape there?

Ben steered his thoughts back to the conversation

at hand. Though he and Joe pursued several lines of questioning, Charlotte continued to deny any knowledge of the whereabouts of Ethan's electronics.

Ben caught Joe's glance. No doubt they were thinking the same thing. *We're done here.* At the front door, Ben turned to Charlotte. "By the way, I noticed a cracked windowpane in the den of Ethan's apartment. Do you know how the glass broke?"

She shrugged. "He told me a floor lamp fell and hit the windowpane. Maintenance was supposed to do repairs. The last time I was there, Ethan had sealed the crack with duct tape."

"Wouldn't have thought of duct tape." Ben kept his voice casual. "Did the tape work well?"

"I have no idea. Ethan didn't say, and I never use the stuff."

Bingo. The color of the tape on Gibbs's collar was the same orange and black print Ethan used on his window. No doubt analysis of the fibers would show a match.

Ben's thoughts raced. Were Ethan and Mindy West working together? Had she deposited money into Ethan's Swiss bank account the day he'd gone to the hospital? Or, was Ethan being set up and wrote the word because he knew he was in danger?

They had their work cut out for them. One thing was in their favor. They knew more than they did an hour ago.

CHAPTER 11

Kate followed Princess Ingrid's security guard along the dormitory hallway. On the day of the CRI ceremony, Ingrid had said she needed to talk. Whatever troubled the princess might have something to do with Kate's stalker. Or not. She had to find out.

"Here we are." The security guard motioned to the last room on the hall.

Ingrid appeared in the doorway. She was barefoot, dressed in sweatpants and a hoodie. Kate smiled. Quite a difference between her outfit now and at the CRI ceremony.

The security guard straightened. "Ms. Peterson to see you, Your Highness."

"Thank you." Ingrid turned to Kate. "I'm glad you called. Come in."

Once inside, the princess gestured around her. "What do you think?"

Kate studied the room. A mahogany desk and upholstered chair stood on one side of a large window.

A leather recliner sat in a corner by an Oriental dresser, and a woven screen partially hid a large bed with a chintz comforter. "Somehow I don't remember dorm rooms being quite this ... elegant."

Ingrid shrugged. "I didn't realize my staff was going to do this. Both the university and our embassy were determined to make me comfortable. Unfortunately, the décor of my room is just one more reason I don't fit in with the other girls on my floor."

"Oh, I don't know. If I lived in the dorm, I'd come over all the time." Kate pointed to a large flat screen TV mounted to the wall. "You have all the comforts of home and then some."

"I never thought of things that way. Maybe I'll invite some people over for popcorn and a movie. Do you think they'd be intimidated by my security?"

"Never hurts to ask." Kate perched on the upholstered chair and Ingrid sank onto the recliner. *Maybe I should ease into the conversation.* "So, how are things going for you?"

Ingrid's face brightened. "I'm enjoying my classes very much. My professors are excellent. The courses are challenging, yet fun. I wish I could stay longer than one semester, but I have a full schedule this summer. My father and I will travel quite a bit."

Kate settled back on the chair. "I can only imagine the responsibility of your family's position."

"My father makes being royal look easy." Ingrid's voice softened. "He's done so much for our country, managing both the good times and bad with such grace. One of the greatest lessons I've learned from him is strength in the face of adversity. He does what he believes is right and doesn't live for everyone else's approval. He possesses true courage." Tears pooled in her eyes.

"What's wrong, Ingrid?" Kate asked gently.

"Thinking of him reminded me of the CRI ceremony."

"Actually, that's one reason I stopped by. You said you needed to talk."

Ingrid stood and walked to the window. She rested her head against the windowpane. "Nine years ago, my uncle was murdered. The killer was captured, but during the trial, testimony pointed to the involvement of another man. He was a trusted family friend." Bitterness laced her tone. "There was insufficient evidence to convict him. Several years later, a witness came forward. When the authorities finally had the proof they needed, he had vanished. Then, at the CRI ceremony …"

Kate tensed. "You saw him?"

"No … I don't know. He doesn't look like the same man, but something about him is so *familiar*—his mannerisms, the way he tilts his head. I know this sounds crazy. I'm only imagining things. Still, the experience was upsetting."

"Have you mentioned this to your security?"

The princess shook her head. "The economists' backgrounds were thoroughly checked before this project."

Ingrid appeared truly shaken. "Has anything else caused you to worry?"

"Not really. I just haven't been able to shake those horrible memories of the murder."

"The man who brought back those memories—what's his name?"

"He was introduced to me on Friday as Victor Schultz."

A sudden knock sounded. Ingrid jerked. "Yes?"

The guard entered. "Your car will arrive shortly, ma'am. You're due at the embassy."

"Thank you." She turned to Kate as the door closed. "I'm sorry. I have to leave."

"I should go to my next assignment anyway. We'll get together again soon." Kate hugged her friend. "Call me if you need anything."

Kate left the dorm and headed to her car. She thought about Ingrid's words. *Was* this the man Ingrid had known? People could change their appearance with plastic surgery. She frowned. No one would go to such drastic lengths for research. The exchange program was simply economics.

Wasn't it?

FEBRUARY 25
TUESDAY, 11:17 A.M.
ALEXANDRIA, VA

Ben pointed the beam of his flashlight under the desk in Charlotte Fitzgerald's study. Good. No cobwebs or spiders. She was a much better housekeeper than her cousin. Dave had taken her to headquarters this morning to get more information on Ethan. He didn't envy Dave the job. Charlotte's outrage was plain with more questioning and another search of her home.

Ben dropped to the floor, then slid beneath the desk. He pivoted the light to the underside of the desk and pushed against the wood. No hidden compartments, nothing attached underneath. Three months ago, they found a photo lodged in the bottom of a desk drawer enabling them to identify terrorists. Not a similar break today.

"See anything?" Joe examined the underside of the sofa across the room.

"No." Ben sat up. He and Joe had crawled under, around, and through every possible place Ethan might have hidden his phone or computer. Ben massaged the muscles in his left shoulder. Maybe Ethan wasn't the one who had hidden his electronics. Maybe Charlotte had taken matters into her own hands to protect her cousin.

"Give me a hand with this, will you?" Joe nodded to the sofa.

Ben helped set the sofa upright. "I wish we had Ethan's computer before we question Mindy West this afternoon. If only we had something more concrete on Sunburst other than the word on a pet's collar. I have a feeling Mindy will come up with an easy explanation for the message on her answering machine."

A door slammed. Ben glanced toward the hall. A scowling Charlotte Fitzgerald strode in, followed by her dog.

"You've had plenty of time to ransack my home." Charlotte stomped upstairs. "You can let yourselves out. Now."

Gibbs trotted into the den. His wagging tail almost knocked over a lamp.

"Hey, boy." Ben stroked Gibbs's sleek fur. The dog's wet tongue slathered over his hand.

Gibbs shook himself, yawned, and ambled over to his bed against the wall. He circled several times. Stumbling, he collapsed in a heap, half on and half off the bed.

"What's wrong, boy?" Ben walked over to the dog. "You must be older than I thought. Arthritis getting you down?"

When he knelt on the bed to help Gibbs, his shin struck something solid. "Ow!"

"What happened?" Joe crouched beside Ben.

"Feels like rocks in here. No wonder he stumbled." Ben slid his hand over the top of the bed and felt a zipper. He unzipped the cover and moved a corner back.

His muscles tensed. He pulled a laptop from the foam inside. "I think we just found what we were searching for. Writing 'Sunburst' on Gibbs collar must have been Ethan's clue to the place he hid his computer—the dog's bed." Ben passed the computer to Joe, zipped the bed's cover, and patted Gibbs's head.

"Good job, Gibbs," Joe murmured. He opened the computer. The screen was black. "Let's get this to headquarters. Once the computer is charged, maybe we'll find the information we need."

FEBRUARY 25
TUESDAY, 12:40 P.M.
HOOVER BUILDING, DC

"The computer's up. Look at this." Susan motioned to Ben and Joe.

Ben strode over to her desk and pulled up a chair beside Joe. An hour had passed since they'd left

Charlotte's townhouse. He was ready to see what Ethan knew.

Susan turned the screen of Fitzgerald's computer toward them.

The words typed on the screen appeared rambling, similar to entries in a diary. Ben read the words aloud.

"People after me.

Still hiding.

Last week decided 2 can play at this game. Followed man who's been tailing me. Lost him in DC near place called O'Reilly's Antiques. Went inside to get out of cold. Ring slid off. Went back days later. Spotted man outside. Chased me to Metro."

Ben paused. "Ethan answered the question of why he went to O'Reilly's when he was in hiding. He tried to follow the man who had been trailing him. If only we could ID this guy." He clenched his hands. "We know he's the same person who posed as Ethan's college roommate. We have photos from his visit to Charlotte Fitzgerald, I chased him at the Metro—"

"I haven't given up on getting an ID." Determination hovered over Susan's features. "We'll find him." She turned to the screen and finished reading the entries aloud.

"Realized my phone bugged. Smashed it.

What is Sunburst? Energy forum CRI created with Liechtenstein? Never heard forum called that.

Note to ambassador didn't help. Research exchange moving forward.

Shot at today! Got to figure this out before they kill me."

Ben processed the words. Ethan Fitzgerald sounded confused, scared—and innocent.

"Look at the fourth entry." Joe's voice penetrated his thoughts. "Ethan admits leaving the note to Margaret Schrader."

"Apparently not as a threat but as a warning."

"I wonder how Ethan got involved in this to begin with." Joe leaned forward. "What did he know that endangered his life?"

Susan propped her chin in her hand and stared at the screen. "When you questioned Mindy West the first time, she said Ethan had asked her to access files. He plainly stumbled onto something that raised his suspicions. Even though he apparently never figured out what was going on, he came too close for somebody's comfort."

Joe gestured toward the computer. "Notice Ethan never mentioned the embezzled funds. We know he didn't deposit them. I wonder if he even knew there was an account in his name until we questioned him in the hospital."

Susan clicked the keyboard of Ethan's computer. "His last entry was dated February tenth."

Ben checked the calendar on his phone. "The day before he was admitted to the hospital. My gut tells me he knew nothing about the missing funds. I have a feeling he was innocent of everything but stumbling onto a crime. Whoever is behind his death was determined to keep him quiet, either by putting him behind bars or in his grave."

Ben clenched his jaw. He hated to see an innocent life taken on his watch. Ethan hadn't been able to beat whoever was after him, but justice would be done.

He stood. The means to justice hid somewhere within CRI. Time to pay another visit to Caldwell Research Institute.

FEBRUARY 25
TUESDAY, 5:47 P.M.
NEW YORK AVENUE, DC

Ben and Joe settled in chairs across from Mindy West. She closed her computer, her hands shaking.

"We need to ask you a few more questions, Ms. West." Ben paused an instant. "What can you tell us about Sunburst?"

She gaped at them. "I—don't know what you're taking about."

"You received a message on your answering machine the day of the ceremony for the Liechtenstein economists. The caller specifically referred to Sunburst."

"I never received any such message." She scribbled something on a notepad. "You must have me confused with someone else." She held up the pad with the words 'Meet me at the coffee shop across the street in fifteen minutes.' "Now, if you'll excuse me, I need to get back to work."

Ben glanced at Joe. Did she think her office was bugged? He flicked his gaze back to Mindy. Or, was she planning to run? He stood. "We'll be in touch."

Once outside the building, Ben turned to Joe. "If you want to hang out here in front, I'll take the back exit."

Joe nodded. "Sounds like a good plan."

Ben strode around to the back of the building. He positioned himself to the side of CRI's back exit to wait. Moments later, the door creaked open. Mindy West stepped into the alley and started in the opposite direction of the coffee shop.

"Do you always leave from the back door?"

Mindy whirled around and gasped. "Sometimes. I—" Her cheeks reddened. "What are you doing? You nearly gave me a heart attack. I can leave from whatever door I please."

"You're absolutely right. Shall we go?" He gestured behind them. "The coffee shop is this way."

Joe joined them. Once inside the coffee shop, they found seats in a quiet corner.

"Ms. West, we need answers." Ben leaned forward. "We can talk here, or we can go to FBI headquarters."

"Please, I can't." Her eyes pleaded. "They threatened my daughter."

Joe frowned. "Who are *they*?"

"I don't know. The message on my answering machine referring to Sunburst said as long as payments were made, I would have insurance. The insurance is the safety of my *daughter.*" Quick gasps punctuated her words. "I work with research grants received by CRI. In January, I received an email with instructions for certain amounts of these grants. The sender was listed only as Sunburst. The email stated my compliance was vital to the continuation of CRI and if I valued my job, I'd follow the instructions. When I sent an email back questioning the instructions, I was told if I cared about my daughter's safety, I would stop asking questions. I wrestled with going to the authorities, but when I picked up my daughter that afternoon, she had a small stuffed bear with her." Mindy's voice shook. "I asked where she'd gotten the toy. She said a man came up to the fence on the playground and gave the bear to her. He told her he'd take her for ice cream sometime."

The faces of Ben's nieces flashed across his mind. "One of the teachers surely saw him."

"I asked. No one noticed him." She swiped at tears filling her eyes. "The man must have lurked nearby—who knows how long he'd watched her—waiting for the moment when the teachers were focused on other kids. My daughter is only four years old." Her voice broke. "Whoever is behind Sunburst was sending me a message. That's why I gave you the address of Ethan's hotel two weeks ago. I thought if you found him maybe this would stop."

"Ms. West, you and your daughter need protection. We can assign agents—"

"No." Her eyes darted around. "No one can protect me. Ethan Fitzgerald is proof."

Ben drew a sharp breath. Was she telling the truth? If so, she was clearly in over her head. "What did the email instruct you to do with the grants?"

"I was to deposit funds in an overseas bank. I was given an account number, nothing more."

Ben blew out a breath. No doubt the Swiss bank account under Fitzgerald's name. "Were you aware Ethan had been accused of embezzlement?"

"Yes. I figured he was being set up. Then he was killed—" Her voice trailed off.

Joe pulled out the photo of the man posing as Ethan's college roommate. "Have you ever seen him?"

She bit her bottom lip. "No."

Ben studied her. Mindy's eyes said yes. He switched course. "How much does Frederick Wilson know?"

"I don't think he has anything to do with Sunburst. As president of CRI, he's concerned about the discrepancies of funds."

Ben quashed frustration. With the death of Ethan Fitzgerald, CRI now employed forty-four analysts. Someone was behind Sunburst. Someone willing to do whatever necessary to get what he wanted. What was the endgame? Could Mindy West be trusted? If she were telling the truth, her daughter was in danger.

He thought back to the pictures of the little girl in Mindy's office. Would they find the perpetrators before other innocent lives were taken?

MARCH 1
SATURDAY, 2:40 P.M.
WASHINGTON, DC

Kate pushed up the sleeves of her sweatshirt. Too bad she hadn't worn something cooler. The temperature outside hovered in the thirties, but inside the soup kitchen large ovens radiated heat. Twenty volunteers chopped, washed, cut, and baked in preparation for the evening meal of vegetable soup, hot bread, salad, and chocolate cake. This was exactly what she needed to take her mind off the disturbing events of the past weeks. She'd talked again with the Shanes and O'Reillys but learned nothing new about Lancaster or Ian. She bit her lip. She would *not* bring this up to Joe or Ben.

Ben slid a pan of potatoes onto the metal workspace. "You're fast. I can hardly keep up with you."

Her eyes met his and her heart flipped. "When you grow up in a family of ten, cooking dinner is science, not art." She picked up a potato and knife. "Especially when five of those ten are guys who are always starved. You learn to move quick."

"I'll give you a hand with the peeling when I finish washing this last batch."

Kate glanced over at him. He was as absorbed in washing potatoes as he had been doing his job as an FBI agent at Caldwell Research Institute. He plainly gave his all, no matter what the task. When he caught her gaze, he winked.

She ducked her head to cover the warmth of her cheeks. "How long have you been a volunteer here?"

He thought a moment. "About three years—maybe a little longer."

"What made you choose a soup kitchen?"

"Several years ago, I always passed a man sitting against a brick building on my way to the Metro. He held out a hat, and sometimes I dropped money in." Ben's voice softened. "One of my favorite memories of my dad happened the year before he died, when I was seven. He had taken me downtown with him to run errands. We decided on lunch at a hot dog stand. A man in ragged clothes approached us and asked for money. He reeked of alcohol, but my dad put an arm around his shoulder and invited him to eat with us. I'll never forget the look on the man's face. My dad taught me a valuable lesson that day on treating people with dignity. Every person has worth." Ben joined Kate in peeling potatoes. "So, one day when I had some extra time, I invited the man I always passed to eat with me. I got to know him, found out he had lived on the streets for two years. We happened to walk by this soup kitchen. We came inside to find out when meals were served. I'd still see him occasionally, but I finally noticed he wasn't sitting on the sidewalk anymore."

Kate blinked. "I wonder what happened to him."

Ben pointed to a man stirring a pot on the stove. "His name is Theo. He decided to get help, turned his life around, and volunteers here every week."

"What a beautiful story."

"Theo is a great mentor to guys on the street. He can relate to them in ways someone like me can't."

The blessings of her life washed over Kate. She'd grown up loved and supported. Her family had always been there to cheer, direct, and comfort her.

She stole a look at Ben. His parents had died when he was so young. He'd trusted God with his tragedy, even forgiven the man who had killed them. The struggle with her own lack of forgiveness surfaced. For the hundredth time.

"Hey, you. You're pretty quiet over there."

"I was just thinking. Ben, how do you define forgiveness?"

Ben sobered. "Well, I'd say forgiveness is granting a pardon for an offense. God's forgiveness is the greatest picture known to man. His holiness wouldn't allow our sin to go unpunished. His love saved us by sending his perfect Son to bear our guilt. All we need to do is receive the gift of his forgiveness."

A deep sigh reverberated through the depths of Kate's heart. "As believers, we should extend forgiveness to those who hurt us. That's where I get tripped up."

"Who hurt you, Kate?" The gentleness in Ben's voice touched her.

She wavered, then plunged ahead. "When I lived in Ohio, I dated a man named Gavin. I cared for him with all my heart. I really thought he was the one for me."

The memory of their last date, before the lies, waylaid her. He'd taken her to a fancy restaurant, had a huge bouquet of red roses delivered to their table, and told her what an exciting future waited for them. How could she have been so blind to the person he really was? She reached for more potatoes. "I thought he loved me. To make a long story short, he didn't. He only wanted me for my contacts in the media. He asked me to cast false allegations on his business competitor. When I refused, things turned ugly. I almost lost my job because of his lies. Needless to say, the relationship ended."

Ben's jaw clenched. "I'm sorry, Kate."

She searched his face. "My hurt is nothing compared with losing your parents. How did you forgive the drunk driver?"

He wiped his hands on a dishtowel, silent for a moment. "I made a choice at a young age to give my hurt and bitterness—and my desire for revenge—into God's hands. Though I've struggled over the years, the thing that's helped me most is praying for the driver whenever I think of him."

Kate absorbed Ben's words. He prayed for the man who had taken everything from him. His forgiveness wasn't dependent on the one for whom he prayed. Her throat tightened. Why was she waiting? Until she let go of her bitterness, she was hurting only herself.

Her eyes stung. She was ready to move forward. She would choose to believe what God said. And she would pray for Gavin. Though she too might struggle, she had settled the issue.

"Hey." Ben turned her to face him, and gently wiped her tears.

She managed a small laugh. "I guess somebody's peeling onions."

Those deep blue eyes searched hers. Could he see inside her soul?

He reached out and pulled her to him. Her heart raced as he bent and kissed her. His tenderness swept through her senses, stopping time.

"Where are those potatoes?"

Theo's voice floated into her consciousness. Laughter echoed through the kitchen.

Her eyes whisked open. "Is everyone watching us?" she whispered.

"I think so." Ben grinned. He touched her cheek, grabbed the pans, and headed to Theo.

Kate gazed after him. Their first kiss. Not roses and a fancy restaurant, but potatoes and a soup kitchen.

Nothing could be more perfect.

CHAPTER 12

MARCH 2
SUNDAY, 4:15 P.M.
FAIRFAX ICE ARENA, FAIRFAX, VA

Ben sipped steaming coffee at a table overlooking the ice-skating rink. Amazingly good coffee. Although after an hour of skating with his nieces, anything warm would taste great. Leah sat across from him, swirling marshmallows in her cup of hot chocolate. Judging from the look on her face, her mind was miles away.

Bonnie and Bekah skated past, waving. How could they still have this much energy?

"They're having fun, aren't they?"

Leah's words startled him. "Absolutely. Remind me not to take them hiking anytime soon. They'd run me into the ground."

She gave a small laugh. A little of the tension he'd carried with him since she fell apart in her kitchen two weeks ago ebbed away. That laugh, no matter how brief, was the first one he'd heard since Rich's funeral.

"Thank you for bringing us here, and for skating with the girls." Her gaze rested on him. "Ben, I wanted you to know I've decided to continue my counseling sessions at church. I need help. I didn't realize how much until I shattered the plate. Then one morning afterward, I woke to the sound of Bekah throwing up. Do you know my first reaction? To pull the covers over my head and let Bonnie take care of her."

She was silent for a moment. Ben waited.

"I've always run to their side when they're sick or something is wrong." Her shoulders slumped. "I caught a glimpse of myself in the mirror, cowering under the blanket. I thought 'What are you doing?' Or maybe the thought wasn't mine. Maybe God was speaking to me."

Ben covered her hand with his. No words came.

She flicked away a tear. "I've never given up on anything in my life. When times are hard, I dig in my heels and fight harder. I think that's why I fell in love with a Marine." She straightened. "I decided I was going to fight again. I know things won't get better overnight, but I'm not giving up."

Relief rushed through Ben. "What can I do to help?"

"Pray for me. Pray about the letter I sent Rich asking for his forgiveness." Her voice trembled. "The letter wasn't in his belongings. If only I knew he read what I wrote, even if the words didn't mean anything to him, I'd know I did everything I could under the circumstances. Maybe I'd get closure." Leah gave a small shrug. "Enough about me. I want to hear how my brother is doing."

He filled her in as much as possible about his work. When he told her about Princess Ingrid, he caught the glimmer of interest in her eyes. He reached back for everything he could remember about her appearance and speeches. Though he couldn't care less about Princess Ingrid's wardrobe, Leah would love hearing every detail. When he mentioned Kate filming the CRI event, Leah tilted her head, a sign she was ready for particulars.

"I'm glad I met Kate at the girls' school play. How are things going?"

The memory of the kiss they shared blasted his senses. Good thing he hadn't thought about their kiss while he was skating. The ice would have melted.

Leah grinned. "Your expression tells me everything I need to know."

"She's special, Leah. Amazing."

His sister's face turned serious. "Ben, I got a call from McKenzie."

His brow furrowed. He hadn't responded to the text she'd sent a little over a week ago. "What did she want?"

"To let me know she moved back to DC. We caught up ... She also mentioned you. She hinted she still has feelings for you."

"She sent me a text and asked to talk."

"Be careful, Ben."

"Don't worry. God used our relationship to open my eyes to things about myself. I'll always appreciate McKenzie, but the feelings end there."

"I'm glad. I've never seen you this relaxed and happy." A hint of mischief danced in her eyes. "I think my big brother is in love."

Bonnie and Bekah skated by. Leah turned to watch. Peace flooded Ben. Leah was back.

She was right on both counts. He'd never been happier. And he had fallen for Kate Peterson. Hard.

MARCH 3
MONDAY, 11:23 A.M.
DC

Martha leaned against the back of the park bench and lifted her face to the morning sun. Warmth radiated through her, chasing away the chill of a sudden breeze. Ah, the promise of spring. Only a few more weeks.

A crunching sound interrupted her thoughts. She looked up in time to see two bikes whiz past on the dirt path surrounding the huge grassy park. Her eyes wandered to a woman passing juice boxes to three children on the nearby playground. A little farther beyond the play area, a gardener trimmed hedges and an elderly couple fed ducks at a pond in the center of the park.

She glanced at her watch. Agent Bradley was late. Did she have the right address? She checked her phone again. This was the park he'd suggested. She frowned. Why did he want to meet in a park in DC instead of at CIA Headquarters in Langley? She had been determined to keep an open mind and not be swayed by Frank's accusations until she examined the evidence for herself. Still, she couldn't shake the uneasiness churning through her.

She punched Bradley's number into her phone. Before she could press the call button, she spotted him. He strode across the grass, his head down. She shoved her phone back into her pocket. *Lord, show me the truth.*

"Ms. Thomas, hello." He grasped her hand with both of his before sitting beside her. "So sorry I'm late. Traffic was ridiculous."

"I was surprised you suggested meeting here. I'd have been happy to come to Langley to save you a trip."

"I couldn't bear the thought of being inside on such a beautiful day. Guess I have spring fever."

She studied him. "You must have a great weather app on your phone. Our meeting was set several weeks ago. How did you know we'd have a beautiful day?"

A startled look darted across his face before he broke into a wide smile. "I do work for the CIA. My connections are the best."

"Can't argue with you there."

His smile faded. "I know you're busy, so I'll get to the point of our meeting. As I told you on the phone, I have information about Frank Edwards."

She nodded. *Here we go.*

"Toward the end of his career in the CIA, Edwards worked as a double agent. At first, he was invaluable in the information he retrieved and in his ability to thwart Russia's attempts to steal and duplicate our military systems. Unfortunately, we have reason to believe he switched loyalties. Among other crimes he committed against the United States, we believe he was an accomplice in the murder of your husband."

Martha stiffened. "Your evidence?"

"A CIA operative witnessed a meeting in Lucerne, Switzerland, between Edwards and Oleg Petrovich, the sniper who shot your husband. This meeting took place one week prior to the murder. We believe Edwards agreed to bring your husband to a prearranged spot so the sniper could kill him." Bradley paused. "As you are aware, your husband's career as a war correspondent made him privy to sensitive information. He made his own enemies who wanted to silence him. Edwards helped them succeed."

"Why wasn't I given this information at the time of my husband's death?"

"We had to protect the identity of our operative."

The identical answer Frank had given her when she asked him the same question. "I'd like to speak with the agent who witnessed the meeting."

"Unfortunately, he died a little over a year ago. Because of that fact, and the amount of time since your husband's murder, proving Edward's involvement would be difficult, if not impossible." Bradley shifted positions to face her. "Another operative, T. J. Moore, was murdered just seven months ago. He had information against Edwards any prosecutor in the country could get a guilty verdict with. My gut tells me Edwards had him killed."

Martha drew a deep breath. Two stories. One truth. "Where do I fit in this?"

"T. J. had a flash drive containing highly classified information, some of which concerned Edwards. He was on his way to give the information to me. Sadly, he was killed before he could make the delivery. Edwards showed up at the scene of the shooting. I'm sure he retrieved the device at the time."

"You said the flash drive contains classified information. I'm guessing you think Frank will sell the information to the highest bidder."

"I have no doubt."

She searched his face. "Do you know where Frank is now?"

His eye twitched. "We haven't been able to apprehend him. Frank Edwards knows how surveillance works. That's why I called you. Given your history with Edwards and the fact he won't trust anyone presently in the CIA, I'm betting he'll contact you. Though we might never prove he was an accomplice in your husband's murder, bringing him to justice would give you some measure of satisfaction, I'm sure." His eyes met hers. "We need Edwards. We also need the flash drive. You were—still are—one of the CIA's finest. I'm counting on you to help us."

"What exactly are you asking me to do?"

"At this point, to wait for Edwards to make his move. I don't think we'll have to wait long. When he contacts you, set up a meeting and call me immediately. We'll do the rest."

"I understand."

"Thank you, Ms. Thomas. I'll check in with you periodically." He stood. "May I escort you back to your car?"

"I'm going to get in a walk before I leave."

With a nod and a wave of his hand, he strode in the direction he came, placing his phone against his ear.

Who was he calling? Frank knew how surveillance worked. She did, too. No doubt she'd been watched ever since Bradley confirmed Frank was in the area.

Her gaze flicked to the gardener, still trimming hedges. Was he assigned to follow her in hopes she'd lead them to Frank? Did they already know he'd contacted her two weeks ago?

Her pulse quickened. Coming out of retirement wouldn't be too bad. For a short while, anyway. She needed to find out what was on the flash drive. Was the information vital to the country's safety?

Or vital to the cover-up of a rogue CIA operative?

MARCH 3
MONDAY, 7:45 P.M.
DC

Kate eased her camera from the bus window and placed her equipment in the case beside her. She should have some good footage. The Washington Monument at sunset, the Jefferson and Lincoln Memorials illumined in the dusk, dots of light around the Potomac …

Laughter and conversations swirled around her. The evening trolley tour of DC had been a hit with the Liechtenstein economists. Judging from the animated conversation, at least. If only she'd taken German in school, she could understand what they were saying. Too bad her oldest brother Tom wasn't here. He spoke German fluently, along with several other languages. He considered eavesdropping on others' conversations simply a way to brush up on his skills. She missed Tom.

Margaret Schrader, the Liechtenstein ambassador, moved down the rows, talking and laughing with her fellow countrymen. She finally reached Kate and eased into the vacant seat beside her.

"Hello, Ambassador Schrader."

"Please, call me Margaret. I think the tour was a success. Everyone seems to be having a wonderful time."

"They certainly are. Seeing the sights in the evening was a great idea."

"One gets a new perspective on the city, don't you think? By the way, how are your interviews coming?"

"I'm enjoying getting to know the men and women working on this project. I've interviewed almost everyone. Fortunately, their English is excellent. They each seem dedicated and passionate about the research and enormous benefits of the project."

"I agree. I had not yet met everyone, so I'm enjoying our time together as well. Do you need any assistance with your story?"

"I don't think so. When we stop for dinner, I'll complete the interviews. By the way, which one is Victor Schultz?" Kate worked to keep her voice casual. "He's one of those I haven't spoken with yet."

Margaret craned her neck. "Ah, let's see. There he is—in the second seat behind the bus driver."

Kate followed her gaze. He looked harmless enough. Thin. A touch of gray in his dark hair. Smiling. Her muscles relaxed. Maybe Ingrid's imagination had gotten the best of her.

The bus pulled to a stop. The tour guide at the front spoke a few words in German. Everyone began gathering belongings.

"I hope the restaurant is suitable. The cuisine is some of the finest in DC." Margaret stood and headed toward the door. "See you inside."

The entourage was led to a private dining room where dinner orders were taken and appetizers served. While everyone mingled, Kate moved to complete the last of her interviews. She waited to interview Victor Schultz last.

She spotted him sitting alone at one of the round tables. Perfect.

"Mr. Schultz, Kate Peterson." She extended her hand. "I've enjoyed hearing from your colleagues regarding the CRI project. I'd love to get your thoughts as well."

He smiled and motioned to the chair beside him. "Yes, I would be happy to speak with you as long as you don't film the interview. Any picture taken of me is unfailingly atrocious."

"I don't have to film our conversation if you'd rather not."

While they talked, she tried to focus on his analysis of the project. His reluctance to be filmed nagged. No one else had refused. She flicked her eyes to the doorway. No sign of servers bringing the entrées. She took a chance.

"I'd enjoy hearing about your life before the research program—where you grew up, other projects you've worked on."

Lines creased his brow, but his smile remained fixed. He detailed his studies and jobs. She listened closely, jotting notes occasionally. Nothing sounded suspicious. According to his story, he never resided in Vaduz, the capital of Liechtenstein and home of the royal family. What did she expect? If he were an accomplice in the murder of Ingrid's uncle, he certainly wouldn't implicate himself.

He glanced at his watch. Suddenly, he shut one eye and grimaced. "I'm terribly sorry. My contact needs attention. I must have something under the lens. If you'll excuse me, I'll attend to the problem."

"Of course. Thank you so much for sharing your experiences."

He strode to the open doorway a few feet away. She caught her breath. On the other side, in the larger dining room, sat Brandon Lancaster. She rose, her heart pounding. No one was with him at the moment. Kate moved out of Lancaster's line of sight and headed toward the door.

Kate passed Margaret Schrader, who stopped her to ask a question. Kate paused to reply, then continued to a serving table filled with water glasses. She snagged a glass and lingered by the doorway.

Lancaster sipped coffee, plainly finished with dinner. Seconds later, he stood. He pulled a large, brown envelope from his coat and dropped the envelope on the table. He glanced around, tugged on his coat, and left.

Lancaster, on his way to the front door, passed a returning Schultz. When Schultz reached Lancaster's table, he picked up the envelope, creased it, and placed the envelope inside his suit pocket.

Schultz looked up. Kate gulped and stepped backward. Had he seen her? She moved to the people closest to her. Schultz entered the room and joined another group.

She blew out a breath. Were Lancaster and Schultz acquaintances? Yet neither looked at the other as they passed.

When dinner was served, Kate only picked at the delicious meal. She probably read too many suspense novels, but what she'd just witnessed made no sense.

Unless Ingrid was right.

The question beat through her. Who was Victor Schultz?

MARCH 4
TUESDAY, 6:59 A.M.
14TH STREET NW, DC

Ben straightened his tie. He'd finished his morning run, grabbed breakfast, and still had time to spare before heading to work. Contentment settled over him. No matter what waited ahead at the Hoover building, the day would end well. He was taking Kate to dinner after work.

He sipped his coffee. Not hot enough. He slipped the cup into the microwave and punched in thirty seconds. The microwave sputtered, stopping at the same moment the apartment lights darkened. Ben leaned over the sink to peer out the window. No lights visible in the shops across the street, either. Another neighborhood power outage. He snapped a lid on his coffee cup. Lukewarm caffeine was better than nothing. He locked the front door, exited the building, and headed to his car.

"Hi, Ben."

He turned. McKenzie.

She ran up to him, a smile dimpling her face. "What a pleasant coincidence."

"McKenzie. What brings you to this area of town so early in the morning?"

She pointed to the apartment building beside his. "I found the greatest apartment. I moved in last week. I guess we're neighbors."

"I guess we are." He dug car keys from his pocket. "Well, I'm sorry I have to run. I need to head for work."

"Ben, I have a huge favor to ask. I'm going downtown, but since the power is out, I'm afraid I won't make my connections on the Metro. Could I get a ride with you?"

He hesitated, then gestured to his car. "Sure. I'm right here."

She smiled as they settled inside. "This is a nice car, but I must confess, I miss your old one. I could hear you coming a block away."

"Yeah, the car was a classic, but I finally realized I was under the hood more than I was in the driver's seat."

He put his key in the ignition. Was McKenzie thinking they could become a couple again? He needed to set the record straight.

"Ben, wait." She touched his arm. "Could we talk for a few minutes? I wanted to tell you something … and apologize. I've had a lot of time to think. I regret the choice I made when I left two years ago. I know I hurt you. I'm very, very sorry." She paused. "I still care about you. I wondered … can you ever forgive me? Could we try to work things out? I think we can reach a compromise on the differences we had. I believe we can both attain the things we want—together."

Her eyes pleaded, her face earnest. These were words he'd longed for, prayed for, after she left. But Kate had come into his life and penetrated the wall around his heart without even trying. Her love for God, her passion for the hurting, her integrity, beauty … God's timing was perfect.

"McKenzie—" Ben worked to keep his tone gentle. "Though I'm grateful for our time together, for all I learned through the relationship, I believe God has moved us in different directions. I know he has someone else for you."

"Oh." A small sob surrounded the word.

Sympathy darted through Ben. He hated to hurt her, yet he had spoken truth.

"Is Kate the reason?" McKenzie wiped tears on her sleeve. "She's beautiful. I hope the two of you will be happy." She turned and reached for the door handle.

"You know, I think I'll take my chances with the Metro. Goodbye, Ben."

As he watched her walk away, he exhaled a long breath. Though he'd loved McKenzie deeply, he never felt the freedom to be himself with her. With Kate, he didn't have to compromise because she valued the same things in life he did.

He couldn't imagine being without her.

CHAPTER 13

"Surpassing last year's fundraiser by seventy-five thousand dollars is quite an accomplishment." Kate smiled across the table at a beaming Liza Tyler. "I love reporting on stories like yours. You're making a difference for so many children and their families." She added a few more notes to those she'd typed on her iPad during their breakfast interview.

"The funds we raised will enable the hospital to forge ahead in both research and purchasing new equipment." Liza heaped orange marmalade on a slice of toast. "I couldn't be more pleased."

"Aunt Martha told me about your work with charities. I admire your caring spirit." Kate finished the last of her hot chocolate. "During my time as a reporter, I've found generosity like yours is rare."

"The business world can be a difficult place. One doesn't know the future. With so much competition, greed can wrap its tentacles around you before you know what happened. Sadly, I speak from experience.

Early in my career, I promised what was, at that point, a sizable donation to a struggling charity. I reneged when the time came to write the check. I was afraid to let go of the money—afraid my company might need the funds." Her eyes narrowed. "Do you know what happened? The charity folded. Many families were hurt because of the closing. Though I wasn't solely responsible, I had a share in the outcome. I made a decision that day to take charge of my money, not the other way around. After all, my sister and I grew up with practically nothing. I can weather poverty again if I need to."

Kate considered Liza's words. "Were you and your sister raised in DC?"

"Yes. Vivien and I always loved the city and made wonderful friends here. I met Martha in elementary school. Though our paths didn't cross for many years, I was glad to reconnect. We promised each other not to lose touch again." She paused. "Old friends are especially important when you lose someone you love. I recently lost my sister."

"I'm so sorry. I have brothers and sisters I can't imagine being without."

"Vivien is all the family I had. Well, if you don't count her husband." Liza visibly stiffened at the mention of him.

Kate hesitated. "I met him the day of the benefit when Aunt Martha and I delivered her artwork."

Liza shrugged. "Vivien and Brandon had a whirlwind courtship. They married after knowing each other only two months. They traveled extensively, mostly using *her* money. They even lived in Europe for a time."

"Really? Where?"

"England, Russia, Liechtenstein. I was glad when they came back to the US permanently."

Liechtenstein. Kate's brain raced. Did Lancaster meet Schultz when he lived there? Yet, the two men didn't acknowledge each other at the restaurant. "Did your brother-in-law conduct business overseas?"

Liza grimaced. "He conducts business wherever he is. Though he's done quite well in real estate, he always seems to want more." She drew a deep breath. "Forgive me, Kate. I shouldn't be rambling on about Brandon. Though we don't get along well, my sister loved him. I need to make more of an effort for her sake." She was silent for a moment. "I enjoyed talking with you about the benefit. I'll look forward to watching the report. When will the interview air?"

"Tomorrow evening on the six o'clock broadcast. Thank you for taking time from your schedule for this interview." An idea sparked. "By the way, I'm doing a series on Princess Ingrid of Liechtenstein. She's studying at Georgetown University this semester. I wonder—do you think Mr. Lancaster would share some of his experiences in the country?"

"One thing I've learned after all these years—don't be afraid to ask. He can only say no." Liza fished out a pen and paper from her purse and scribbled something. "Here's his number. Feel free to tell him I thought talking to you would be a good idea." The corners of her mouth pulled up. "Perhaps give him a little extra push. He's hoping for a job in my company."

"Thank you. I'll call him this morning."

They finished breakfast and said goodbye. Kate walked to her car, her mind racing. If only Lancaster would agree to talk with her. Maybe she could find something to explain the strange encounter with Schultz. Perhaps she could also get information regarding his dealings with the Shanes and O'Reillys.

Kate settled into her car and pulled out her phone. Was contacting Lancaster the right thing to do? She didn't want to cause more trouble for her friends. But Ian had threatened Max, maybe even hit him, and Ingrid was shaken by her encounter with Schultz. Both problems involved Lancaster. *Lord, help me with this.*

She punched in Lancaster's number. After several rings, a woman's voice answered.

"Lancaster Reality."

"I'd like to speak with Mr. Lancaster, please. This is Kate Peterson."

"You are calling regarding …"

"I'm a reporter with WOTN. I'm currently doing a series on Princess Ingrid of Liechtenstein. I understand Mr. Lancaster lived in the country for a time. I'd like to hear some of his experiences."

"One moment, please."

Kate swiped a hand across her forehead. Would he go for this?

"I'm sorry, Ms. Peterson. Mr. Lancaster is quite busy. Perhaps if you could try again in a few months."

Kate straightened. "Please assure Mr. Lancaster I wouldn't take much of his time. His sister-in-law, Liza Tyler, told me about his stay in Liechtenstein. She recommended I speak with him."

"One moment."

The change in the woman's voice was unmistakable. Liza's name carried weight.

"Mr. Lancaster just found an opening in his schedule. If you could be in our office at one-thirty today, he will be happy to speak with you."

Perfect. She could use her lunch hour to meet him. "Yes, I'll be there. Thank you."

Kate ended the call and blew out a breath.

Game on.

MARCH 4
TUESDAY, 8:20 A.M.
HOOVER BUILDING, DC

Ben studied the photos on the board in front of his desk. *Ethan Fitzgerald. His cousin Charlotte. Mindy West. Frederick Wilson. The man posing as Ethan's college roommate. The two CRI employees who had accused Ethan of embezzling.*

He almost pulled the pictures of the CRI employees off the board. He leaned back. No, not yet, though questioning them had yielded little. They appeared to believe Ethan was guilty and had just been doing their job in reporting the missing funds.

Two weeks had passed since Ethan's murder. Ben's gaze pivoted to Fitzgerald's photo. Serious eyes behind wire-rimmed glasses stared back. *What did you know, Ethan? Who found out?*

He turned to his computer and clicked onto details they'd gathered regarding Fitzgerald's past. Ethan and his cousin Charlotte had grown up next door to each other in a small South Carolina town. Ethan's father died when Ethan was twelve. Ben shifted positions. Wouldn't a young boy have spent time with a close uncle after the death of his dad?

He found information on Charlotte's family and scanned facts regarding her father. Bank president, active in his community, church deacon. An obituary contained many accolades regarding Fitzgerald's business and community endeavors. A description of his personal life included his enjoyment of fishing and hunting. Ben looked closer. "He loved nothing more than fishing with his nephew Ethan and hunting with his daughter Charlotte. His greatest pride was in Charlotte's ability to shoot. She was the Junior Division Skeet Champion three years in a row."

Ben searched for newspaper articles on skeet shoots fifteen years ago in South Carolina. Photos of Charlotte with her father were everywhere, along with glowing reports of Charlotte's ability to handle shotguns. He dug deeper. More articles, more awards. Her skills extended to rifles and handguns. She continued to compete during her high school and college years.

Ben ordered his thoughts. Charlotte was an expert shot. She possessed the ability to hit a moving target from a distance. Maybe even from a parking garage to the front of St. Michael's Hospital.

Would she kill her last remaining relative? Sadly, he had seen the scenario before. If she *had* killed him, what was her motive?

"Find anything?"

Joe's voice penetrated his thoughts. He pointed to the computer. "Read this."

His partner's expression changed as he studied the material. He looked at Ben. "What do you think?"

"Being an expert shot doesn't make Charlotte a murderer, but the fact does add a new dimension to things."

Joe leaned against Ben's desk. "For the sake of argument, let's say Charlotte is guilty. Any ideas for motive?"

"Just wondering the same thing. No family fortune waiting to be claimed. No long-standing disagreements we know of."

"If Charlotte is the murderer, the timing doesn't make sense." Joe ran a hand through his hair. "Ethan stayed with her while he was on the run. Why wouldn't she have killed him then instead of waiting until he was surrounded by security at the hospital?"

"Good questions … motive and timing. Maybe the answer to both is found in whatever Ethan knew about Sunburst. If he and Charlotte were working together on Sunburst—which I doubt—she might have decided she could do without a partner."

"What if Charlotte was involved in Sunburst and Ethan found out? We were planning to question him as soon as he was released from the hospital. She could have been afraid he would implicate her. Or, she could have tried to kill him earlier and failed. Someone shot at Ethan a few days before he was admitted to the hospital. Although in light of the articles we just read, her missing him seems unlikely."

"If Charlotte is involved in Sunburst, who would have drawn her in? Her only contact from CRI other than Ethan is Mindy West. So far, Mindy has been cooperative in the investigation. According to ground surveillance, she isn't venturing anywhere other than home, work, and her daughter's school." Ben twirled a pen through his fingers. "The man posing as Ethan's college roommate visited Charlotte at her townhouse. Maybe the two of them are in this together."

Joe groaned. "Mystery man. We need a break finding this guy's identity."

"You got that right. I also think we need to return to the clothing store where Charlotte works to speak with the employees again. They corroborated her story of doing inventory on the day of the murder, but in case someone is lying, a second visit by the FBI makes the idea a little more unpalatable."

"I agree. I have several meetings today, but we can go tomorrow morning if you're free. Janet is working on scheduling interviews with the remaining CRI employees. Hopefully, we can speak with most of them this week."

"Good. My gut tells me Sunburst isn't limited to the Liechtenstein project."

Joe stood. "What's on your agenda for the rest of the day?"

"Chasing information on the drug ring we're surveilling. We're getting close to moving in." He massaged the muscles in his shoulder. "If only we could deal with one case at a time. Juggling multiple cases gets dicey."

"I hear you. Unfortunately, since months of surveillance and research go into the majority of our work, we don't achieve the one-hour wrap-up most people see on TV."

Ben grinned. "Don't tell me, tell the press."

Joe left, and Ben turned to his computer. While he worked, his thoughts drifted to Charlotte. She was the last person he'd peg for Ethan's murder, yet this latest information painted a picture of possibilities. Charlotte possessed the needed skills. But motive? Timing?

Where did Sunburst fit in?

They needed answers. More than anything, they needed to catch a killer.

MARCH 4
TUESDAY, 1:35 P.M.
LANCASTER REALTY, DC

"Vivien and I enjoyed all of our travels in Europe. Liechtenstein was especially beautiful." Brandon Lancaster paused to sip coffee from a mug. "Are you sure I can't get you anything?"

"Thank you, I'm fine." Kate glanced at the list of questions she'd prepared. They'd almost completed the interview. She pressed closer to the real purpose for her visit. "Were you and your wife settled in one city during your stay there?"

"We traveled as much as we could. One of the highlights for me was visiting Gutenberg Castle. The fortress was built in the Middle Ages. The gardens are magnificent. My wife loved the Schadler Pottery in the town of Nendeln. We also attended the Liechtenstein Festival in Schaan—delicious food. Business kept me in Vaduz most of the time."

Vaduz—Ingrid's home. "Did you ever glimpse the royal family?"

"No. However, I did mingle with many prominent people. Some knew the royal family quite well." A self-satisfied smile lingered.

"I assume you're aware of the research exchange project between Liechtenstein and Caldwell Research Institute here in DC. I filmed a story for WOTN regarding the exchange, as well as interviewed the Liechtenstein economists."

He nodded. "I saw your story and interviews. They were excellent. I certainly hope both countries benefit."

"Do you know any of the economists?"

"Haven't had the pleasure."

His expression never wavered. Before she could push further, Ian stepped through the door. When he glanced in her direction, a cold stare replaced his smile.

"Sorry, didn't know anyone was here."

Her muscles tightened. He never took his gaze from her.

"Ms. Peterson and I won't be much longer."

Ian finally broke eye contact. He slid a large brown envelope across Lancaster's desk. "I checked the information you requested."

Kate caught her breath. The envelope had a crease down the center. Was this the same one Schultz had taken at the restaurant—and now had returned to Lancaster?

"Thank you. We'll talk later." Lancaster opened the envelope and scanned the contents.

Kate's thoughts churned while he read. He denied knowing any of the economists. Should she tell him she saw him at the restaurant? If only she'd caught Schultz and Lancaster's transaction on film. As things stood now, he could simply tell her she was mistaken. Besides, better to keep her observation quiet. His denial confirmed her suspicions. He couldn't be trusted. The insurance fraud and extortion sounded more plausible all the time. Was Schultz connected to his schemes?

Lancaster turned back to her with a smile. "Pardon the interruption. I'm afraid I have some pressing business to attend to. Perhaps one more question?"

She steeled herself. "I understand some of the buildings you own have been vandalized at least twice over the time they've belonged to you. Any idea who's behind the crimes?"

His eyes narrowed. "You're asking a question for the authorities. As far as I know, they have made no arrests."

"Except in the case of the attempted robbery, of course." She studied him. "I wonder if he acted on his own."

"We'll probably never know." Frost edged Lancaster's tone. "If you'll excuse me, I have work—"

His cell phone rang. He swiveled his chair to turn his back to her. She heard Liza's name. Lancaster's manner shifted a hundred and eighty degrees. He could turn charm on and off quicker than anyone she'd ever met.

"Yes, Vivien would be pleased. I think you'll find I'll make a wonderful CFO for Tyler Wealth Management. Thank you for placing your confidence in me."

He got the job. Strange Liza would give him the position when she seemed to dislike him so. Lancaster stood and strode to the window, still gushing, his back toward her. Kate gathered her things. Her eyes fell on the information Ian left. Dollar amounts. Large ones. With names of— Her eyes snapped to Lancaster. Still turned away. She leaned closer. Names of businesses? Maybe his real estate investments ... with the money he made through fraud and extortion? She studied two lines highlighted in yellow at the bottom of the sheet.

Motion caught her eye. Ian stood at the door. Watching her. Blocking her exit.

Was he her stalker?

"If you think you can make trouble for Brandon Lancaster, you'll find the idea a bad one."

She met his gaze. "Pardon me, I'm leaving now."

Seconds passed. He moved to allow her to exit. Would he follow? The thought of being on an elevator alone with him unnerved her. She ducked through the doors to the stairway. Unlike the parking garage a little over a month ago, no footsteps echoed behind.

Her breathing slowed. She played the information on Lancaster's desk back through her brain. The dollar amounts were in the hundreds of thousands. If only she could have looked more closely at the names beside the amounts. She tried to picture the sheet. Someone had highlighted "Smithsonian Station, twelve-thirty p.m." in yellow. What was the date written underneath? Wait—March eighth, her brother Tom's birthday.

She exited the building and squinted against the bright sun. She couldn't quit. Certainty coursed through her. She was close to uncovering a crime. What was her next move? Maybe enjoy a little sight-seeing around the Smithsonian on March eighth? This time, she'd be sure to bring a camera.

MARCH 5
WEDNESDAY, 5:37 A.M.
CAMILLA AVENUE, FAIRFAX, VA

"Good kitty, Shadow. Come and eat your breakfast."

The gray and white cat hopped onto the dryer, meowing.

"What's all the yowling about? I'll bet you want me to turn on the dryer while you eat." Martha moved his food dish closer to him. "Sorry, buddy, today isn't spa day. I have other things on my mind."

She peered around the curtain of the laundry room window. Taking care of her friend's cat for a week couldn't have come at a better time. She'd established the routine of leaving her apartment before five a.m. to come here. She chuckled. Ted Bradley's surveillance team was probably outside asleep. She'd parked in the driveway each day and spent about three hours here before returning home. All in preparation for today.

She filled Shadow's water dish. She'd cleaned the litter box and brought in yesterday's mail. She tugged on a light jacket. The sun would be rising soon. She needed to hurry.

She zipped her keys into her pocket. Today she'd give the guys watching her the slip without them ever knowing she left. She hoped. She checked the blinds throughout the house. Everything closed. Several lamps on. She opened the back door and stepped out.

A dog in the yard next door barked. She froze. He barked again, this time farther away. She peered through the darkness. Maybe something else had distracted him. She moved quickly along the back yard, through an empty lot, and across a quiet street. She drew a breath and glanced behind her. Everything still.

She checked her watch and headed two blocks north. At the corner bus stop, several figures loomed in the darkness. She closed the distance between them. Two teenagers with backpacks, an elderly lady with a shopping bag, a younger woman wearing the uniform from a local fast-food.

Moments later, a city bus squealed to a stop in front of them. She paid the fare and chose a seat midway down the aisle, careful to survey the passengers she passed. People heading to work or returning home—no one appeared out of place. She pulled her phone from her pocket. According to her GPS, she would arrive at her destination in five minutes thirteen seconds. Frank would meet her at the back entrance.

She settled against the cracked vinyl of her seat. The office building where she would meet Frank belonged to a trusted friend of his. Frank would show her the information from the flash drive in the secure location. At last. The flash drive T. J. Moore, the murdered CIA operative, had in his possession before he died. The flash drive he'd hidden in her niece Jenny's car when she stopped to help him. Jenny had given the flash drive back to Frank. Martha was ready to see the contents.

The bus rolled to a stop half a block from the office building. Martha got off and glanced around her. The sidewalks were not yet filled with pedestrians. She turned toward her destination. A smattering of raindrops splashed her face, then the heavens opened. She slipped on her hood. Maybe a torrential downpour was a good thing. The deluge would make visuals more difficult if anyone were watching. She reached the office building and hurried to the back entrance. On cue, the door swung open. She stepped inside.

"Saw you coming." Frank grinned down at her. "Sorry I didn't bring towels. You're drenched."

She peeled off her dripping coat and hung the garment over a chair by the door. "I was so busy trying not to be followed I never bothered checking the weather. Let's see the flash drive."

"Just like the old days—ready to work."

He led her down a hall. Their footsteps echoed in the deserted building. They turned into a large conference room and entered a door to a smaller office. A computer sat on the desk. Frank offered her a chair, pulled up another one, and clicked the computer. Martha held her breath.

"Here's what we've got."

She scanned the information. Pages of bank records, travel itineraries, emails … all concerning Ted Bradley. She glanced sideways at Frank. Was this T. J.'s flash drive? She wanted to believe her friend.

Martha studied the bank records. "The salary of CIA operatives apparently increased drastically after I left the agency."

"You would think so, based on deposits made to Bradley's account." Frank clicked onto another page. "Look at these records of trips taken over the last three years—Europe, Asia, South America. Bradley was tracking something … or someone. Notice this email regarding passports being taken care of. His or someone else's?"

"Anyone out in the field you can trust to conduct some fact-finding expeditions?"

"A few. I've already contacted them. They're going to get back with me as soon as possible."

Martha studied the dates in the travel itinerary for a moment. "Large deposits appear in Bradley's account exactly a month after his return from each of these trips. We need to find the source."

"T. J. was working on tracking the source before he was murdered." Regret filtered through Frank's voice. "Look at this video he included on the flash drive." Frank clicked the play button.

A serious young man appeared on the screen. Martha recognized him from several photographs included in the newspaper article she'd read at Jenny's apartment six months ago. She listened closely to the evidence he cited from the case he was building against Bradley, much of the information in the pages she'd just seen.

"Hope this answers some of your questions, Frank." T. J.'s voice lowered. "I'll expect to hear from you in a few days. Watch your back. Bradley's in this too deep to let anyone get in his way. He's trying to frame me, or worse. He'll probably do the same to you once he figures out how much you know. Be careful."

The video ended. Her insides churned. A young man had lost his life in his quest to uphold the law. The sadness never lessened though she'd seen this tragedy in the past. Yet, thankfulness mingled with the sorrow. Because of this video, doubts about Frank could, at long last, be put to rest. He had not gone rogue. Bradley had leveled false accusations against Frank to cover his own crimes. She blinked back tears. Now Frank's life was in danger just as T. J.'s had been.

"Martha? Are you okay?"

She looked into Frank's weathered face and steadied herself. "I—" Her voice caught. "I don't want to lose you."

A slow smile spread across his face. "You won't. After all, someone has to stick around to watch out for you." His tone turned serious. "Things could get rough."

"We'll get through this. We've tackled tough cases before."

"You always were one for understatements."

The alarm on Martha's phone sounded. "Almost time to head back." She turned her attention to the information on the computer. "I remember the newspaper article I read at Jenny's apartment mentioned T. J. was engaged."

"Yes, to a sweet, courageous young woman who is a zoological veterinarian. T. J.'s murder devastated her."

"I'd like to speak with her. Maybe she knows something significant, something she doesn't even realize. Do you have her number?"

"I do." Frank wrote down the information.

Martha glanced out the window. Rain still pounded. She'd try to call T. J.'s fiancée once she arrived home.

They left the office and headed to the back entrance. Frank pushed the door open a crack, then wider. He scanned the area and nodded. "I'll look into Bradley's email regarding the passports. As soon as I hear from my contacts, I'll get in touch with you."

With a wave and smile, she stepped out into the downpour. Though rain drenched her, she didn't care. A weight had lifted from her shoulders. Frank was who he'd always been—loyal, trustworthy, a man of integrity. Finding the name of her husband's killer. Seeking justice for T. J.

She'd missed him. Now all she had to do was keep him alive so she could enjoy having him back.

CHAPTER 14

Ben tried to breathe through a haze of perfume permeating the office of Charlotte Fitzgerald's employer. He and Joe were in for a tough time if they returned to the Hoover building smelling like gardenia blossoms.

Marci, the clothing store manager, pushed a clipboard across her desk. "I located the inventory record for February eighteenth since you apparently didn't believe me when you previously came to question us. As you can see, Charlotte Fitzgerald inventoried handbags on the third floor, jewelry on the second. Each employee was responsible for different areas. Like I told you before, she was in the store working the day of her cousin's murder."

Ben studied the information. "I don't see notes regarding start and completion times of the inventories. Were breaks and lunch hours scheduled?"

"Each employee had assigned areas. They worked until they finished them. They were free to move back and forth between departments. They were also allowed to take breaks and lunch whenever they wanted. We had other employees taking care of customers, so the timing wasn't important."

Ben glanced up from the clipboard. Maybe timing hadn't been important to her boss, but if Charlotte killed her cousin, timing would have been everything. Only a small window existed while Ethan was escorted out of the hospital.

Marci stood. "Anything else? I really need to get back out on the floor."

"We'll contact you if we have further questions." As she left, weariness settled over Ben. No changes in the stories of Marci or the other employees they'd spoken with again today. Everyone assured them Charlotte was in the store. Were they only assuming she was there? No one worked with her every minute. Would they have noticed if she'd slipped out for a couple of hours?

"Nothing we didn't know before," Joe mused. "An alibi filled with holes."

Ben nodded. Joe's voice mirrored his own fatigue. They exited the building and headed toward the car.

While they walked, his phone beeped. He slid the device to his ear. "Ben Anderson."

"Ben, guess what?" Susan's voice rose with each word. "We have the murder weapon used to kill Ethan Fitzgerald."

Energy surged. "Hold on, Susan. Joe and I are almost to our car. I'm going to put the phone's speaker on."

Once inside their vehicle, they resumed the call.

"Two parking garage workers found the gun used to kill Ethan Fitzgerald this morning. They were checking a blocked trash chute located by an elevator. When they cleaned out the garbage stuck in the chute, they found the rifle lodged there. The bullet that hit Fitzgerald was a match."

"Great news." Joe slapped Ben's shoulder. "The break we needed."

"I just checked the owner registration," Susan continued. "The gun is registered to—"

"Susan?" Ben checked his phone. Still connected.

"I'm here. Just trying to figure out … The owner of the gun, Simon Ford, is deceased. His wife resides in an assisted living facility." The staccato of Susan's fingers on her computer keyboard filtered through the phone. "A house in Arlington is listed in their name. I need to find relatives, see who is responsible for the property. Someone in the family must have keys."

"We're on our way back to Headquarters now. What do you need us to do?"

"I'll pull the information together. We'll talk when you get here."

"Okay, see you soon." Ben disconnected the call and glanced at Joe. "The plot thickens."

"Inevitably." Joe blew out a breath. "What do you think? A random home invasion, or someone with a key?"

Ben considered the options. "Both scenarios leave us with headaches. If there are no fingerprints, finding the perpetrator of a home invasion could take time we don't have. If we did find the thief, he wouldn't necessarily be the killer. The gun could have changed hands."

"Same with the second scenario. A key could have been used by someone other than the owner's family."

Joe maneuvered the car to the next exit ramp. "We might be in for a long afternoon and evening. Let's grab food on our way back. We'll get something for Susan, too."

They had their work cut out for them. What connected Sunburst, Ethan Fitzgerald, a deceased man, and a killer? Or, maybe the most important question wasn't *what*. The most pressing question was *who*.

MARCH 6
THURSDAY, 2:27 P.M.
ARLINGTON, VA

"This is the house." Ben pulled out his badge. He and Joe climbed the front steps to the home of Simon Ford, the deceased owner of the murder weapon.

Joe rang the bell. "I'm thankful we were able to track down Mr. Ford's brother, and that he was in town today."

Before Ben could reply, the door opened.

"Afternoon, gentlemen. I'm Chuck Ford."

Piercing blue eyes under a shock of white hair swept over them. Wearing a black Stetson, boots, jeans, and a plaid shirt, Mr. Ford could have stepped out of the Westerns Ben loved as a kid. "Hello, Mr. Ford. I'm Ben Anderson. This is Joe Peterson." They flipped open their badges.

"Not every day a fella gets a visit from the Feds. Hope I haven't done anything wrong." His lined face crinkled into a slow smile. He led them inside to a comfortable living area and gestured to the sofa. He removed his hat and settled in a rocking chair across from them. "Even though I try to keep up with the taxes and payments on my brother's house, traveling between here and my ranch in Montana wears me down sometimes. Not as young as I used to be."

Ben nodded. "Mr. Ford—"

"Chuck, please."

"Chuck. The reason we're here is because a rifle registered to your late brother was used in a crime."

The elderly man's eyes widened. "I don't see how—like you just said, my brother is deceased."

Joe leaned forward. "Has the house been broken into recently?"

"Never had any problems with burglaries in this area."

"Anyone else besides you have a key?"

"No need for anybody else to have a key. I usually come here around the first of each month, stay for a few days to take care of any work to be done. Of course, I was here twice in February because I needed to sign some papers at the bank two weeks ago."

Ben straightened. Ethan was murdered on February eighteenth—two weeks ago.

"The exact dates of your stay?"

Chuck reached in his pocket and pulled out a checkbook. "Let's see, according to my calendar, I arrived in DC on Friday the fifteenth and departed Monday the seventeenth." He chuckled. "I almost missed my flight on Monday afternoon. Charlotte and I stayed at the shooting range a little longer than we intended."

"Charlotte?" Caution hung in Joe's voice.

"Yes, Charlotte Fitzgerald. I grew up with her dad in Montana. When he moved away, I kept in touch with the family. I was delighted to find Charlotte and her cousin Ethan in DC. I know how much she loves guns, so sometimes when I'm in town we spend an afternoon at the shooting range. The day I flew out, we visited Ethan in the hospital—he was in a bad accident—then we did some shooting."

Ben processed the information. Did Chuck know Ethan was dead? "Have you spoken with Charlotte recently?"

"Not since the afternoon I left. We stopped by the house to return the guns and get my suitcase, then Charlotte drove me to the airport. I've been so busy I haven't contacted her this visit."

How would Chuck react to the news of Ethan's death? Ben cleared his throat. "I'm sorry to have to tell you this, sir. Ethan Fitzgerald was murdered on February eighteenth—the day after you left."

The man blanched. "I don't understand … Why didn't Charlotte call me?" Bewilderment glimmered in his eyes.

Ben paused a moment, then continued. "The gun used to kill Ethan was registered to your brother."

"My brother is dead." Sudden fire replaced confusion. "Are you accusing me? Because you can check with the airline to verify that I boarded the plane, as well as interview the twenty-three ranch hands I worked with every day afterward."

"We simply have to explore every lead in order to do our job." Ben kept his voice even. "May we see where your brother's guns are stored?"

"This way." He stalked down a hall into a large bedroom. A solid walnut cabinet stood in a corner. He reached into the top drawer of a nightstand, then lifted out a key. "This will put such nonsense to rest. The two guns belonging to my brother are right here."

He opened the cabinet and stilled. One of the racks was empty. "We returned both of the guns." He spoke softly, almost to himself.

"Were you both in the room or did Charlotte return the guns while you got your suitcase?"

Chuck visibly stiffened with Joe's question. "We were both in the room, the guns were returned, and I locked the cabinet."

Ben surveyed the surroundings. "Have you noticed any doors or windows that might have been tampered with?"

Chuck shook his head. "I haven't been looking. Like I said, this area doesn't have problems with crime."

"Do we have your permission to check?"

"Go ahead." He sank onto the edge of the bed. "I can't believe this. Maybe I'll wake up to find everything was a bad dream."

They pulled on gloves and began the search. The locks on the first-floor doors and windows proved secure. Ben gestured toward the basement door. "Let's see what we find down there."

He switched on a light and led the way down the wooden stairs. Expecting a basement the size of his sister's, he prepared to duck. He'd hit his head more than once on the low beams. but when they reached the bottom of the stairs, he stood upright. The room was spacious, with a ceiling around seven feet. High windows slightly above ground level allowed the waning daylight inside. They started on opposite ends of the room and checked each window.

Ben reached the corner. The latch of the last window was broken. "Bingo."

Joe joined him. "A tight squeeze, maybe, but doable."

Ben peered through the glass. The sun had set. "I'd like to check the ground outside. I'll get a flashlight from the car."

"I'm going back to the gun case to have a closer look at the lock."

Moments later, Ben shone a light on the ground outside the basement windows. Level, with one exception. The dirt at the bottom of the corner window had been pushed up to one side. Time for the guys at the lab to dust for fingerprints inside and out. He looked closer. Maybe bits of torn clothing or skin could be found on the rough windowsill.

He joined Joe and Chuck inside. Joe answered the question hovering on Ben's lips.

"The gun case lock hasn't been tampered with. Whoever stole the gun used the key."

Ben turned to Chuck. "Were you aware a window in the basement has a broken latch?"

"No." His shoulders sagged. "What's going to happen next?"

"A team will dust for fingerprints, both inside and outside the house. I'm certain we'll have more questions for you in the coming days, so you'll need to stay in town until further notice."

Chuck led them to the front door. "Wish I could say meeting you has been a pleasure, but you fellas sure ruined my day."

As they headed to the car, Ben pulled out his phone. He'd text Susan to verify Chuck's travel information and to notify the lab. His thoughts swung to Charlotte.

No doubt her fingerprints would be found on the firearms and the gun cabinet. If her prints were lifted from the cabinet key and the basement window, their search for Ethan's killer might be drawing to an end.

MARCH 6
THURSDAY, 5:31 P.M.
BENCHMARK FITNESS, DC

"Welcome to Benchmark Fitness." A petite blond in bright pink workout clothes stood behind the front desk. "You're Dr. Carly Bennett's guest for this afternoon, correct?"

Martha nodded. T. J.'s fiancée had suggested they meet here after her job ended for the day. Martha jumped at the opportunity. A gym for women only cut down the possibility of surveillance by Bradley's team considerably. Unless, of course, he had female operatives trailing her. She scanned the room, filled with machines and women of all ages. A chance she'd have to take.

"Carly is on the treadmill against the wall. There's an open one next to her."

Martha's gaze rested on Carly Bennett. Her auburn hair was tucked into a braid. She wore an absorbed expression, plainly working hard. No one would be close enough to hear their conversation. Martha murmured her thanks and headed over.

Carly looked up, slowed her pace, and offered a warm smile. "From the description you gave me over the phone, I'd guess you're Martha Thomas. I wouldn't have guessed you're a CIA operative, though."

"Was." Martha returned her smile. "I'm retired. A pleasure to meet you, Carly." Martha stepped onto the treadmill, programmed her workout, and matched her stride to Carly's. "Thank you for being willing to talk with me." A small shadow passed over the young woman's features. Martha's heart went out to her. She needed to make this as painless as possible. "Do you come here often?"

"Every afternoon after work. Exercising here is a good way to unwind. This morning's surgery on one of our lions had some stressful moments."

Martha grimaced. "You've brought a whole new meaning to the word 'stress.' How long have you worked at the zoo?"

"Three years." She paused. "I met T. J. there. The lions fascinated him. He kept coming back whenever he had a day off. One evening he asked me to dinner." Tears brimmed in her hazel eyes. "He proposed six months later."

"Carly, I'm so sorry."

They were silent for a moment, their steps on the treadmills the only sound between them.

Carly lifted her shoulders in a small shrug. "I try very hard to focus on the time we had together. T. J. was a wonderful man. I'm thankful for the privilege of loving him—and having his love in return."

Martha reached across the equipment and gave her a hug. Grief forged quick friendships. "Tell me some of your best memories of T. J."

"He loved learning, hearing new ideas. He read a book a week, always retaining the knowledge. I joked he had a photographic memory. He enjoyed hearing about my days at the zoo. He had the gift of making me feel I was the most important person in the world when I talked with him."

"What did you enjoy doing together?"

"Simple things, like popping popcorn and sitting outside under the stars. We enjoyed each other's company. T. J. had a great sense of humor. We'd laugh until our sides hurt. Sometimes I'm afraid I'll never find someone to laugh with like that again."

"Losing your best friend is hard," Martha said gently. "You wonder if life will ever be good again. The process takes time, yet God has a way of turning darkness back to light."

"I used to tease T. J. because he was so cautious in those last few months. I'm sorry I did. He was a great CIA operative. I hope he didn't listen to me and let down his guard."

Martha's thoughts darted back to her own time in the CIA. "Please don't worry, Carly. A CIA operative's training doesn't allow him to let down his guard." She smiled. "Even in retirement. Do you have any idea why he was so cautious?"

"No. T. J. discussed his work with me only in generalities, never specifics. I just noticed he searched his car and apartment—and mine—more than usual. I wondered if he were looking for bombs."

Or tracking devices, if Bradley hoped T. J. would lead him to Frank. "Did T. J. talk about the other operatives he worked with?"

"I met Frank Edwards. They worked together when T. J. first came to the Agency. I understand Mr. Edwards is retired now. We also went to dinner with a few of his friends from work, but I don't know them well. His supervisor, Ted Bradley, was very helpful to me around T. J.'s birthday. Mr. Bradley helped me find a particular watch T. J. wanted. He even had the piece delivered to me."

"Did T. J. know?"

Carly shook her head. "Mr. Bradley didn't want anyone to find out, said he didn't want to give the impression of partiality."

Alarm snapped through Martha's senses. T. J. had switched vehicles on the day of his murder. Yet, Bradley still managed to find him. What if Bradley put a tracking device in T. J.'s watch? The one place T. J. wouldn't have suspected because it had been a gift from Carly. "Do you have the watch?"

"Yes, I received it, along with a ring he always wore." Carly flicked a puzzled look her way. "Why?"

Martha chose her words carefully. "CIA operatives can get very creative with places they leave critical technology."

"You mean you think something inside the watch or ring might have a connection to T. J.'s murder?"

"Possibly. May I take the pieces for a few days? I'd like to have a friend from the FBI examine them."

"Of course, if you think that might help find T. J.'s killer. You're welcome to come to my apartment when we leave the gym."

Martha glanced outside. Going to Carly's apartment would be a bad idea. Most likely, Bradley had no clue she had met with Carly today. She wanted to keep things that way. "If you're coming here tomorrow, perhaps you could bring them then."

"Absolutely. I hope that means you're planning to join Benchmark Fitness. I think we could become good friends."

"I couldn't agree more."

They both increased their paces to a jog and ran in a comfortable silence. Martha glanced around the facility. Who cared if she already had a gym in her apartment building? Now she'd get twice as much exercise.

A little extra endurance was a good thing. If she found what she suspected in T. J.'s watch, they would be one step closer in the chase.

MARCH 8
SATURDAY, NOON
NATIONAL MALL, DC

Kate adjusted her sunglasses and tugged the brim of her baseball cap lower. *Blend in. Just blend in with everyone else.*

People filled the National Mall. Would Lancaster and Schultz show up today? Had she interpreted the information she'd seen in Lancaster's office correctly? Her eyes flicked over the tourists walking next to her. Would she be able to spot them in the midst of the crowds?

She sucked in a breath. Whatever took place, if anything, wouldn't happen for another thirty minutes. Might as well find a place to wait. She finally chose a bench near the Smithsonian Metro stop. She perched beside a family with two kids in strollers.

While she checked her camera, a giggle sounded. She looked up into the smiling face of the little boy sitting closest to her. Curly blond hair framed blue eyes and a mouth smudged with peanut butter.

"Mama," he cooed, eyeing her.

"Ah, no. I'm Kate."

His mother reached over and handed him a plastic cup with a lid. She beamed at Kate. "He already knows two words—'mama' and 'daddy.' Isn't he smart?" She turned back to her other child without waiting for a reply.

Kate busied herself checking her watch and picking up the little boy's cup each time he pitched it to the ground. At twelve twenty-five, she smiled goodbye to her curly-haired friend and started in the direction of the Metro.

She walked to the opposite side of the stairs leading up from the train. She stood next to a concession stand selling ice cream, searching the faces of those who passed. No sign of Lancaster or Schultz. She bit her lip. Or Ian.

Minutes stretched to an hour. Frustration surged. She'd make a terrible spy. She should have gotten surveillance tips from Ben or Joe, but to do so would require talking to them about the situation. Which she hadn't.

"Can I help you, lady?" The man selling ice cream leaned out the window of his stand.

"No, thank you." Probably her cue to make room for paying customers. She ambled along the path away from the Metro stop. She'd walk a few more minutes, then leave.

A large group of teenagers wearing fluorescent green shirts meandered in front of her, finally wandering in another direction. She was alone except for two men a few feet ahead. Some German words from their conversation floated in her direction. Something about them seemed familiar.

One of the men turned slightly. Of course. Two of Ingrid's security guards. Perhaps they had the day off and decided to explore the city. She almost called out to them but stopped. They probably wouldn't remember her. Besides, they had picked up their pace.

Should she head home? She glanced around. A figure striding across the grassy center of the mall caught her eye. Her pulse quickened. *Lancaster.* Had he seen her?

She slowed. Lancaster wasn't coming toward her. He veered off the path, crossed the street, and settled on a low brick wall surrounding the entrance to a museum. Something on his phone absorbed his attention.

Options bounced in her brain. She couldn't stop in front of him, but she needed to stand close enough to see what he would do next. She looked past him to the courtyard in front of the museum. Perfect. She could photograph flowers and watch Lancaster at the same time. She continued walking, then circled back behind him into the garden. Two Japanese maples shielded her from view.

Thirty minutes passed. She squinted through her viewfinder. Two men suddenly joined Lancaster. She frowned. Ingrid's security guards. What business would they have with Lancaster? Had they met while Lancaster lived in Liechtenstein?

She focused the camera and shot successive photos. Her skin prickled. Ian was in the pictures, standing off to one side. Thankfully, he wasn't looking in her direction. In less than two minutes, the group parted, heading in opposite directions.

Kate stared after them. What could they discuss in such a short time? The information she'd seen in

Lancaster's office contained names along with large dollar amounts. Was he hiring the guards to provide security for someone? Or was he bringing them into his real estate dealings?

She exhaled a long breath. She'd expected to see Schultz today. Hoped to find something to explain his transaction with Lancaster at the restaurant. Something to prove Lancaster's guilt or innocence in dealing with the Shanes and O'Reillys. Instead, a whole new set of questions hammered her. She grabbed her phone and sank to the wall occupied by Lancaster moments ago. One question could be answered now. She punched in Ingrid's number.

"Hi, Kate," the princess croaked.

"What's wrong? Are you sick?"

"Just a terrible cold. I sound awful, but I'm over the worst. One of my guards just brought me delicious chicken soup. I'm sure I'll feel better once I eat some."

"I won't keep you long, then. Speaking of your security guards, I have a question for you. Are they allowed to engage in business while in America with you?"

"They must follow a strict code of ethics and regulations while employed by our family. Personal business ventures aren't restricted, as long as they are discreet and legal, of course. Why?" A fit of coughing echoed through the phone.

Poor Ingrid. This wasn't the time to bombard her with questions. "I'll explain later. I hope you get well soon."

"Thanks." Another wave of coughing ended the call.

Kate picked up her camera and clicked through the photos she'd shot. Though she'd only captured profiles, intensity etched the men's expressions. Her interview with Lancaster whirred through her brain. He hadn't met the royal family. Was he using the guards to gain a foothold with Ingrid and her father?

She was scheduled to accompany the princess to one last interview at CRI. She'd have a chance to observe Schultz again. If things went her way, maybe the two security guards who'd met with Lancaster would be on duty.

She lifted her eyes to the cloudless blue sky. Whatever Lancaster was a part of, she had a feeling the stakes were high. Judging from the expression on his face today, he planned to win.

CHAPTER 15

MARCH 8
SATURDAY, 4:37 P.M.
DC

Ben studied Charlotte Fitzgerald from across the table. In the two days since her arrest, she had refused to talk, look at them, acknowledge their presence. She probably knew the exact number of tiles in the jail's interrogation room. She'd stared into space long enough.

Joe pulled up a chair. She continued to stare at the floor.

"I checked on your dog earlier today," Ben said. "Your neighbor assured me Gibbs is doing well. She said her son taught him to roll over."

Charlotte shifted in her chair—eyes downcast. The slump in her shoulders hadn't been there earlier. Was she finally ready to cooperate?

She lifted her eyes and, at last, looked at him. Tears splashed down her cheeks. "Why won't you let me go home? I didn't kill my cousin."

"Then help us prove your innocence by answering our questions."

A scowl dried her tears. "I was under the impression a person is innocent until proven guilty."

Joe tapped a folder on the table. "Right now, our evidence points to you as the perpetrator of the crime."

"Your evidence is faulty."

"The latch on a window in Simon Ford's basement is broken. Your fingerprints were lifted from both the inside and outside of the window. Can you explain why?"

She straightened. "Simon's brother Chuck takes care of the property. He and I are close family friends. I try to help him whenever I can because he has such responsibility with his brother's home as well as his ranch in Montana. When I visit, I usually walk through the house to see if anything needs attention. The afternoon before Ethan was killed—" She swiped a hand across her eyes. "I'd planned to drive Chuck to the airport. While he finished packing, I checked the first floor and basement. When I noticed the broken latch, I tried to fix the piece."

Ben glanced at Joe. "Did you tell Mr. Ford about the latch?"

She shook her head. "He was already afraid he would miss his flight. I didn't want to trouble him. I knew he'd be back in two weeks, so I decided to wait until then to tell him."

"Why were your prints lifted outside?"

"After I drove Chuck to the airport, I started wondering whether someone could get in the house through the window. I went back and tried from the outside. I was able to open the glass an inch or two. I didn't think anyone could open the window high enough to climb through. Obviously, I was wrong. I was planning to tell Chuck about the latch—and Ethan—but you had other ideas for me."

"Did anyone go back with you to the house? Talk to anyone in the neighborhood while you were there?" Ben searched her eyes. They'd already questioned neighbors, who claimed they'd seen nothing out of the ordinary.

"I didn't see anyone. After I left the house, I went back home, ate dinner, and spent the rest of the evening watching TV."

Ben switched course. "Talk to us about the following day, the day of Ethan's murder."

"I went to work, inventoried merchandise, then received the worst phone call of my life."

"Which employees did you speak with during the day? Eat lunch with anyone?"

"I said good morning to everyone, then started work. I ate lunch in the break room, which, by the way, was empty."

"Is there anything else you can tell us? Anything to corroborate your account?"

Her face reddened. "How ridiculous! I was in the store from nine a.m. until I received the call about Ethan at five p.m. Period." Anger seethed. "You know what I think? I think because you've botched the investigation, you're trying to pin this on me. I demand to know whether you've checked the murder weapon for prints."

"Three sets of prints were lifted from the gun," Joe answered. "Yours, the garage attendant who retrieved the weapon, and Chuck Ford. Both Mr. Ford and the attendant had witnesses with them at the time of Ethan's murder."

"You found my prints on the weapon because I used the gun at the shooting range the day before Ethan died. I didn't murder my cousin. The killer must have worn gloves."

She crossed her arms and slouched in her chair. Was she retreating into silence again? Ben changed tactics. "Tell us about Sunburst."

Disgust hovered over her features.

Ben placed Gibbs's collar on the table, the duct tape with 'Sunburst' facing up. "Why is this on your dog's collar?"

Her eyes widened. "I have no idea." She looked closer. "This looks like Ethan's handwriting."

"Did he ever mention Sunburst to you?"

"Never. He was probably working on some experiment or project. He loved testing unusual theories—like whether dogs could learn through osmosis."

"What about the quarter of a million dollars in a Swiss bank account under Ethan's name? Which, by the way, was transferred from the account to an untraceable location."

Charlotte's mouth dropped open. "That's crazy. You're all crazy. You're making up bizarre things to cover your incompetence."

"So, you're telling us you know nothing about these funds."

"That's exactly what I'm telling you."

"Then let's talk about something you do know. How did Mindy West find out Ethan was in the hospital? You said she just showed up. She said you called her."

Charlotte sighed. "Okay, so I called her. I lied to you because she left work when she wasn't supposed to. I didn't want her to get into trouble. I thought having her in the hospital might help Ethan. Is one lie such a crime? I've answered your questions. Can't I go home now?"

Joe laid an envelope on the table. "You've lied to us more than once, Ms. Fitzgerald. We found this plane ticket to Mexico in your possession. You neglected to tell us you were planning to leave the country."

"You never asked."

"Because of this ticket, you are considered a flight risk."

Defiance flashed. "I was planning to return home in three weeks. I purchased a return ticket."

"You're still considered a flight risk."

"I have nothing more to say."

They tried several lines of questioning. This time, she was true to her word. After she was escorted out, Joe turned to Ben.

"Let's head back to the office and process what we've got."

A short while later, they settled in an empty conference room at the Hoover building.

Ben leaned back in his chair. "Let's go with Charlotte's story first and argue for her innocence. She leaves prints on the murder weapon because she spends the afternoon at the shooting range with Chuck Ford. Back at the Ford home, she notices a broken window latch. She tries unsuccessfully to fix the latch. Later in the evening, she checks the window from the outside, thereby leaving more fingerprints. She works the following day at her job until she receives the news about Ethan. She knows nothing about Sunburst or the money in the Swiss bank account. She buys a plane ticket to Mexico to get away from the stress and grief of her cousin's murder." He straightened. "The problems lie in the fact she has no one to corroborate her whereabouts the evening the gun was stolen, nor during the time of Ethan's murder. We also have no evidence of a home invasion—no fingerprints besides hers, no locks tampered with. She had access to the murder weapon. She's also lied to us on multiple occasions."

Joe stood and paced. "On the flip side, let's argue she's guilty. She spends the afternoon with Chuck Ford to gain access to the Ford home. While he packs, she heads for the basement. She breaks the latch on the window as an alibi for a home invasion. She returns to the house later in the evening, crawls through the window, and steals the gun. She goes to work the next morning as usual, then slips out with no one noticing, murders Ethan, gets rid of the weapon, and returns to work to continue inventory. She or someone she's working with transfers the money from the Swiss bank account to an undisclosed location, possibly Mexico, the destination of her plane ticket." He paused. "The difficulties with this argument are no solid evidence linking her to Sunburst. Also, her prints were not found on the key to Ford's gun cabinet."

"In her haste to enter the house, she forgets to wear gloves, then puts them on once inside?" Ben furrowed his brow. "A stretch, with no proof."

Joe sank into his chair. "She possesses the skill to commit the crime, had access to the murder weapon, but motive?"

"Unless we can connect her to Sunburst, motive is the big question." Ben drummed a pen on the table. "Susan is working on tracing the money. If the funds turn up in Mexico, we'll have our answer." He thought back over the arguments for her innocence and guilt. "We know she sold a gun two years ago. No weapons are presently registered to her. If she's guilty, why use the gun of someone whose family is linked to hers?"

Joe rubbed his eyes. "Good question."

"Let's revisit the theory of Charlotte's innocence. We believe Ethan was set up. Let's say the same of Charlotte. Someone who wanted to implicate her would choose a family connected to her. If the person had done his homework, he would know Charlotte's skill with guns, be aware of her trips to the shooting range with Chuck Ford." Ben leaned forward. "Was Charlotte's trip to the shooting range the day before Ethan's release from the hospital mere coincidence, or did someone arrange the trip to highlight her access to the murder weapon?"

"The timing would be difficult to plan, but not impossible."

"Especially if you were—"

Joe's eyes narrowed. "Chuck Ford. Even though he has an alibi during the time of the murder, he could be working with someone else."

Ben nodded. "We need to dig deeper."

Weariness penetrated his muscles. Maybe they were heading down a dead-end path, but the possibility of Ford's involvement was an avenue they couldn't afford to ignore.

MARCH 10

MONDAY, 10:47 A.M.

PINE VALLEY ASSISTED LIVING, ARLINGTON, VA

"Mrs. Ford will be pleased to have company today." The receptionist at Pine Valley Assisted Living smiled. "She's one of my favorite residents. Most days her mind is sharp as a tack."

"That's good to hear." Ben signed the visitor clipboard and passed the pen to Joe. "Do many people stop in to see her?"

"Her brother-in-law visits whenever he's in town. She also has friends who come." The receptionist gestured toward a hall to their left. "Follow the corridor past the nurses' station. Mrs. Ford's room is the first one on the right."

They thanked her and headed down the wide hall. Ben's pulse quickened. Visiting Simon Ford's wife might yield something to aid their investigation. Though Susan's background check on Chuck had come up clean, they needed to rule out any possibility of his involvement in Ethan's murder.

Her door stood slightly ajar. Ben knocked.

"Come in," a warbly voice called.

They entered a large, cheerful room. Mrs. Ford sat in a recliner facing a window. Outside, bright red cardinals hopped between two bird feeders.

"Mrs. Ford, I'm Special Agent Ben Anderson. This is Special Agent Joe Peterson. We spoke with your brother-in-law Chuck last week."

She turned and squinted at their identification. Snow-white hair framed a lined face still beautiful. "Won't you sit down?"

"Thank you."

She pulled a white sweater with tiny pearl buttons closer around her and studied them. "What nice-looking young men you are. You remind me of my late husband Simon. We were married sixty-five years."

"What a wonderful legacy." Ben returned her smile. "Mrs. Ford, the reason we're here is—"

"Simon's family owned a ranch," she continued. "We lived there for a decade."

Ben nodded. Mrs. Ford plainly had more to say.

"He and his brother worked together. Because Simon loved to travel, he finally decided to take a job with an insurance company. His employers sent him to corporate offices in several states. We finally ended up here in Virginia and decided to stay. Simon died almost two years ago." Some of the light faded from her smile. "I miss him every day. His brother comes to visit whenever he's in town."

The TV remote slipped from her lap. Ben picked up the device. "I would imagine they were close since they worked together on the ranch for ten years."

"Oh, yes. They hit a rough spot in their relationship when Simon gave up ranching, but they patched things up. Simon's death was hard on Chuck. When I moved here last year, Chuck promised to take care of the house until I was ready to sell. I know I can always call on him if I have a problem."

Joe leaned forward. "Does Chuck have other business ventures besides the ranch?"

A silvery laugh sounded. "Goodness, no. When you own a ranch, some days you hardly have time to breathe."

"I can imagine. I grew up on a farm in Kansas. There was always work to do." Joe paused. "Mrs. Ford, Ben and I are looking for information on something called 'Sunburst.' Has Chuck ever mentioned the name to you?"

"Not that I remember."

"A friend of Chuck's, Ethan Fitzgerald, was also trying to get information on Sunburst. Do you know Ethan and his sister Charlotte?"

"I know the names. Chuck talks about going to the shooting range sometimes. I believe he visited the young man in the hospital recently. I never met the family personally."

A nurse appeared in the doorway. "Almost lunchtime, Mrs. Ford. I'll return in just a moment to help you to the dining room."

"Thank you." Mrs. Ford turned back to Ben and Joe, her blue eyes twinkling. "The meals here are okay, but the desserts are scrumptious. So, I always eat dessert first. Aren't I terrible?"

Ben grinned. "I think you're delightful. I might try your plan myself. Thank you for visiting with us."

"My pleasure. I hope you'll come again."

Ben couldn't remember his own grandparents. He'd enjoy another visit with her. As they stood, his eyes rested on a set of keys hanging on a hook by the door. "Mrs. Ford, I wondered … most people have more than one key to their home. Do you keep an extra key to your house here?"

"Yes, I do. Usually. I gave my key to the electrician."

Ben stilled. Chuck Ford said he took care of any work that needed to be done. "When did the electrician come by?"

"The days sometimes run together. A month ago, maybe? He told me he needed to repair some wiring in the house."

"Did he show you any identification, tell you which company he worked with?"

"No. I assumed my brother-in-law arranged for him to come. I keep meaning to ask Chuck when he visits. He's planning to come by tomorrow. I'll ask him then."

Ben's mind raced. They now had a third person with access to the murder weapon. They needed to contact Chuck Ford, get his story. If Ford hadn't sent anyone, determining the man's identity could be a nightmare.

An idea hit. A long shot, but … Ben pulled out his phone and scrolled through photos. He turned the screen to Mrs. Ford. "Was this the man who came?"

"Yes. Has he done electrical work at your house?"

Before Ben could answer, the nurse entered.

"Ready to eat?"

They walked with Mrs. Ford to the dining room. The men said goodbye and headed to the lobby.

Joe turned to Ben. "I'm betting the electrician was the man who posed as Ethan's college roommate."

"One and the same."

"We need to find him. Now."

"He's going to get careless at some point. Let's speak with the staff, get records of the visitors, check security cameras."

"I'll call Chuck Ford. Meet you at the front office."

Ben nodded and strode toward the offices. Whoever killed Ethan Fitzgerald wasn't going to get away with murder. Not on his watch.

MARCH 11
TUESDAY, 12:45 P.M.
NEW YORK AVENUE, DC

Kate finished the last bite of a peanut butter and jelly sandwich and brushed away crumbs. She shivered. In the few minutes she'd sat in her car to eat lunch, the heat from the ride over had dissipated. She gathered her camera equipment. Fortunately, Caldwell Research Institute was only a block away.

She shivered again as she walked, this time the cold was inside. Today was her last interview with Ingrid at CRI. The catered luncheon for the Liechtenstein economists and the princess should be wrapping up by now. Kate would film the analysts as they gave detailed explanations of their work. Schultz had refused to be filmed in their earlier interview. Would he refuse again?

She approached the building and slowed. People were filing out of the front entrance, briefcases in hand. Were they leaving? She frowned. Had she misunderstood the date of the interview?

She wove through the stream of economists and approached the glass doors. Frederick Wilson stood in the lobby with Ingrid. Two security guards hovered behind them. Kate's heart hammered. *The guards who met with Lancaster.* She stepped inside.

"Again, please accept my deepest apologies. I had hoped the problem would be corrected by the time we finished lunch. We will reschedule as soon as possible."

Ingrid smiled at Wilson. "I certainly understand. I enjoyed the meal immensely."

Wilson glanced in Kate's direction. "Ms. Peterson, we're experiencing problems with our internet services, so our analysts will be working from home this afternoon. My administrative assistant will contact you with a new date for the interview." His tone was not nearly as apologetic toward her.

His attention shifted back to the princess. "Your Highness, I believe your car is ready."

"Thank you, Mr. Wilson."

She turned to Kate on the way out. "Do you have a few minutes?"

"Of course."

She followed Ingrid to the sleek limousine situated over two parking spaces. She carefully slid her camera case onto the black leather seat.

Once settled, Ingrid addressed the guards. "Gentlemen, I need a moment, please."

"Yes, ma'am."

The men exited the vehicle. With the click of the car door, Ingrid whirled around to face Kate, her eyes dark.

"He's here."

Kate blinked. "Do you mean Victor Schultz?"

"Schultz—or whatever his real name is. The person who murdered my uncle." Ingrid twisted her hands in her lap. "I suspected him before because of his familiar mannerisms. But after today, I have no doubt."

"How can you be sure?"

"The man I knew had one brown eye and one blue eye—a condition called heterochromia iridis. Today, I looked into those same eyes. Evil stared back at me."

Kate processed the information. "I've spoken with Victor Schultz. His eyes aren't—" She stopped as his words at the restaurant rushed back. *I'm terribly sorry, but my contact needs attention. I must have something under the lens.* She drew a sharp breath. "He wears contacts."

"At the luncheon today, we were seated across from each other. When he was served, soup splashed on him. He rubbed his eye, and his contact apparently slipped out. He immediately excused himself, but not before we locked eyes." She shuddered. "He knows I recognized him. I could see it in his face."

"He's surely aware he's a wanted man. What would motivate him to undergo major plastic surgery and come to DC?" Kate's blood chilled, and she grasped her friend's arm. "Are you his target?"

The princess didn't flinch. "I don't believe so. He could have killed me by now if he'd wanted."

"Ingrid, I need to tell you something." Kate related the meeting between the security guards and Lancaster, as well as the exchange between Lancaster and Schultz at the restaurant. "Brandon Lancaster also lived in Vaduz for a time."

"Who is this man?"

"He's in real estate. Recently, he became the CFO for Tyler Wealth Management. I have friends who lease his buildings. From what I've seen, he can't be trusted. I thought he wanted to draw Schultz and your security guards into his business dealings, or maybe use them to gain an audience with you. I believe Lancaster might be guilty of extortion and insurance fraud. Based on what you've told me, I'd bet a year's salary he's involved in something more."

Ingrid didn't reply. She appeared deep in thought, yet unshaken. Was she truly unafraid, or was she relying on the skill of masking her feelings?

The princess finally spoke. "I need to get to our embassy, speak with my father in a secure location and tell him about Schultz. We also need the authorities in our country to find out what Lancaster's business dealings involved when he lived in Liechtenstein."

Kate straightened. "I'll come with you."

Ingrid smiled at her. "I'll be fine. I imagine my father will insist I stay at the embassy until this matter is dealt with." She glanced out the window. "I need to be careful how I voice my suspicions. I can't embarrass my country. I'm also a guest of the United States. I refuse to jeopardize the research exchange program unless there is no other choice."

The realization of her friend's responsibilities struck Kate again. Shouldn't her safety come first? "If Schultz knows you recognized him, you're in danger. Two of your security guards might be working with him. Please, let me call the FBI. My—"

Ingrid held up a hand. "Calling the FBI isn't necessary. The embassy is a short distance away. I'll call our head of security now to request his presence immediately upon my arrival. I'll even text you later. Of course, I won't be able to disclose anything I learn …" She grinned. "I have an idea. At seven o'clock this evening, I'll send a message about setting up another time to go horseback riding. Like a code—you'll know I'm perfectly fine, and we'll satisfy your passion for intrigue at the same time."

Kate considered the plan. "Okay—deal." Another reason she liked Ingrid. Her friend could joke in the face of … She sobered. Grave danger. She opened the car door, careful not to look at the faces of the guards.

As the convoy merged into traffic, Kate gripped her phone. Fine. She'd wait until seven o'clock. If Ingrid didn't text, she didn't care if she started an international event. She was calling the FBI.

CHAPTER 16

Ben filled his mug with fresh coffee, then stirred in a packet of sugar. Surely sweetened caffeine was more potent than plain. He hoped. He rubbed his eyes and headed back to his desk. His team had worked through the night without success. They were still chasing after the identity of their imposter. Janet, Curt, and Dave were searching for everyone who'd passed through the doors of Pine Valley Assisted Living. He was wading through home security videos from the Fords' neighbors with Joe and Susan.

Joe looked up. "Even though we haven't found anything yet, at least everyone in the Fords' neighborhood has been cooperative with the investigation."

Susan yawned. "We'll get him. We just have to keep looking."

Ben eased the mug onto his desk and focused on the videos. He checked a black Honda parked eight doors from the Fords' house against the homeowner's registration. A match. The next frame of the video, an hour later, showed a different car. He looked closer. Blue, maybe a Mazda, with only part of the license plate visible. He made a notation, then forwarded the information to Susan. She was working with partial numbers, along with models and color, to determine the owners.

The office was quiet, everyone working. An hour passed.

"Yes!" Dave's voice broke the silence. "We found our guy at Pine Valley. A hall security camera shows him outside Mrs. Ford's door. Of course, I doubt he was stupid enough to sign in, but at least we have the timeframe."

Susan leaned back and propped her feet on her desk. A huge grin spread across her face. "He was stupid enough to park his car eight doors down from the Fords' house."

Ben spun around to face her. "The blue Mazda?"

"Yep. Registered to Ian Dunbar. The photo is a match to those Joe shot at Charlotte Fitzgerald's townhouse."

Adrenaline bit back Ben's fatigue. "We're on it. Send us his info, then get out an APB."

She sat upright, fingers clicking computer keys. He and Joe grabbed Kevlar vests and headed for the door. *Thank you, Lord.* One step closer to solving Ethan's murder and figuring out why someone thought Sunburst was worth his life.

Minutes later, Ben programmed Dunbar's address into his GPS and merged into traffic. They were twenty minutes away from Dunbar's apartment when Joe's phone buzzed.

"Peterson." A pause. "Don't let him out of your sight. We're on our way." Joe switched on the flashing dashboard light. "Head west." He punched in a new address.

Ben pressed his foot against the gas pedal. "Dunbar's been spotted?"

"Yes." Joe's voice sounded grim. "He's parked now, sitting in his car outside Springview Academy."

Springview—the school Mindy West's daughter attended. Ben flicked a glance to the dashboard clock. Four thirty-five. Around the time Mindy would pick up her daughter?

"I think we can safely assume Dunbar gave Mindy's daughter the toy in January. I wonder if this is another intimidation tactic, or if he wants Mindy to do something more regarding Sunburst."

"If things go our way, we should be able to ask him in about ten minutes."

Seconds before they reached Springview Academy, Ben switched off the flashing light. He turned into the parking area and slowed. He spotted two unmarked vehicles from ground surveillance. One sat near the exit of the parking area. The other waited next to the side of the school.

He maneuvered his car a few yards behind Dunbar's and scanned the parking area. The lot was about one-third full, with no foot traffic. "Let's get the agents by the side of the school to enter the building to keep anyone from coming out. The guys waiting near the street can block the exit until we apprehend Dunbar."

"Got it."

While Joe made contact with the other agents, Ben studied Dunbar. He sat with his arm out of the driver's window, occasionally flicking away cigarette ashes. A moment later, he tossed the cigarette to the pavement. He pulled his arm into the car, leaving the window down.

The two agents closest to the school got out of their vehicle and walked inside. Wearing slacks and sports coats, they appeared to be dads coming to pick up their kids. Ben glanced in the rearview mirror. The exit was blocked.

"Everything's in place." Ben grasped his weapon. "Let's go."

A blur of color across the parking area drew his eye. Mindy West strolled toward the school. He froze. Had she been waiting in her vehicle until time to pick up her daughter? Dunbar hadn't seen him. He eased out of the car and signaled Joe. They'd wait until Mindy was inside to take Dunbar.

Ben fixed his gaze on Dunbar. He appeared to watch Mindy. Ben edged nearer. Exhaust fumes burned his nose.

Suddenly, sun hit metal. Dunbar pointed a gun at Mindy.

"FBI!" Ben shouted. "Drop your weapon."

Tires squealed as Dunbar's car lurched forward. Ben fired.

The vehicle swerved, slamming into a parked car. He ran closer, Joe steps behind. One of the agents positioned at the exit sprinted toward Mindy, yelling for her to hit the pavement. Dunbar jumped from his vehicle and crouched behind the open door.

Bullets from his gun sprayed around Ben and Joe. They lunged for the grass and flattened themselves behind a brick sign.

Ben edged around the sign in time to see Dunbar turn his gun toward Mindy. Ben tracked Dunbar in his weapon's sights and squeezed the trigger. Dunbar collapsed.

Ben and Joe moved forward with guns trained on the motionless form. The other agents approached his vehicle from behind. Seconds later, Joe took Dunbar's weapon and checked his pulse. He shook his head.

Ben lowered his gun. The what-ifs deluged his thoughts. This was a *school*. Children might have seen this. Or worse. He breathed a scattered prayer.

A woman's moans invaded his senses. Mindy West huddled on the sidewalk, holding the arm of the agent beside her. Ben moved toward them. When she tried to stand, she nearly collapsed. They helped her to a bench by the door.

"He almost … killed me. He almost killed me." She turned to Ben, anguish flooding her eyes. "When you showed me his picture, I was afraid to tell you he'd threatened me before. He said I'd better cooperate or his boss would make me regret it—just like Ethan." Sobs punctuated every word.

Sirens sounded in the distance. Questions for Mindy would have to wait. She needed to be checked by paramedics and placed in protective custody with her daughter.

Hours of work still stretched ahead. Ian Dunbar had attempted to kill Mindy for someone else. That someone else was still out there.

Judging from Ethan's murder and the attempt on Mindy's life, Dunbar's boss wasn't planning to leave any witnesses.

MARCH 11
TUESDAY, 6:59 P.M.
WOTN, DC

Kate stared at her phone. Seven o'clock. No text.

She held her breath. Waited one minute. Then two.

"That's it." She touched the call icon and almost pressed the number when a text pinged.

She exhaled. Frowned.

I have more information. Meet me at my dorm. Hurry.

Kate reread the text. Had Ingrid been joking earlier about the coded message? Maybe in the urgency of finding something new, forgotten their conversation? Her insides churned. Was her friend in trouble?

She snatched up her purse. She wasn't taking chances. She'd head to Ingrid's dorm and call Joe and Ben on the way. She swept up her hair into a ponytail, then jogged through the night to her vehicle.

She unlocked the door and slid inside. Seconds later, she darted through traffic toward Georgetown. She sped through two intersections, traffic lights still yellow … in her brothers' words, pink around the edges.

Another intersection loomed ahead. The light turned red well before she reached it. She slowed to a stop, fumbling in the dark for her phone.

Sudden heat fluttered across the side of her neck. She reached up.

A face met her fingers.

Every nerve screamed. She lunged for the door handle. An arm whisked around her throat.

"I wouldn't try that."

She pounded the horn. Nothing. She fought to reach the hazard lights. He tightened his grip. She punched behind her with one hand and stretched for the interior lights with the other.

Sharp, cold metal pricked her neck. She stilled.

"You're going to do exactly as I say. Understand? Stay in this lane. Continue driving until I tell you to turn."

Her breath puffed out in shallow gasps. Still pressing the knife against her, he pulled his arm from her throat. She gripped the steering wheel.

The traffic light blurred. *Dear God, don't let me pass out.* Green swirled through the haze. A horn honked behind her.

Raw pain pulsed across her skin. She pressed the accelerator.

"If you try something like that again, I'll make more than a tiny cut," he snarled.

Warmth trickled into the back of her shirt. She forced air into her lungs. One deep breath. Another. Her vision cleared, and the ice freezing her brain slowly melted.

She lifted her eyes to the rearview mirror. A streetlight illuminated for an instant the form behind her. He wore a ski mask. A tie stuck out from his coat.

She wiped damp palms on her jacket. Her stalker wasn't Ian. The man behind her was bigger.

Traffic slowed. Police car lights flashed in the distance.

Her heart hammered. Help was near.

"Turn at this exit. Now."

She pressed the accelerator harder for a split second, then eased off. Ramming into cars ahead was pointless. Innocent lives might be taken, and her stalker could still get away. She wouldn't be in any shape to stop him. He'd kill her before he fled.

She turned at the exit. The highway narrowed into two lanes. Buildings stood farther apart. Fields lined the road. They were moving away from the city. Away from people.

Her eyes darted to the rearview mirror. With no streetlights, she could only see a silhouette. "Who are you? What do you want with me?"

"Shut up and drive."

The knife pressed harder. Her stalker was in no mood to talk.

How much farther? When they arrived wherever they were going, he would probably kill her. If only she could call for help.

She swallowed hard as she thought of her family … and Ben. His faith, his strength, the depth of his heart, the gentleness of his kiss. She'd even begun to dream of a future with him.

She gritted her teeth. She might not come out of this alive, but she would *not* go down without a fight. She glanced at her surroundings. No other vehicles were near. She had nothing to lose.

She breathed a desperate prayer and jerked the steering wheel to her left. The car spun.

He swore and came over the seat. His weight landed on her. She struggled for air.

He wrenched the wheel hard, gaining control. "What a stupid thing to do."

She fought to free her pinned arms. He raised his fist. Searing heat radiated through her jaw, and darkness crawled across her vision.

MARCH 11
TUESDAY, 9:40 P.M.
VIRGINIA

"Pick up your feet and walk."

Kate strained to hear. The voice seemed to echo from a tunnel. She struggled to wake up. She couldn't remember falling asleep.

Her jaw throbbed. She reached up to touch her cheek. *The stalker.* A surge of adrenaline blasted her grogginess. Her knees buckled. She pitched forward and landed hard.

He cursed. "I said *walk.*"

Spitting out a mouthful of dirt, she crawled to her knees. Fingers dug into her shoulders, pulled her up, and shoved her forward.

Her eyes focused. Moonlight filtered through tree branches, illumining the dirt path in front of her. A short distance ahead, an open field bordered a house. A very dark house.

When they reached the clearing, he twisted her arms behind her, dragging her as he ran across the field. She battled to free herself, but his hold was too strong. She strained to see ahead. If he were planning to take her in the house, he'd have to use one hand to open the door. That would be her chance to break free. If she failed …

He pulled her to the side entrance. The door swung open. A shadowy figure stood inside. She gulped air as his grip relaxed.

She jerked free and sprinted toward the back of the house. A large building loomed in the shadows. A barn? She darted toward the door, pivoted, and kept running. Even if she managed to pry open the door, she would be trapped if her stalker found her.

Her eyes swept over the area. More open fields surrounded her. She flung a glance over her shoulder. The beam of a flashlight danced toward her. He was gaining ground. She sped away, forcing oxygen into her lungs.

A bright light split the darkness in front of her. Shielding her eyes, she cut to her left. Strong arms tackled her and threw her to the ground. An instant later, her stalker joined the man standing over her.

"You think you can escape from me, do you? That little stunt will be your last."

A long blade glimmered in the beam of the light. He lifted the knife over his head.

The second man grabbed his wrist and said something she couldn't understand. He picked up Kate and slung her over his shoulder. She squeezed her eyes shut to keep from throwing up.

When he finally slowed, she opened her eyes. He started through the door of the house. She grabbed for the doorframe. He jerked her inside, then dumped her on the floor in front of a second door. Panic welled up. Her stalker shone the flashlight on the lock and shoved a key in. The light fell across his tie.

She fought, making contact. Cursing, they pushed her through the door, slammed and locked it.

She slumped over, her heart racing. She forced air through her lungs. She couldn't give up. She had to escape.

She stretched her hands in front of her. She wasn't in a closet. The blackness in front of her slowly softened to gray. The faintest light came through cracks in the wood floor. Shapes against the walls resembled cabinets. Maybe this was a large pantry, or a storage room. She stood and stepped forward.

A *whoosh* of air sounded. She stilled. Something in this room besides her was breathing. A minute passed. Then a quiet plea.

"Help me. Please."

The accent was unmistakable. Ingrid. "It's Kate. I'm coming." She gingerly stepped toward the sound of her friend's voice. Ingrid slumped in a corner. "What have they done to you?"

"I'm okay." Her words slurred slightly. "I have a bad headache."

Kate knelt beside her. "Can you remember what happened?"

"I … remember riding in the limousine. After you left, we drove away from CRI. I think we turned a corner. I'd just pulled out my phone. One of the guards said there was a problem." Anger strengthened her voice. "He took my phone before I could get a call to the embassy. They must have bugged the limousine, because they knew what you and I had talked about. The guards discussed sending you a text at seven. They covered my face with a cloth. Something on the cloth smelled sweet. I don't remember anything afterward."

"Chloroform."

"What?"

"They must have drugged you with chloroform."

"I'm sorry I couldn't stop them from sending the message to you. The text was a trap."

"I was afraid you were in trouble. I couldn't call for help because the man who's been stalking me was hiding in my car."

A soft gasp sounded. "Someone's been stalking you?"

"Yes. I thought I knew his identity, but I was wrong." Kate's mind skimmed over the events of the afternoon.

"When did you find out about the internet problems at CRI?"

"During lunch."

"After you recognized Schultz?"

"A few moments after. Why?"

"The internet excuse must have been a set-up. Once Schultz realized you'd recognized him, he needed to make sure you didn't let anyone know."

"Oh, Kate, if I hadn't asked to speak with you on the way out, you wouldn't be involved in this. I should have known something was wrong by the way Frederick Wilson acted. He insisted on calling my car immediately after we left the dining area. He must be involved as well."

The image of Wilson standing in the CRI lobby flashed through Kate's mind. Sudden chills iced her spine. "Frederick Wilson is my stalker."

"Did you glimpse his face when he was in your car? Or identify his voice?"

"He wore a ski mask, and he kept his voice raspy when he spoke." Kate exhaled a shaky breath. "When he shoved me in this room, the flashlight beam fell on his tie. The same one Frederick Wilson wore this afternoon. I just made the connection."

"You remembered a tie? I'm not sure I would have noticed."

"Trust me, if you'd grown up with four brothers who loved outdoing each other in their choice of clothes, you'd notice."

"Kate—" Ingrid's tone turned grave. "They're going to kill us."

Kate pushed away the memory of the blade Wilson had lifted over her. "Not if we get away first."

She stood. There must be a way out.

The problem would be finding it in time.

MARCH 12
WEDNESDAY, 6:37 A.M.
DC

"Read this." Frank moved the computer closer to Martha.

She studied the information on the screen. A pang of nostalgia whisked through her. She missed her old job. "Looks like your contacts in the field came through. They provided proof Bradley accepted bribes and tampered with evidence in at least two cases."

"Likely more than two. He also has provided illegal documents for passports."

Frank nodded toward the watch she'd laid on the desk. "I feel certain the FBI will find a tracking device. With the evidence on the flash drives, Bradley's arrest and prosecution are imminent. Once he's in prison for T. J.'s murder, maybe I'll get closure. I can only imagine what Carly has been through."

"I hope she'll be able to let go of everything except the good memories." Martha's voice caught. "Maybe the process won't take as long for her as it did for me."

Frank squeezed her hand, then turned back to the computer. "We'll deliver T. J.'s flash drive, along with this one, when we take his watch to the Hoover building."

Martha stared at the screen. One of the names linked to Bradley sounded familiar. She shut her eyes. Victor Schultz. Where had she heard his name? The knowledge danced just outside her memory.

"Well, well, looks like we have company."

Frank's voice interrupted her thoughts, his tone the one he used when trouble loomed. He stood by the window, peering out.

"I'm assuming the windows are tinted so our company can't see in?"

"Thankfully, yes.

"Do we have a plan?"

"We'll make things up as we go." He reached for the computer and ejected the flash drive.

She smiled inwardly. Not that different from the old days. She hurried to the window. Two men stood outside the back entrance. One drew his weapon. "They're shooting the lock."

Frank pressed a small bag into her hand. "The watch and two flash drives are in here. Put these in your purse. In case we need to split up, you head for the Hoover building. I'll keep Bradley's men busy."

She slipped the purse around her shoulder holster and zipped her coat over the precious cargo.

Frank grabbed her hand. "Head for the front door."

They sprinted down a dark corridor. Running shoes had been a good choice. As they slid around a corner, lights illumined the hall they'd just run through. Great. Motion sensor lights would announce their location to Bradley's men. But the reverse was also true.

She spotted an office with a glass window at the end of the hall. "Left or right?"

"Right."

They turned and skidded to a stop. Lights blinked on in a stairwell ahead.

Frank pulled her in the opposite direction. Footsteps pounded behind them. The front lobby was just ahead.

Overhead lights gleamed. They were cut off from the front door.

A dark stairwell stood to their right. They darted underneath the staircase seconds before lights switched on.

"This way," one of the men yelled. "They're upstairs."

"Go after them," the other replied. "I'll wait here."

Martha held her breath. The echo of footsteps stopped. A door slammed. With the light sensors, he would need only seconds to realize she and Frank weren't there.

Frank eased his weapon from the holster. He held the gun by the barrel and edged from underneath the stairway. A thud sounded, followed by a soft moan. Martha darted from her position at the instant the man, still moaning, hit the floor.

Seconds later, she and Frank burst through the front doors onto the sidewalk. "The Metro stop is directly across the street. Lose yourself in the crowds. I'll wait in my car until they spot me. With any luck they'll follow me, and you'll already be on a train."

She lifted her hand in a wave. Though she hated leaving him to face Bradley's men alone, they'd worked together too long for her to argue. She jogged to the Metro. They both knew the risks inherent in the job. They would see the task through.

She ran down the escalator and swiped her Metro card. Morning commuters filled the platform. She wove through toward the line headed to the Federal Triangle stop. She looked at the lighted board above her. Twelve minutes until the next train.

She perched on a bench beside students with backpacks and watched the people around her. Bradley's men would be on the streets by now. Would they figure out she was headed to the Hoover building? If they switched on sirens and dodged traffic, they might get there before she did. If they followed Frank—

The rumble of the train filled the station. She jumped up to join others waiting to board. The doors opened and she slid into a seat. When the train started moving, her muscles relaxed. Safe—for the moment.

She leaned back against the seat. Once she exited the Metro, a five-minute walk stood between her and the Hoover building. Pedestrians would fill the sidewalk at this time of the morning. She would blend in, or duck into a building if she got into trouble.

She counted the stops. Six more. Each time people boarded the train, she held her breath.

"Next stop, Federal Triangle."

The muffled voice over the speaker registered in her brain. She stood, grasping the edge of the seat in front. The train lurched to a stop. *Here goes.*

She stepped through the doors. Her eyes flicked across the platform. No one appeared to watch her. She strode to the escalator. When she reached the sidewalk, she shoved on sunglasses and pulled up the hood of her black coat. She'd almost worn a bright pink jacket this morning. She grimaced at the image. She would have been spotted a mile away.

She quickened her pace to reach a group of businessmen. Opinions of political parties swirled around her. If only this group would continue to her destination.

A car in the lane closest to the sidewalk slowed. She kept her eyes ahead. The car stayed in her peripheral vision. She peeled away from the group and ducked into a coffee shop.

She got in line and pulled out her phone. Her fingers skimmed over the keypad. Horns honked outside. She strained to see. The vehicle had stopped, blocking traffic. The passenger door flew open. One of Bradley's men jumped out. He bolted toward the coffee shop.

She pushed through the crowd and headed out a side door leading into a shopping mall. None of the shops were open yet, only the huge lobby. A lone maintenance worker disappeared through a door at one end of the mall. An exit sign glowed at the opposite end. She sprinted to the sign, almost there, when the outside door opened.

Frank walked in, holding a gun.

Pointed at her.

She swallowed against the burning in her throat.

Footsteps sounded behind her. The man chasing her took her weapon. He and Bradley's other henchman joined Frank.

Frank looked at her. "Don't you want an explanation?" He blinked rapidly three times.

"I assumed you'd give me one." She gathered herself and followed his lead. "Unless you're planning to kill me first. Then I guess an explanation won't be necessary."

"I'm sorry, Martha. Bradley made me an offer I couldn't refuse. Money. A lot of money. With a flight out of the country. Give me the bag." His voice hardened with each word.

She reached for her purse.

"Slowly."

Her fingers closed over the evidence.

"Slide the bag to me."

She did as he said.

When Frank stooped to pick up the watch and flash drive, one of Bradley's men raised his fist and struck Frank on the back of the head. Frank's knees buckled. He struggled to remain on his feet. "Are you crazy? We have a deal."

"Sorry, Frank."

The voice sounded behind Martha. She whirled around. Ted Bradley.

"Not the way things are going down." He strolled over to Frank and stuffed the evidence into his pocket. "The police will rule the deaths of you and Ms. Thomas as a murder-suicide—with your gun, of course. Don't worry. We'll wipe off our fingerprints." He looked at his men. "Cuff them, get them out of town."

Movement outside caught Martha's eye. She drew a sharp breath. They were here.

Bradley and his men looked down, their attention on the handcuffs, their backs to the door. She gestured to Frank.

An instant later, shouts and pulses of light exploded around them.

"FBI—freeze!"

She hit the floor, praying Frank did the same.

She squinted through haze. Bradley and his men had let down their guard a split second too long. They never had time to react. The agents subdued them without firing a shot.

A moment later, one of the agents gave her a thumbs-up. She pulled herself to her feet while Frank covered the distance between them. He wrapped her in a hug, then pulled back and peered into her face.

"Are you okay?"

"Fine."

"When Bradley's men caught up with me, I was hoping to buy us a little extra time to get out of this. I should have known you'd have everything under control. When did you call the FBI?"

"I sent a text at the coffee shop. I didn't wait for a response, but Joe plainly was on top of things to get cars here so quickly."

"Are you mad at me for pointing a gun at you?"

"Was the weapon loaded?"

"No."

"Then I'm not mad."

He smiled at her. "You know, I think we should come out of retirement to work together again. As private investigators."

Before she could reply, two of the agents stepped over to them. She tucked away the idea.

They did make a pretty good team.

CHAPTER 17

"You've reached Kate Peterson. Sorry I can't come to the phone. Please leave a message."

Ben smiled at the sound of her voice. Must be on a story. He had missed talking with her yesterday evening. After leaving Springview Academy, he and Joe worked late into the night. He'd try again this afternoon. He turned back to the information he'd gathered on Ian Dunbar. He was deep in thought when Susan called his name.

"I have news." She pulled a chair over to his desk. "By the way, is Aunt Martha still here?"

When Susan had been assigned to guard Jenny during a threat against her life several months ago, she'd become friends with Aunt Martha.

"Yep." Ben gestured toward the conference room. "She's with Joe and Frank Edwards. Quite a morning with Ted Bradley."

"No kidding. I'm glad they were able to stop him."

Ben glanced at the time on his computer screen. "They'll probably be finished soon. What's up?"

"I just heard from the guys at the lab. In the preliminary sweep of Dunbar's vehicle, a receipt was found underneath the driver's seat."

"Please tell me this is the break we need."

Susan smiled—her satisfaction obvious. "The receipt showed payment of a parking garage ticket. The date with time of entry to the garage across from St. Michael's Hospital were stamped on the paper, as well as an expiration time. Dunbar arrived at the garage one hour before Ethan's murder. The expiration time was two-thirty p.m.—exactly seven minutes after Ethan was shot."

Ben rocked back in his chair. "He had the timing planned down to the wire. For a man as skilled in breaching security as he was, leaving the receipt was pretty careless."

"I'd guess the receipt slipped between the seats. Dunbar probably forgot about it."

Adrenaline pumped. With Mrs. Ford's identification of Dunbar and the video of his car in the Fords' neighborhood, the receipt was the final link to Ethan's murder. But who was his boss?

"According to Mindy West, Dunbar worked for someone else." Ben reached for a marker and leaned over to the whiteboard beside his desk. He wrote Dunbar's name at the bottom, then drew a question mark above. "Our focus now is who ordered Dunbar to kill Ethan Fitzgerald."

"We know Ethan was killed because he came too close to discovering something about Sunburst. Since Sunburst is connected to Caldwell Research Institute, Dunbar's boss is connected to CRI. Finding that relationship might prove problematic. Though the person Dunbar worked for could be a CRI employee, he might also be someone in a corporation utilizing CRI, or a benefactor, or a university professor applying data obtained from CRI—" Susan's voice trailed off.

"Let's start with what we already have." Ben wrote the names of Chuck Ford and Charlotte Fitzgerald on the board. "With the evidence found in Dunbar's car, we can rule out Charlotte as the killer."

"Could she be Dunbar's boss? You saw him at her townhouse."

"For once, I believe she was telling the truth when she said she knew nothing about Sunburst. We have no proof to indicate otherwise."

"What about Chuck Ford?"

"Dunbar wouldn't have needed a key from Mrs. Ford if he and Chuck were working together. My gut tells me Ford was an innocent bystander in a plan to set up Charlotte Fitzgerald."

"Makes sense. When Dunbar's boss decided to kill Ethan, he needed someone to take the heat. A relative would be a logical choice. Given Charlotte's skill with guns, the idea would be even more plausible. They apparently trailed her, found out she and Chuck Ford periodically visited the shooting range. Maybe the trip to the range the day before Ethan left the hospital was coincidence, but Charlotte's recent access to the murder weapon would fit perfectly into the plan." Susan paused. "Should I begin the process to release her, with the stipulation she not leave the country yet?"

"Let's meet with Joe—" His phone vibrated. "Just a second, Susan." He answered as the conference room door opened.

"Ben Anderson."

"This is the Liechtenstein Embassy. Ambassador Schrader needs a word with you. It is imperative she speak with you now."

"Of course."

"Please hold while I connect you."

Ben waited. Joe strolled over, and Susan hugged Aunt Martha when she and Edwards joined them.

Seconds later, Margaret Schrader spoke. "Agent Anderson, I'll come right to the point. The princess is missing."

Had he heard correctly? He switched on the phone's speaker, and motioned to Joe and Susan. "How long has she been missing?"

"She was due at the embassy for a tea this morning. When the car arrived at the university to pick her up, she didn't answer her door. The guard gained entry to her room. The window overlooking the courtyard outside was open. Nothing in the room was out of place, and the window did not appear to have been forced open."

"When was the last time anyone spoke with her?"

"Yesterday afternoon. She attended a meeting at Caldwell Research Institute. Afterward, the guards took her back to her dormitory. She told them she was writing a paper and didn't wish to be disturbed until time for the tea this morning."

"Were the guards posted outside her room as usual?"

"Of course." She hesitated a beat. "In full disclosure, I must tell you Princess Ingrid has been known to strike out on her own occasionally. As you can imagine, the pressures she faces are enormous, but she's never disappeared for more than a few hours. The guards did tell me they overheard the princess speaking with Kate Peterson from WOTN. Ms. Peterson was also at the Institute yesterday. Ms. Peterson asked Princess Ingrid to fly out west for a ski trip. She said she'd loan her ski clothes. I do hope," she added, her words measured, "that Ms. Peterson would not use the princess to gain an exclusive story in order to further her own career."

Ben bristled. He flicked a glance at Joe, whose clenched jaw communicated his feelings. Ben drew a breath and continued the conversation. He jotted down information regarding the progress of the embassy's security team and their current location, his brain already formulating a plan of action. Moments later, he ended the call.

"Kate doesn't ski."

Joe's voice penetrated Ben's thoughts. "I know. Something's wrong."

Joe pulled out his phone. "You call her cell. I'll call her work."

Voicemail. Again. Ben left a message for her while listening to Joe at the same time.

"She didn't call or come in today? At seven last night? If you hear from Kate, please ask her to contact me. Thank you."

Ben's muscles tightened. Kate took her job seriously. She would never miss work without calling.

Joe turned to Aunt Martha. She plainly knew the question without his asking. "I talked to Kate at breakfast yesterday."

"You didn't see her last night or this morning?"

She shook her head. "That's not unusual, though. Our schedules are different. I'll head home immediately to check the apartment and her parking spot."

Ben longed to go, but Aunt Martha would notice anything out of the ordinary sooner than he could. His unit needed to meet with the security team in Georgetown to question the guards who had last seen Kate and Ingrid.

Scenarios surged over him. He quashed the fear.

Maybe a simple explanation existed, but nothing he came up with made sense.

Kate, why haven't you answered my calls? Where are you?

MARCH 12
WEDNESDAY, 11:57 A.M.
GEORGETOWN UNIVERSITY, DC

Ben's eyes swept over Princess Ingrid's dorm room. Their search had yielded little. "I'd have to agree with the embassy security team's assessment. No sign of a struggle or forced entry."

Joe nodded. "Since the sliding glass window has a blocking bar, no one could access the window from outside unless they broke the glass."

"There's also no evidence she packed anything to leave." Ben pulled off his gloves and stuffed them back into his pocket. "Dave and Curt should have joined up with the embassy team by now. Let's head outside to look around while we wait for contact."

They nodded to a campus policeman, who locked Ingrid's door after them.

Ben's thoughts turned to Kate. For the hundredth time. Aunt Martha had called on their way to Georgetown. The clothes Kate wore yesterday were not in her closet, no damp towels hung in her bathroom.

As far as Aunt Martha could tell, she had not returned to the apartment after work yesterday. He ran a hand through his hair. They'd notified ground surveillance to search for her car. So far, they had heard nothing. *Lord, keep her safe. Help us to figure this out.*

He rounded the corner and collided with someone carrying two large baskets of laundry. Towels and sheets cascaded to the floor.

"I'm so sorry." A girl wearing an athletic shirt with the name 'Mia' stitched on the front bent to gather towels. "I shouldn't have tried to carry so much at once. I couldn't see where I was going."

Ben knelt to help her. "Wednesday must be laundry day."

"Laundry day is whenever I have spare time. This morning just happens to be a day with no papers or tests." She pointed down the hall. "I saw you go into Ingrid's room on my way to the washing machines. Is she okay? I was worried when I saw campus police here."

Joe added towels to a basket. "Are you a friend of hers?"

"Yes. We get together when we can. I'm a first-year student. Ingrid has been really nice to me."

"Have you talked lately?"

"A couple of days ago. Then last night, I stopped by her room to return a book she loaned me, but she didn't answer. She must have been out, because no security guards were posted by the door."

Ben stilled. "What time did you come by?"

She shrugged. "Around seven-thirty, I think. When I went out for pizza later, I saw the guards return. The princess wasn't with them—I'm not sure why." She gathered the baskets in her arms. "If you happen to see Ingrid, let her know Mia asked about her."

She waved, almost dropping her load again, and headed down the hall. Ben and Joe strode to the front door and onto the sidewalk.

Ben clenched his hands into fists. "If the security guards know where Ingrid is, they know where Kate is. Let's head to their location."

"Anderson—wait up."

Ben turned. Pete Sanders of the Metropolitan Police Department walked toward them. Could his presence here have something to do with Kate and Ingrid?

"Pete." Ben shook hands. "Were you looking for us?"

"I'm here for a meeting on campus. I called your office earlier with some information. Janet said I might run into you."

"What do you have for us?"

"The kid who held up Shane's Jewelers finally talked."

Joe's eyes widened. "Angelo?"

"Yep. His grandmother convinced him to give up his boss. His name is Brandon Lancaster. He's the new CFO of Tyler Wealth Management. He also owns the building the Shanes and O'Reillys lease. Based on the evidence we found, Lancaster could face a long list of criminal charges relating to his realty business."

Ben frowned. "He hired Angelo to rob the Shanes? Why would an investment company's CFO, who also owns real estate, need to rob a jewelry store?"

Pete shrugged. "Bottom line? An insatiable desire for wealth. He wants something, he takes it. He vandalized several of the buildings he owns to collect insurance money. Angelo told us Lancaster also hired another man to extort money from tenants of his buildings. His name is—was—Ian Dunbar. I heard what happened at Springview Academy yesterday," he added.

Ben sucked in a breath. "Is Lancaster in custody?"

"Not yet. He's gone off the grid. I'm afraid he's your problem now. With alleged fraud and extortion, the case belongs to you guys." Pete checked his watch. "I need to go. Keep in touch."

Pete left, and Joe turned to Ben. "Dave just texted me. Lancaster's not the only one off the grid—so are the two guards who last saw Ingrid. He and Curt are working to find them."

"Then we need to get to Tyler Wealth Management. If Brandon Lancaster ordered Dunbar to kill Ethan, he has a big stake in Sunburst. I'd bet he's the top guy, or one of them." Sudden realization blasted Ben's senses. In Kate's series on Ingrid and CRI, she did a story on Brandon Lancaster.

His heart hammered. Had Kate learned something about Lancaster during her interview, or even during the robbery attempt at Shanes? Was Sunburst a plot to kidnap the princess for ransom, and Kate had been sucked in because of their friendship? He shoved away images of Ethan Fitzgerald.

He prayed he was wrong. If he wasn't, Kate was in the hands of a killer.

MARCH 12
WEDNESDAY, 12:27 P.M.
VIRGINIA

Kate paced the length of her prison. Light streamed through a hole in one of the walls. At least she and

Ingrid weren't stumbling in darkness. She looked at her watch. Captive for over twelve hours.

They had checked every inch of the room for something to cut, saw, or hammer their way out. She'd even spent an hour trying to dismantle a rusted pipe of the sink in the small adjoining bathroom. Not that a rusted pipe would be much use, but the idea sounded good when they had nothing.

"I can't hear anyone." Ingrid moved her ear from the door. "Do you think they left us alone?"

"I don't know." Kate resumed pacing. "I wish we knew their plans."

Ingrid opened cabinet doors. Something she'd done almost hourly. "I can't believe there's nothing in here except old plastic storage containers. Along with one rusted cake pan." After she examined the pan, she returned it to the shelf. "Somebody must have cleared everything else out before the house was vacated."

"If only—" Kate caught her breath. "Look."

"What's wrong?"

"The floorboards. They run vertically except over one small area in the corner. I just noticed the different pattern when light fell across that part of the room." She moved closer. Her pulse quickened. "Ingrid, there are two hinges over here."

"Meaning ...?"

"This might be a way out." She stooped and wedged her fingers between the cracks of the wood floor. "The house must have a cellar. I think this is an access."

Ingrid hurried over and knelt beside her. Together they pulled the trapdoor open and peered down to a dirt floor below. Light filtering through slats of an old louvered door revealed wooden crates, glass bottles, several rusted rakes, and a chair with no seat.

"I saw a glow through the floorboards last night. Someone must have been down here with a flashlight."

"If this is an access from the pantry to the cellar, I wonder why there are no steps."

"Look in the corner." Kate pointed to a tall ladder, most of the rungs missing, leaning against a wall. "Probably what's left."

"Suppose we can't get out once we jump down?"

"I don't think we'll be any worse off than here. The door looks pretty rickety. Maybe we can force it open. Do you want me to go first?"

Ingrid shook her head, a wry grin spreading across her face. "Royalty always goes first, even if we kill ourselves in the process." She swung her legs over. "Learn from my mistakes." She hesitated an instant, lowered herself through the opening, and let go.

Kate held her breath. Her friend landed with a thud. "Are you okay?"

Ingrid eased to her feet. "I think so. I can still move everything."

Kate dangled her legs over the cellar. "I'll try to shut the trapdoor as I jump." She maneuvered herself down and clutched the side of the opening with one hand, holding the trapdoor with the other. Inhaling, she dropped. The unyielding floor jarred her whole body.

"Kate?"

"I'm fine." Ignoring the pain, she propelled herself to her feet. "Let's try the door."

They hurried over and pushed against the slats. The door moved an inch.

Hope surged through Kate. "I don't think there's a lock. The door seems stuck against the packed dirt."

They continued to push and pull, working the wood over the floor. Finally, the door scraped open. Fresh air flowed into the musty cellar.

"Kate, we're free! Maybe we can find help."

"We need to figure out a way to get to the woods. Open fields are all around the house." Kate gathered herself. "I'll take a quick look outside."

"Be careful."

She squeezed through the doorway. The barn faced her. Good. They were at the back of the house. The distance to the woods appeared to be a couple of miles. Should they hide in the barn until dark? Every muscle screamed for her to run. Now.

She eased along the house. Birds chirped. A train whistle echoed in the distance. She held her breath and continued to the corner.

No vehicles in sight. Surely the guards would still be here. She scanned the area. If she and Ingrid headed for the woods behind the barn, they would be shielded from view of anyone at the house. She hurried back to the cellar.

"What did you see?" Lines etched Ingrid's forehead.

"No cars, but they could be parked somewhere else. I can't imagine that no one is here. We could hide in the barn behind the house until dark, or take a chance now. We have about two miles of open fields before we reach the woods."

"If they realize we're missing, we might not get another chance. Let's go now."

Kate nodded. The moment of truth. "Help us, Jesus," she breathed aloud. As she started outside, Ingrid stopped her.

"Before we go, I need to tell you something." Ingrid's features softened as she put her hand over her heart. "I'm a believer now. I belong to Jesus. Remember what you told me?"

Tears sprang to Kate's eyes. "Heart knowledge." She hugged her friend. Even if her life ended now, God had graced her with seeing the answer to her prayer for Ingrid.

"Where are they?"

The muffled shout overhead surged through Kate's senses. "Go!" She pushed Ingrid through the door.

Kate bolted toward the barn, Ingrid matching her stride. They raced around the building and sprinted ahead.

Kate sucked in air and fixed her gaze on the woods. Two miles? More like three. They should reach cover in about twenty-five minutes. She snapped a glance over her shoulder. No one followed. Yet.

Cows grazed in a field to her left. Water shimmered in the distance. She pressed forward as she looked toward her destination. Her legs must weigh a hundred pounds. She ransacked her brain for something else to think about.

Her sister Ann had seen two bears on a hike last fall. Were bears in these woods? She shook herself inwardly. Not a good subject.

Sharp pain shot through her side. *Deep breaths, Kate. You can do this.* Moments later, she glanced at her watch. Halfway to the goal.

Ingrid's gulps for air pushed into her consciousness. Kate shifted her pace to her friend's. Finally, Ingrid shook her head and slowed to a stop.

"Sorry," she gasped. She bent over, breathing hard.

Kate forced air into her lungs. "Not much farther."

She wiped sweat from her eyes and looked across the fields. A vehicle sped to the front of the farmhouse. Her sweat ran cold. "The guards must have called for help. We need to go."

Her muscles cramped as they ran. Stopping was a bad idea. Running hard with nothing to eat for fifteen hours wasn't great, either, but they were almost there.

At last, they plunged into the cover of the forest. A wave of nausea rolled over Kate. She steadied herself against a tree and glanced over at her friend. Ingrid stooped to the ground, her face white.

"Ingrid—don't pass out on me."

"I won't. I just need a minute."

Kate sank onto a log. Dense woods stretched around them. Progress would be slow. "We'll sit here for a little longer, then start moving again."

The urge to cry washed over her. The woods might extend for miles. They'd had nothing to eat or drink for hours. How long could they continue?

Finally, she pulled herself up. They had to get started.

"Kate." Ingrid whispered her name.

She followed Ingrid's gaze.

"Look—across the field. They're coming for us."

March 12
Wednesday, 1:30 p.m.
Pennsylvania Avenue, DC

Ben stared out the window of Liza Tyler's office. Kate had been missing almost nineteen hours. What if she were hurt? What if … He shoved away the possibilities. He sank into a chair and flicked a sideways glance at Joe. His friend looked ready to explode.

Liza Tyler hurried into the room. "I'm so sorry to keep you waiting. My assistant said your business is urgent."

Ben and Joe showed her their badges. She perched on a chair behind her desk.

"We need to ask you about Brandon Lancaster." Ben worked to control his voice. "We understand he's recently taken the position of CFO in your company."

Liza's features tensed. "He's had the position less than two weeks and has done a lousy job. I can't wait to have the pleasure of telling him to his face he's fired." She removed her glasses. "Brandon is my brother-in-law. I hired him only because my deceased sister would have wanted him to work here. I don't trust him any farther than I can throw him. Judging from the fact I have two FBI agents in my office, my feelings are apparently valid."

Joe leaned forward. "Do you have any idea where he is?"

She shook her head. "Since he also owns a realty business, he might be at one of his properties—on my company's time, of course. If you'd like, I can show you a list of them." She reached for her computer. "I did some research recently to see how he'd spent my sister's money." Her fingers skimmed over the keyboard. "As you can see, he owns properties in DC as well as northern Virginia." She moved the screen in their direction. "I also have a list of real estate he owns outside the US."

Ben scanned the information. Around thirty properties in the area. They'd need manpower to search them. Along with time—time they didn't have.

Joe pointed to a separate column at the bottom of the screen. "What are these?"

"Listings he's sold or leased during the past year."

Ben studied the screen. "Joe, the third listing from the bottom ... Lancaster sold property in northern Virginia to Frederick Wilson."

"Most likely as a tax deduction." Bitterness crept into Liza's voice. "That property was my grandmother's home. Since Frederick Wilson is the CEO of Caldwell Research Institute, I doubt he needs an old farmhouse. CRI is executing an economic analysis for our company. Brandon's first, and only, project," she added.

Ben's breath hitched. An economic analysis Lancaster initiated with CRI. Was this Sunburst? "We'll need immediate access to your financial records, Ms. Tyler."

"Of course." Her face suddenly flushed. "I manage millions of dollars for a large number of clients. Are you saying the security of my company might have been compromised?"

"Once we examine your company's data, we'll be in a better position to answer your questions."

She swore under her breath. "If Brandon has stolen one dime from my clients, he'd better hope you find him before I do."

Ben's phone pinged. He looked down. A text from Dave stared back at him.

Kate's car found.

CHAPTER 18

Kate wedged herself beneath dense underbrush. Briars gouged her arms and face. She fought to lie flat.

Damp earth penetrated her senses. The smell of the farm ... the fragrance of home. Would she live to show Ben where she'd grown up?

A car engine hummed. She stilled. Ingrid hid several yards away. Had they concealed themselves well enough? The engine's drone grew louder, then stopped. Doors slammed.

Muffled voices floated on the breeze. Leaves crackled as footsteps shuffled closer.

A branch snapped. Kate shifted her eyes to the left. Boots stood two feet from her.

"They have to be here." A thick German accent laced the man's words. "I glimpsed them just before they disappeared into the woods."

"I'd think a trained security guard would never have let them get away."

"They can't have gone far. They're probably right under our noses. Why don't we start shooting?"

"Once we get to the plane, we'll get rid of them. If we don't find them, you'll be skydiving without a parachute."

The guard cursed. Rhythmic *swooshes* sounded around Kate. Was he using a machete to slice through the brush?

A lizard skittered across her arm. She jerked.

Sudden pressure gripped her ankles. She dug her fingernails into the dirt but was powerless to stop the force raking her body from the underbrush. She lifted her head. Lancaster stood over her.

"Ms. Peterson, we meet again." Hardness glimmered in his eyes. "Where is the princess?"

Kate coughed dirt from her throat. "We separated. She's found help by now."

His boot kicked the breath from her. Gasping for air, she struggled to her knees.

"Answer me. Where is she?"

"Leave her alone." Ingrid scrambled from the underbrush and stood before them, glaring. "I'm the one you want. Take me."

Lancaster scowled at Ingrid. "I didn't want either of you. Unfortunately, you recognized Schultz. We've worked too hard to let you stop us." He turned back to Kate. "As for you, Ms. Peterson, you should learn not to ask so many questions. You brought this on yourselves. Too bad you won't live to regret it." He pointed his gun at them. "Get in the car."

Fight, Kate. You've got to fight.

Walking took every ounce of strength she possessed.

The car sped to the farmhouse. Moments later, Kate and Ingrid huddled on the kitchen floor, hands and feet tied with thick rope. Lancaster and the guard sat at a table across the room.

Kate rested her head against her knees. Getting away now would be nearly impossible. Once they stepped on the plane, there would be no escape.

A doorknob rattled, and Schultz sauntered in.

The guard rocked back in his chair to face him. "Where are the others?"

"Wilson should arrive any moment. Your buddy is waiting with the plane." Schultz glanced toward Ingrid. "Your Highness."

Ingrid's dark eyes flashed. "You murdered my uncle."

"I only arranged for him to be in—shall we say—the wrong place at the right time. Your uncle died because he knew too much. He was going to take the information to the authorities."

"He was a man of integrity—unlike yourself."

"He was a man of stupidity. If he had continued working with me, he could have gained more wealth and power than he would ever have attained on his own." Schultz's eyes narrowed. "At the risk of tainting your image of him, I assure you he did work with me for a time. Why do you think we named our cyberattacks Sunburst?"

"How dare you." Ingrid's voice shook. "He called me Sunburst as a child."

"Such a pity he isn't here to enjoy what could have been his. We have everything we need now to siphon millions of dollars from companies both in America and Europe."

"Wealth is worth taking a life?"

"Wealth is worth taking as many lives as we need to."

Lancaster joined Schultz's laughter.

Kate shuddered. Evil permeated the room.

MARCH 12
WEDNESDAY, 2:30 P.M.
VIRGINIA

Ben steadied himself at the sight of Kate's Camry. Though her vehicle showed no outer signs of damage, someone had concealed the car deep in the woods. If a hunter out training his dogs had not spotted it, the vehicle might have gone unnoticed for weeks. Ben forced himself to shut out images bombarding his mind. He would find her.

"The lab confirmed Frederick Wilson's fingerprints are all over her car." Quiet rage bit through Joe's words. He pointed to fresh tire tracks. "An analysis of these tracks is also being processed."

Ben slammed his fist against the hood. How had they missed this? "He must have followed her or waited at her car, then brought her here to switch vehicles—" He turned toward the forensics team combing the area, unable to speak. So far, the team had found nothing in the immediate vicinity. If Kate had struggled, bits of clothing or crushed branches would have been left behind.

Joe gripped Ben's shoulder. "My sister is smart and tough. We'll find her."

Smart, tough, gentle, beautiful. The woman I want to spend my life with …

Ben's phone buzzed. He snapped back to the present and scanned the text. "It's Curt. Our men are in place at Caldwell Research Institute and at Wilson's house in DC. A helicopter has been dispatched to the property Wilson bought from Lancaster, along with thermal imaging equipment. If Wilson stayed in the area, the house would be a hiding place. Let's go."

Seconds later, Ben sped toward the highway while Joe fielded a phone call. When he ended the conversation, he turned to Ben.

"A Liechtenstein economist, Victor Schultz, entered the country with an illegal passport courtesy of Ted Bradley. Schultz has used multiple aliases. He's also had extensive plastic surgery. He's wanted in connection with the murder of Ingrid's uncle years ago."

Ben processed Joe's words. Had Ingrid somehow realized who Schultz was? Had Kate put the pieces together during research for her series? The players of Sunburst had added another member—Lancaster, Wilson, two security guards, and now Schultz. Ben tightened his grip on the steering wheel, praying for wisdom and skill. For the safety of Kate and Ingrid.

For strength to face what waited ahead.

MARCH 12
WEDNESDAY, 2:50 P.M.
VIRGINIA

"Please, we need water."

No response. Kate repeated her request. The men continued to ignore her. They sat around the table, eating something that smelled heavenly. Frederick Wilson had arrived a few minutes earlier.

She glanced at Ingrid. Her friend hadn't spoken since her exchange with Schultz. Her will to fight seemed to have dissolved.

Kate gritted her teeth. Time to do something. Anything. "If you don't give us food and water, you'll have to carry us to the plane." She spoke louder with each word. "I'm sure people at the airport will notice. If you get to the airport, that is. Your faces are plastered all over social media by now. Every law enforcement officer in the area is looking for you. You might as well give yourselves up."

Wilson banged his fist on the table. "Somebody get them something to eat just to shut her up."

Lancaster scraped his chair away from the table, muttering. He placed two bottles of water and a sandwich on the floor between them. He hesitated, then untied their hands. "Remember, we're armed. You aren't." He joined the others.

Ingrid rubbed her wrists but made no move toward the provisions.

"You need to eat something," Kate whispered.

"What difference does it make?"

"Don't give up. We're not on the plane yet."

Ingrid shrugged, then opened a bottle of water. Kate breathed a sigh of relief. They had to stay strong.

She sipped her water and took a few bites of food. Did anyone know she was missing yet? Surely the embassy was aware of Ingrid's disappearance, but how would they know where to look? She certainly had no clue where they were. The time between Wilson hitting her and reaching the farmhouse was a blank.

"We should be leaving soon." Schultz's words interrupted her thoughts. "Our private jet is scheduled for takeoff in two hours."

"Let's leave now." Wilson looked around the table. "The sooner we're on the plane, the better."

After further discussion, the men finally agreed. While they gathered their possessions, Lancaster strode over to Kate and Ingrid. He untied the ropes binding their ankles and pulled out his gun.

"Get up."

Kate stood, her legs tingling. She scanned the room for a weapon. Lancaster shoved her toward the door.

A breeze cooled her skin. Time suddenly moved in slow motion. Lancaster pushed them inside an SUV parked at the front of the farmhouse. The men climbed in, and the engine rumbled to life. Lancaster settled onto the seat in front of Kate's, his weapon out.

The vehicle bumped along a dirt road bordering open pastures. Kate leaned her forehead against the window. The fields stretched as far as she could see, horses grazing in the distance. At least her last memories would be those of home.

Wilson cursed as he slammed on the brakes.

Kate leaned around Lancaster to see ahead. Her mouth dropped open.

Cows. Fifteen or twenty, completely blocking the road. A farmer stood in their midst.

"Go around them," Lancaster snarled.

"I can't. The woods on either side are too dense. I'll turn around and head out another way."

"There is no other way."

Schultz pounded the back of Wilson's seat. "This is insane. Drive through them."

"You're an idiot. We'd need a tow truck to take us to the airport."

The farmer strode over to their vehicle. Lancaster concealed his gun as Wilson lowered the window.

The middle-aged man smiled. "Sorry about this. Part of the herd broke through my fence. I'm afraid I'll need your help to corral them if you plan to use the road." He turned back to the animals.

Wilson opened his door and started to get out.

"Are you crazy?" Schultz sputtered. "Stay here. Let him deal with this."

"We're scheduled for takeoff in less than two hours. I don't plan to be late. Get out and help."

Doors opened. Lancaster turned to Kate and Ingrid, his eyes steel. "If you try anything, I'll kill the farmer."

Once Lancaster left, Kate spun to Ingrid. "Search the seats and floor for anything sharp we could use as a weapon."

Ingrid bolted to the front of the vehicle. Kate dropped to her knees and swept her hands under each seat. Nothing. The carpet even smelled clean.

She glanced out the window. The cows lumbered off the road and through the pasture. Cold sweat trickled down her back. They had no way to convey their plight to the retreating farmer. Lancaster strode toward the vehicle with the other men. If she and Ingrid ran now, they would be easy targets.

Schultz climbed in first. "What do you two think you're doing? Sit down."

Once the others were inside, Wilson jerked the car into gear. The tires spun and the vehicle lurched ahead. When they reached the highway, a helicopter off to the left caught Kate's attention. Hope surged.

"We've got company," Wilson growled, pointing up.

"Relax." Lancaster shrugged. "Probably just relaying traffic reports."

The minutes stretched in silence. Finally, Wilson headed up an entrance ramp and merged onto I-95.

Despair settled in the pit of Kate's stomach. How much time did she and Ingrid have left?

MARCH 12
WEDNESDAY, 4:15 P.M.
VIRGINIA

"Wilson's vehicle is on the move. Ready with coordinates." The voice of the chopper pilot filtered into Ben's earpiece.

Ben sucked in a sharp breath. Susan had once again come through with the break they needed and located the car Wilson had rented—a silver Lexus SUV. Where was Wilson heading?

"Did you get a count of the passengers when they entered the vehicle?" Ben almost shouted the words.

"Picked up the SUV already in transit about a half mile from Wilson's farmhouse. Only visuals were four men who briefly exited. Can't determine if other passengers are in the car. They're heading north now on I-95, possibly toward Dulles."

Ben shoved his foot harder against the gas pedal. What had they done with Kate? Were she and Ingrid in the vehicle or at Wilson's property? If the men had decided they didn't need them anymore and left them at the farmhouse … He swallowed hard against the bile burning his throat. He would not let his mind go to the possibilities.

Joe swore. "Stay with the Lexus and give us the coordinates. We'll alert SOG." He punched the "We're taking a different route."

"This doesn't lead to the airport. I'm turning the car around."

Lancaster swung his gun up and jabbed the weapon against Wilson's temple. "No, you're not."

Kate gripped her seat. What was going on?

"Are you crazy?" Wilson jerked the car to a stop. "What are you doing?"

"Time to get rid of excess baggage before boarding the plane. You're no longer useful to us. I see no reason Schultz and I should split millions of dollars with you."

"You wouldn't *have* millions if I hadn't arranged for CRI to be your cover, along with making sure these two women didn't talk."

"You're absolutely right, so it's only fitting that your gun should be the one to kill them … and you. You'll get all the credit."

Wilson lunged for Lancaster's weapon. The security guard in the seat behind whisked his arm around Wilson's throat and wrestled him to the floor of the SUV. Lancaster slid into the driver's side. He sped toward a long, low building. Heavy machinery, concrete cylinders, huge metal bins, and massive piles of sand filled the area.

An orange barricade blocked the remainder of the road. Lancaster slammed on brakes, switched off the engine, then turned to Schultz and the guard. "Let's get Wilson and the women inside the building."

Adrenaline coursed through Kate, but with the cold metal of a gun jammed against her, she had no escape. Once outside the car, Lancaster twisted her arm behind her. He shoved her toward the building. Schultz jerked Ingrid from the vehicle and followed them.

Seconds later, metal whipping air muffled, then exploded into a deafening roar above them. A low-flying chopper darkened the sky. Wind from the blades swirled the mounds of sand on the ground into clouds of dust. Kate struggled to turn her head against the pelting grains stinging her eyes, but Lancaster still gripped her throat. If the chopper was FBI, she and Ingrid would be human shields for Lancaster and the others.

The helicopter dipped lower. When Lancaster raised his weapon to fire overhead, his hold on Kate loosened. She twisted away and shoved him hard against Schultz. They staggered, and Ingrid wrenched free.

"Run," Kate screamed, her cry swallowed by the pounding blades above.

They sprinted toward a huge backhoe and darted behind the machine's massive tires. Lancaster and his men exchanged fire with the chopper. Both Schultz and the guard crumpled to the ground. More shots were fired. The helicopter lurched wildly, then whirred toward a clearing on the other side of the building.

Gulping air, Kate scanned the area. Even if the chopper landed safely, Lancaster could kill them before anyone from the helicopter reached them.

Ingrid gripped Kate's arm. "What should we do?"

"We can't stay here. We need to find someplace safer to hide."

Kate pivoted. The barrel of Lancaster's gun gleamed in front of her. Her knees buckled.

He cocked his weapon.

She braced. "You won't get away with this."

"Watch me."

"Drop your gun, Lancaster." Wilson appeared behind him. "Move away from the women."

Lancaster lowered his weapon but didn't move. "So, you're going to play knight in shining armor—kill me, rescue them. They'll put you away for life when they talk."

Movement off to Kate's right caught her eye. She dared not turn.

"I'm not rescuing them," Wilson sneered. "I'm keeping them alive to make sure I get on that plane. You *are* right on one count—I'm going to kill you."

"FBI!" a voice shouted.

Both men froze.

"Drop your weapons."

Kate held her breath. Wilson tossed his gun to the ground and dropped to his knees. In one swift movement, Lancaster raised his weapon and pointed it at Kate. Her pulse pounded in her ears. A shot rang out.

Lancaster's eyes widened, then glazed. He collapsed into her. His blood dripped onto her hand. She screamed.

Strong arms caught her just before she fell.

The terror suffocating her brain eased its hold, and she buried her head against Ben's shoulder.

MARCH 12
WEDNESDAY, 5:40 P.M.
VIRGINIA

Kate sipped water while the paramedic packed his stethoscope and talked with Joe. She'd promised to force fluids if she didn't have to go to the hospital.

Satisfied that she and Ingrid were okay, Joe planted a kiss on her head before he strode over to his FBI team.

The paramedic studied Kate a moment. "Didn't we just do this two months ago?"

Kate grimaced. How could the same medic who treated her after the robbery attempt at Shane's Jewelers respond here in Virginia? "Last time we were in DC. How can you cover this area also?"

"I don't work in the city now. My wife and I moved away because I was ready for a slower pace." He glanced around at the maze of law enforcement personnel, flashing lights, and crime scene tape. "I think we might need to consider moving farther." He stood. "Remember, keep forcing fluids. And please, take things easy. Your life is way too exciting."

She watched him leave. Maybe she should take his advice.

She walked over to Ingrid and sank on a bench beside her. "How are you?"

"Good." She raised her water bottle in a toast. "Like you, I promised to force liquids if I didn't have to get an IV."

Kate turned to Ingrid. "I just heard the other security guard was arrested at the plane. Interesting twenty-four hours."

"No kidding." Ingrid finished the rest of her water. "I've been thinking a lot about my uncle. I loved him so much. He was kind to me when my mother died, took me on trips to the zoo and parks. He understood the demands being royal places on a child." She hesitated. "I've also thought about Schultz's accusations. As I grew older, my uncle and I talked about everything except his work. I heard bits of conversations I didn't understand, saw things that didn't make sense at the time. He was always quick to cover his computer when I came into the room. I also heard him talking on the phone once when he used the word 'Sunburst.' I assumed he was talking about me because that was his name for me." A tear trickled down her cheek. "I think Schultz was, incredibly, telling the truth about my uncle's involvement in his crimes."

"I'm sorry, Ingrid. Yet his decision to go to the authorities took courage. He must have had a change of heart."

"I hope so." She paused. "My father will be devastated if these allegations are true. Realizing someone you love isn't the person you thought is difficult."

Her relationship with Gavin flashed through Kate's mind. "It's difficult, but truth brings the chance to forgive and heal." Her eyes wandered to the surreal scene around them. "Truth also allows the freedom to move forward."

She caught sight of Ben and her heart skipped a beat. She couldn't wait to move forward with this man in her life.

CHAPTER 19

MARCH 22
SATURDAY, 12:35 P.M.
SHANE'S JEWELERS, DC

"Quiet, please." Max O'Reilly clinked a knife against his coffee cup. "Time for my speech."

Beaming, he made his way over to Levi and Nelda. Kate joined the circle of friends around Max and the Shanes. A little over a week had passed since her kidnapping. Nightmares still haunted her sleep. Time with friends was a welcome distraction.

"Does everybody have food on their plates?" A broad grin spread across Levi's face. "Once O'Reilly has an audience, he can go on for hours."

Max clapped Levi on the back. "I go on for hours because you keep interrupting."

"Levi, Max." Nelda shook her head. "Behave yourselves."

Those three. Kate lifted her phone and snapped a picture.

"All kidding aside, congratulations. Thirty years in business is a great accomplishment." Max gestured toward his audience. "As we've worked side by side over the years, we've had great times and hard times, but we always came through. Even if we have to close our shops in these next months—" His voice caught.

Kate glanced at the door. Now would be the perfect time for her surprise to arrive.

"No matter what happens," Max continued, "we'll always be a family. Sophie, do you have the gift?"

Sophie handed her uncle a large striped bag.

"All of us chipped in to get this." Max presented the gift with a flourish.

Levi and Nelda, murmuring their thanks, removed the tissue paper. They pulled out a beautiful mantle clock.

Applause rippled as Max stepped forward. "Katie, will you do the honors of cutting the cake?"

"Of course."

She took her place behind the table laden with sandwiches, potato salad, fruit, and dessert. Sophie joined her as she cut slices of triple-layer chocolate cake.

"Thank you for helping us with the party, Kate. The Shanes were really surprised."

"My pleasure. I've missed everyone during the weeks since I've visited. Are Levi and Max still playing their daily checker game?"

"Without fail. Levi and Nelda even decided they aren't ready to retire yet." Sophie added forks to the cake plates. "If we have to close the shops, Uncle Max and the Shanes will be crushed. With Lancaster's death, we're haven't heard what will happen to his property."

Before Kate could reply, the bell over the front door jingled. "Excuse me, Sophie." She wiped her hands on a napkin and hurried over.

"Ms. Tyler, I'm so happy you're here."

"Please, call me Liza." Her eyes darted around the shop, plainly taking in every detail with a single glance. She furrowed her brow. "The building needs work. Water damage on the ceiling, peeling plaster …"

"Also, some of the lights don't work. During the robbery attempt, a bullet hit an electrical panel. I can show you the other shop in this building if you'd like. The card shop and dress shop are located next door."

Max, Sophie, and the Shanes strolled over. Kate introduced them. "Brandon Lancaster was Liza's brother-in-law," she added.

Liza jumped into the awkward pause with both feet. "Though we were related by marriage, I assure you that's the only thing we had in common. I'm sorry for all the trouble Brandon caused you. Kate told me your situation. My lawyers are gathering information for me on the possibility of buying these two buildings. In the meantime, I'd like to use my own funds to repair them and keep things running smoothly. We'll keep you open for business. You have my word."

Sophie threw her arms around her uncle as the Shanes hugged Liza. Surprise and pleasure mingled on Liza's face. Apparently, her other clients weren't quite as demonstrative. "I also have some marketing ideas for your businesses. Perhaps after you introduce me to Stephanie and Cynthia, I could tell you my thoughts."

As the others ambled away, Levi put a frail arm around Kate. "Thank you for talking with Ms. Tyler. Your help means more than you know."

She returned his hug. "Sophie said you and Nelda decided you weren't ready to retire yet."

"Staying in business is the only way O'Reilly and I will keep out of trouble." Levi limped over to the table and brought back two glasses of punch.

Kate raised her glass. "May you and Max enjoy many more checker games in the back room."

Levi grinned. "With Nelda's fudge brownies."

"With lots of love and laughter."

"With me winning more games than O'Reilly."

"With me there to cheer you both on." She blinked back sudden tears. *For many years to come.*

MARCH 22
SATURDAY, 4:40 P.M.
N. TROY STREET, ARLINGTON, VA

Kate pushed the vacuum over the living room carpet. Aunt Martha was away for the weekend visiting friends, and this was the perfect time for chores. For something normal.

She needed normal. Her emotions were still strapped to a roller coaster.

She finished cleaning, then headed to her bedroom to put away laundry. When she opened the dresser drawer to stack folded shirts inside, her hand slid over something long and ridged. A belt? She couldn't remember putting one there. She grasped the object and drew out her hand.

A snake dangled from her fingers.

She pushed down a scream and slung the disgusting thing across the room. The snake hit the floor but didn't slither away. She exhaled a long breath and inched nearer. Living on the farm, she'd seen her share of snakes, even killed a few. They usually didn't scare her, but they weren't usually in her dresser drawer.

She looked closer. Great. A copperhead.

At least the poisonous snake was dead. She turned back to the dresser. How on earth did a snake find its way there? She licked her lips. Maybe she should check the other drawers in case he brought a friend.

She eased open the next drawer and froze. Printed on a white sheet of paper, *What Will I Do Next?* stared back. Adrenaline coursed through her veins. Wilson was in prison. Who had invaded her *home*?

Dread flooded over her. What if he were still here?

She whirled to run. Gavin filled the doorway.

"Hey, sweetheart." He took a step toward her. "I've missed you."

Realization dawned, and nausea swept over her. "You? You've been stalking me?" She clenched her fists. "When did you start working for Wilson and Lancaster?"

"I don't know anybody named Wilson. Or Lancaster." His expression shifted. A look she couldn't read settled over his features. "I'm sorry, Kate. I had to punish you. You didn't help me with my business proposition. I kept waiting for you to come back to tell me you're sorry. When you never came, I tried to get you out of my mind. I couldn't, so I've come to take you home with me. I love you." His face contorted as fury erupted. "I hate you!"

Kate gulped a breath. Insanity glittered in his eyes. She slipped her hand toward her pocket. Panic hit. She'd left her phone in the other room.

"Lose something?"

Gavin held up her phone, then dropped the device to the floor and ground the heel of his boot into the screen. "Don't worry. I already sent a text from your phone to your friend Ben. He's coming over soon." He moved his jacket to reveal a sidearm. "When he walks through the door, I'm going to kill him."

MARCH 22
SATURDAY, 5:00 P.M.
HOOVER BUILDING, DC

Ben forced himself to focus on work while his team's conversations hummed around him. He was having trouble putting the ordeal of Kate's kidnapping behind him. He couldn't wait to see her this evening. The fear of losing her had hit hard. The deaths of Lancaster, Schultz, and the guard played through his mind. Wasted lives never stopped being a tragedy.

"Everybody did a great job on the case." Joe's voice interrupted Ben's thoughts. "Thank you for keeping my sister safe." Joe turned to Curt. "How are things going with the interrogation of Wilson?"

"He's been quite cooperative in hopes of a lighter sentence. He's given us invaluable information on Sunburst. He's also confessed to his own crimes." A frown etched Curt's forehead. "Though he's adamant he didn't stalk Kate until the night he waited for her in her car."

Ben's gut clenched. The thought of her dealing with the threats alone stabbed. If only Kate had confided in him earlier. Joe's expression mirrored Ben's feelings.

"Lancaster or Schultz might have been responsible, or Lancaster could have hired Ian Dunbar." Susan glanced at her computer screen. "The crimes of these men would fill volumes—cyberwarfare, fraud, murder ..."

Janet refilled her coffee mug. "We know Lancaster and Schultz met in Vaduz. How did Wilson meet the two of them?"

"Wilson spent time in Vaduz preparing for CRI's research exchange program with Liechtenstein," Ben answered. "While he was there, he crossed paths with Lancaster, whom he'd met years ago in DC. Lancaster and Schultz brought Wilson into their scheme of hacking financial institutions. They decided the research project would be the perfect cover."

"Though the background checks on the Liechtenstein economists were stringent, Schultz was added at the last possible moment." Susan clicked her computer. "Remember the man arrested for tampering with Prince Alexander's brakes two months ago? I received word yesterday the Liechtenstein authorities found evidence he was framed. He was one of the economists scheduled to fly to the US. After his arrest, Schultz took his place."

"With a background check and passport provided by none other than CIA operative Ted Bradley. Make that ex-CIA operative." Joe capped his water bottle. "Bradley apparently gained a reputation in the crime world as someone who'd do anything for the right price. He even arranged the killing of one of his own operatives. A tracking device was found in a watch he had sent to T. J. Atkinson. T. J. was building a case against Bradley."

"Just like Ethan Fitzgerald was trying to figure out the meaning of Sunburst," Susan said softly.

"That's why—" A ping from Joe's phone interrupted him. When he glanced down, the color drained from his face.

317

Ben stood. "What's wrong?"

"My friend in the Cleveland office found information linking Kate's ex to the DC area. According to Gavin's business partners, he was fired from his job several months ago because of irrational behavior. Kate needs to know."

Ben's chest tightened. She was still struggling to recover from the past weeks. "I'm going to her apartment now."

Joe already had his phone against his ear. "I'm contacting the Cleveland office. I'll be right behind you."

Ben headed to his car. Should he call her? Maybe the news would be easier if he told her in person.

He and Joe would figure out a plan. They would keep her safe.

So why couldn't he quell the unrest churning through him?

MARCH 22
SATURDAY, 5:40 P.M.
N. TROY STREET, ARLINGTON, VA

Kate hovered in the kitchen doorway while Gavin strode up and down in front of her. He raged about her, his business, his family. Though his gun had remained by his side, she had no doubt he would use the weapon.

Lord, help, she breathed. Ben would be here at any moment. She had no way to contact him. Her only option was to stop Gavin

She eased backward into the kitchen. He halted, glaring.

"What are you doing?"

"I'm hungry, and I'll bet you are too." She opened the refrigerator and forced a smile. "I'll heat up a big pot of homemade soup for us."

He calmed. "I guess that will work. If we eat now, we won't have to stop on our way home." He unlocked the back door. "Your friend will come to this door." He touched his gun. "When he knocks, tell him to come in."

Kate pushed down the panic welling up inside, filled a pan with soup, and switched the burner on high. Gavin rambled about the home he'd bought for them in Ohio, vacillating between love for her and hate.

She stared at the pot. The liquid simmered. At last, the soup began to boil.

Gavin moved closer. Her skin prickled. She grasped the handles of the pot, but he turned away. She inhaled a deep breath. She had one chance.

A knock on the back door pounded through her being. "Kate?"

Gavin ripped out his gun and glared at her. "Tell him to—"

She flung the scalding soup in Gavin's face. A cry of agony pierced the room.

Ben exploded through the door. He kicked the gun from Gavin's hand. In one swift movement, he jerked Gavin to the floor and jammed his knee into the man's back, holding him motionless.

"Kate." Ben's voice shook. "Did he hurt you?"

She drew a ragged breath. "I'm ... okay."

Ben whipped out his phone and called for backup. While he answered the dispatcher's questions, Kate pushed a towel under cool water. Despite everything, she hated to see Gavin in pain.

Kneeling, she gently placed the towel over his burns and prayed once again for him.

When backup arrived, Ben rushed over and enveloped her in his arms. Her tears flowed. "Gavin was going to kill you."

"You stopped him," he murmured, his lips against her hair. He leaned back and looked at her, the depth of feeling in his eyes stealing her breath. "Thank you for risking your life for me."

His words spoken months ago at Shane's Jewelers flowed back, warming her. She slipped her arms around him. "Your life was worth the risk."

APRIL 5
SATURDAY, 9:55 A.M.
MEADOW DRIVE, FAIRFAX, VA

"See you later, Uncle Ben—wish you were coming!"

Ben smiled and waved at his nieces. Kate's car pulled out of the driveway. The girls bounced up and down in the back seat, huge grins lighting up their faces. They were thrilled to be going to the zoo with Aunt Kate. He hoped she didn't mind being called "aunt." He loved the idea.

As he turned toward Leah's house, his smile faded. How would this morning go? He drew a deep breath and headed inside. Leah stood at the kitchen sink, staring out the window.

He walked over and hugged her. "How are you doing, Sis?"

She shrugged. "Feeling a hundred different emotions at once. I don't know what to expect. To get a call from a Marine who was deployed with Rich—" Her voice quivered. "He said he had something to tell me, that he would have come sooner if he could have. I wonder why he waited this long?"

Leah had been doing so well this past month. If only he'd spoken with Rich's friend before he came to see her. Would this visit be a step backward?

Leah looked at the clock over the stove. "He should arrive any moment. Did I tell you his name?"

Ben nodded. "Mark. I'll see if he's here yet."

He made his way to the front porch and sank into a rocking chair. *Lord, help us through this.*

A short while later, a vehicle drove slowly past the house, backed up, and turned into Leah's driveway. Ben walked over to the car.

The door opened. A golden retriever jumped out, his eyes focused on the person inside. The owner slid from the vehicle. He stood with his prosthetic leg next to his service dog and grasped the dog's harness.

Ben extended his hand. "Good morning. I'm Leah's brother, Ben Anderson."

"Mark Matthews."

Mark appeared close to his own age, with the build of a linebacker on a pro football team. His gaze was direct, his handshake firm.

"My dog's name is John-Luke." Mark grinned. "Had to get all four gospel writers between our two names. I just call him Luke for short."

"What a beautiful dog."

"He's a rescue—intelligent, loyal. We've only been together a short time, but he can sense what I need sooner than I can."

They neared the porch steps.

"Mark, can I help you in any way?"

He shook his head. "Just be patient. I'm still new at this."

Together, he and Luke maneuvered the steps. Ben opened the door and led him to the den.

After introductions were made, Leah gestured toward a chair. Once Mark was seated, she perched on the sofa beside Ben. Mark chatted easily with her about the landscaping in her front yard. Slowly, her clenched hands relaxed.

During a lull in the conversation, Luke's snores brought the welcome sound of her laughter. "Mark, would you care for coffee? Or lemonade?"

"Maybe later, thank you." His expression turned serious.

Ben studied him. This plainly wasn't any easier for him than for Leah.

"I'm sorry I wasn't able to speak with you sooner—" He glanced at his leg, then back to Leah. "Rich and I became good friends during deployment. I'm sorry for your loss, ma'am."

She looked down. "Thank you."

"Though Rich and I only came through three months of deployment together before the attack, he saved my life. Twice, actually."

Ben glanced at his sister. Something stirred in her eyes.

"If the experiences aren't too difficult to talk about, I'd like to hear how he helped you."

Ben turned his attention to Mark. *Please, give her something to hold on to.*

"The first time he saved my life was a few weeks into deployment. During early morning combat, my weapon malfunctioned. I panicked, but Rich put himself between me and enemy fire. If he hadn't been there to cover me, I would have died. No question in my mind." He paused. "We talked a lot after that day—about life, our families."

Ben drew a breath. What was coming?

Leah flinched. "I don't know how much he told you. We had serious problems before he left. I wrote him a letter telling him—" Her voice caught. "Telling him I loved him, that I wanted to save our marriage. Do you have any idea if he ever received the letter?"

Mark hesitated, then shook his head. "I'm sorry. Because of our position during those first months of deployment, outside communication wasn't possible."

Her tears fell.

Ben grasped her hand. Mark waited, stroking his dog's head, plainly willing to give her the time she needed.

When she finally looked up, Mark leaned forward. "I need to tell you how he saved me the second time. After the attack that took Rich's life, I was brought to the States for more surgery and rehab. I struggled with overwhelming depression. I had no desire to live the rest of my life with one leg. I came very close to giving up. But as I'd lie there in a dark room, refusing to see my friends and family, one conversation I'd had with Rich played in my mind. I couldn't get away from it. Since he was gone, I knew there was something he'd want me to do for him. I couldn't do it lying in a hospital bed." He paused. "I finally made the decision to pour everything I had into getting better. The recovery was the hardest thing I've ever done, but a lot of great people helped me. I got Luke, and I found out there can be hope on the other side of agony."

The ticking of the clock on the wall was the only sound for several minutes.

"I can't even imagine what you've been through. I'm so glad you had the strength to keep going." Leah bit her lip. "You said Rich would want you to do something for him. What did he want?"

"For me to find you." He paused a beat. "Rich told me about the arguments the two of you had before he left, but only in the context of saying what a fool he'd been." Mark shrugged. "His language was a lot stronger in describing himself. He told me you were everything to him, and he wasn't going to lose you. You should have heard the plans he was making." A smile flickered over Mark's face. "He wanted to take you to a cabin in the mountains—the same place you'd spent your honeymoon. He planned to fill every room with roses. Then he was going to get down on his knees, ask you to marry him all over again, and give you—" Mark fumbled in his pocket and brought out a small box. "He bought something special for you in a port on the way to our destination. Later—the day he died—we were standing by my bunk while he showed this to me. When we heard bombs exploding, we ran to our positions. His gift wound up in my belongings." He handed the box to Leah.

She held the small box for a moment. Finally, she opened the lid and looked inside. A soft gasp sounded. She turned the box for Ben to see. A gleaming silver band etched with tiny hearts held a beautiful white pearl.

"This is perfect, perfect," she murmured. "Rich and I once heard a pastor compare the struggles of life to abrasive grains of sand in an oyster. Over time, the sand becomes a pearl. And ultimately, God works our heartache into beauty. We reminded each other of the truth many times." She lifted her gaze to Mark. "Words can't express how much you coming here means to me." She was silent a moment. "If only Rich had been able to read my letter ..."

"He never doubted your love, ma'am. I promise."

As she slipped on the ring, her tears flowed.

Ben put an arm around her shoulders and nodded his thanks to Mark.

At last, healing had begun.

APRIL 12
SATURDAY, 3:55 P.M.
VIRGINIA

Jenny slowly turned as Aunt Martha arranged her veil. Kate caught her breath. She'd never seen a bride more lovely.

Aunt Martha stood back and whisked out a tissue. "Jenny, you look absolutely beautiful."

"Thank you, Aunt Martha." Jenny beamed. "I can't believe I'll be Mrs. Joe Peterson in a little over an hour."

A knock sounded. Kelly, the maid of honor, poked her head in. "Your wedding photographer is here."

Kelly and the photographer entered, along with Kate's sisters and the mothers of the bride and groom.

"Jenny, you're gorgeous," exclaimed Kate's mother.

"I can't believe you're getting married today." Abigail Thomas hugged her daughter.

"This is you in six months," Rachel teased Christy.

"Okay, ladies, time for photographs. The Greens' home is lovely, so we'll start with some indoor shots, then move outside. Don't worry—I made sure the groom is still in the guest house."

As they followed the photographer, Kate's phone pinged. She glanced down at a text from Joe.

Tom is late.

She grinned and replied. *Tom is always late.*

Don't tell Jenny yet. What will we do if we have four bridesmaids and three groomsmen?

One of the groomsmen can escort two bridesmaids. He'll love it.

I'm going to kill Tom.

"Kate? Is something wrong?"

She looked up. Nine pairs of eyes were fixed on her. "Everything's great. Where should I stand for the picture?"

An hour and a hundred photos later, Kate took her place on the garden path. She lifted her face to the gentle breeze. Spring was turning out warm and beautiful in DC. Today was no exception. Blue sky reflecting in the pristine lake made a stunning backdrop. Guests sat in white chairs placed in rows before a rose covered arch. Beds of pink tulips bordered by pink and white azaleas surrounded them. Farther down, a huge reception tent waited on the spacious lawn.

Music from a string quartet floated through the air. She spotted Ingrid walking to her seat. The princess looked rested and relaxed. Kate was glad her friend had joined them.

Almost time. Her stomach fluttered. She hadn't seen Ben yet. He would already be standing up front when she walked down the aisle.

The hum of an engine in the distance suddenly drew her attention. Kate glanced around. Surely the neighbors hadn't picked this exact moment to mow their lawn. The hum grew louder. The sound wasn't really that of a lawn mower. Maybe a— She turned. Motorcycle.

Tom was here. Kate glimpsed him roaring up the circle drive. He disappeared from view for a moment. Seconds later, he sprinted across the yard, tossing his helmet on the grass and smoothing his tux as he ran.

He waved to his sisters. "Had to help a grandma change a flat tire."

Kate returned the wave as he ran past. Only Tom could change a tire in a tux and still look good. Joe's choice of black hadn't hurt.

Moments later, the music changed, and the processional began. When her turn came to walk down the aisle, she lifted her eyes to Ben. Her heart fluttered at his smile. She drew a deep breath and took her place with her sisters.

The ceremony began. Tears sprang to her eyes more than once. If only she'd remembered to stick a tissue in her bouquet. Her sister Ann finally nudged her elbow and passed her a lace handkerchief. She nodded slightly. Ann was always the most prepared of the whole Peterson clan.

The ceremony concluded with a radiant bride and a beaming husband. The bridal party and guests strolled to the reception. After the first dance, Joe and Jenny invited everyone to join them.

Someone touched Kate's shoulder. She turned and looked into Ben's blue eyes.

"May I have this dance?"

Her heart skipped a beat. "My pleasure."

He slipped his arm around her waist and led her toward the other couples. Something wet dripped on her hair. Then on her hand. Was this going to be the romantic dance in the rain she'd always dreamed of? She looked up. Nope. Hues of pink and gold streaked the clear evening sky.

Sudden mists of water surged across the lawn, drenching everyone.

"Oh, no!" Mrs. Green shouted. "We forgot to reset the automatic sprinklers."

Kate and Ben burst out laughing. They ran with the others toward the tent. As music and laughter floated around them, Ben took off his coat and slipped it over Kate's shoulders.

He stepped closer and smoothed her damp hair. She stilled at his touch. Drawing her to him, he tilted up her chin and looked deep into her eyes. "I love you, Kate Peterson."

Could he feel the pounding of her heart? Love for this man enveloped her soul. God had brought him into her life at the perfect time, and gratefulness settled over her. She melted into the warmth of his kiss, dreams of their future dancing in her heart.

About the Author

With a love of suspense fueled by years of reading and a commitment to authenticity rooted in over thirty-five years as a pastor's wife, Kim Teague brings faith-through-fire suspense to her readers. She portrays characters facing real-life challenges while striving to live their faith in an imperfect world. Kim's passion lies in bringing her characters, along with her readers, to a deeper trust in God and his unfailing promises.

Kim is the author of *The Secret of Jenny's Portrait*. She also contributed to *The Wonders of Nature: 365 Devotions Celebrating God's Beauty*. She is a member of American Christian Fiction Writers.

Kim is married to Barry, senior pastor of Brices Creek Bible Church. They enjoy spending time with their grown children and being outdoors. They make their home in North Carolina.

IF YOU'VE ENJOYED *DEADLY PRETENSE*, YOU'LL ENJOY THE BOOK THAT STARTED IT ALL, *THE SECRET OF JENNY'S PORTRAIT.*

www.ingramcontent.com/pod-product-compliance
Lightning Source LLC
Chambersburg PA
CBHW051528280626
47161CB00021B/425